Winter's Poison

The Winter Murders, Book 1

E.L. Johnson

ARE YOU SIGNED UP FOR DRAGONBLADE'S BLOG?

You'll get the latest news and information on exclusive giveaways, exclusive excerpts, coming releases, sales, free books, cover reveals and more.

Check out our complete list of authors, too!

No spam, no junk. That's a promise!

Sign Up Here

www.dragonbladepublishing.com

Dearest Reader;

Thank you for your support of a small press. At Dragonblade Publishing, we strive to bring you the highest quality Historical Romance from some of the best authors in the business. Without your support, there is no 'us', so we sincerely hope you adore these stories and find some new favorite authors along the way.

Happy Reading!

CEO, Dragonblade Publishing

Additional Dragonblade books by Author E.L. Johnson

For Uncle Larry and Aunt LeAnn,
whose love is an inspiration

Chapter One

In the year of our Lord, eleven hundred and forty-one, the first month, in Lincoln. Anno Domini Rex Stephani.

ON A COLD January morning in the city of Lincoln, Bronwyn Blakenhale wiped her brow, feeling beads of sweat dot her skin. She'd been up for hours already, kneading and preparing dough in the large, wooden trough and worktables in her family's workshop. The air smelled of yeast and dough, and loaves sat proofing on the workspace—small loaves and big ones, covered with damp cloths as they sat in the warm room.

"Bronwyn!" her stepmother, Margaret, called. "Bronwyn Blakenhale, you come inside this instant. And tell your father to come right now. Where's he gone?"

"I don't know." Her voice bordered on mocking and she rolled her eyes. She didn't care. Her father was gone, but he would be back. Nothing ever changed in their city.

Her stepmother, a shrill-voiced, middle-aged woman with a head full of wispy, brown hair with a few strands of grey, nudged her aside and took over, raking coals and adding more firewood to the mix, stoking the black coals so that the big oven grew hotter. "Find him, would you? We need to make sure these loaves are weighted properly. Don't want to get fined again."

She was right. Baking was a serious business, and if their

loaves didn't meet the exact weight required by law, they could be fined or worse, her papa could be imprisoned or forced to wear a faulty loaf around his neck and be marched through the streets. It would be a more serious punishment for such a crime, but not unheard of. She'd seen it once before and had never forgotten the sight.

It had happened to a neighbor of theirs, Thomas Nell, who'd added iron rods to his loaf to give it the proper weight, but when he'd been found out, the city's watch had had him up on a charge and ordered a public punishment. No one had bought his loaves in the days since, and he'd had to start all over again elsewhere, out of town. Her papa had been fined once, and since then, they hadn't dared get the measurements wrong again.

Now that dawn had come, the workday properly began. Bronwyn wore a stiff, woolen housedress and apron, her dirty-blonde hair tied back in a kerchief. It was hot, tiring, and sweaty work, baking, but she loved it. It was her one relief from the world outside.

She did like the stark, black spidery limbs of the trees in the wood that gleamed against the white, winter skies as she would gather herbs and mushrooms, and she liked the contrast of the wildness of the forest outside to the city of Lincoln, full of buildings, tall and thin, squat and fat, leaning and ever-growing, towering over each other, and above them all, atop Steep Hill, Lincoln Castle.

But recently, the city stood in an uneasy peace, stuck between two masters. The townspeople of Lincoln found themselves in the midst of an ongoing war between King Stephen and Empress Maud, who battled for the English crown. Bronwyn had never thought the war would come her way, but shortly before Christmas, Ranulf de Gernon, the Earl of Chester, and his half-brother, William de Roumare, had taken Lincoln and the castle in a daring trick.

The rumor went that the wives of de Gernon and de Roumare had paid a friendly visit to the wife of the chatelain of the castle. When their husbands had come to collect them, dressed in ordinary clothes and unarmed, only escorted by three knights for protection, the men had attacked and with a small force overwhelmed the few men inside, claiming the castle and the city. The battle had changed Bronwyn's life overnight.

The townspeople of Lincoln had sent word to King Stephen in London that two of his men had holed up in the castle and were mistreating people. In January, the king had reclaimed the fair city with his knights and mighty siege engines, great towers of war. Bronwyn had not seen them but heard them outside the walls.

Word was that de Gernon had escaped, but no one knew to where. They said it was a matter of time before his master, Robert of Gloucester, and perhaps even the lady herself, Empress Maud, come to claim the city in her name. Since then, people looked over their shoulders and kept strangers at arms' length. Fights had broken out in the taverns over which side was right, and whilst Stephen had taken residence in the castle and kept the peace by way of armed guards, it was an uneasy peace at best.

Bronwyn had never felt unsafe walking outside before, but now… Armed men boldly walked the streets like never before, and rumors of war weren't just muttered in passing—they hung on the tip of every tongue.

Bronwyn brushed dough off her dress and headed out of the workroom, away from the delicious smells of beer, yeast, dough, and fermentation, and hurried outside, her eyes drinking in the darkness before dawn. It wouldn't be long now. In winter, their working hours were short and the nights were long; in summer, it was the opposite. Her papa came walking through the street, along with Wyot, their ten-year-old oafish apprentice.

Their arms were full of firewood, but Bronwyn knew they'd go through it within hours. Her father brushed some of his dirty-blond hair from his eyes and greeted her with a smile. He liked having a young person to show around the bakery and he hefted an axe over his shoulder as he carried a bundle of wood in his other hand. "So you're up."

"I've been up for ages," she said.

"So you are. Helping your ma?"

"She's looking for you. She wants to get the weights right."

He nodded and led the way inside. The air was cold with a morning chill, and dawn's early light began to shine over the buildings. She joined them back inside the bakery, shutting the wooden door closed behind her.

Father and Wyot laid down their bundles as Papa hung up his axe and greeted her stepmother with a kiss. Margaret Blakenhale giggled and batted his hands away, then put her hands on her hips. "Can you measure out the loaves? I can never trust they're right."

He tied a work apron around his waist, wiped his hands, and set to feeling the small, round loaves of dough that were proofing beneath the damp cloths. He held them up by hand, measuring each. "This one is too light. Add more flour."

Margaret did what he'd instructed, adding a dusting more flour to the wet loaf. "And now?"

"Better." He went through all the loaves, big and small, on the tables. "The rest are good."

"Will you make oatcakes today, Master Alan?" Wyot asked. A cheerful boy, he often stuffed his mouth with any burnt or poorly baked goods that weren't good enough to sell, and despite being thin, he was already outgrowing his clothes. In no time at all, they knew he'd be as tall as a beanpole.

Bronwyn and her father grinned. They all knew Wyot's love of oatcakes made with honey. "Maybe, boy. If there's honey to be had."

He surveyed the loaves, examining those made with a mixture of peas and beans. He supervised as Margaret and Bronwyn cut pretty designs into the dough and began adding them to the oven with the peel—the long, wooden, flat board at the end of a pole—and shoveling them onto the hard, stone shelf for baking.

Once they had several loaves in, they sat back and watched,

turning them when necessary. Bronwyn's father gave each roll a final measure on the scales, satisfied they met the required weight for sale, and as the first shaft of daylight lit up the outside, they threw open the shop doors.

Wyot and Bronwyn began loading the shop's wooden cart with rolls, round loaves that smelled heavenly. Once the cart was fairly stacked and covered, they began to wheel the cart out. Bronwyn and her father walked into the city proper, whilst Wyot stayed back and helped Margaret with the cleaning and baking. It being Saturday, they walked toward the city center toward the weekly farmers' market, where hundreds of people from nearby would come to purchase wares and food. They could buy from the shop directly, but there was always more to be had on market days.

Bronwyn stood by as Papa purchased a stall in the market center and together they began unloading the breads, placing them for sale on the stall with the cart behind them. The first batch sold quickly, and it was a flurry of activity as they sold half loaves, cheap loaves made of grain husks, others made of peas and barley, and even some oat ones made with a drop of honey.

An inspector came by and weighed one of the loaves. Bronwyn held her breath as he held up and set it on his scales. He tapped the loaf and broke off a tiny piece to eat, eventually chewing and nodding his assent. She let out a breath as he packed up his scale and walked away.

Her father watched him go. "We need some sort of regulation."

"What do you mean?" she asked.

"We need a group. A body to govern us and our craft. I'm all for a fair price, but I don't like these stories I hear about bakers messing about with their loaves. It makes it harder for the rest of us who do an honest day's work."

"You'll get fair pay now that King Stephen is here," a stranger said, drawing Bronwyn's and her father's attention. "There'll be fair work and pay for all honest craftsmen. More so than if that

French wench were inside the walls."

He stood tall and heavyset, with a trimmed, black beard and tanned face. He was dressed in plain clothes, but something about him gave away a military bearing, a readiness to arms, and a skillful hand at weaponry. His voice held a note of testing, comment, and curiosity.

Her father bowed his head. "Interest you in a loaf of bread, sir?"

"Yes." The man took a loaf, tore off a hunk, and popped it in his mouth. "This is good, but I need better. Where's your white bread?"

"I've only made brown bread this morning but can bake you the white. How many loaves do you need? One?"

"Ten," the man said. "No, better make it more. Fifteen ought to do. I'll need them tonight."

Her father blinked. "Tonight?"

"Unless you are unable to do this? I can go elsewhere."

An expensive order like that would set them up nicely. Bronwyn raised an eyebrow at her father. She knew the right answer. "Yes, sir. We can do that. Where should I deliver them?"

"To Danesgate, by the castle. Tell the guards that Hugh de Grecy sent you."

"Very good, sir." Her father paused. "I will need payment before I begin, to purchase the flour."

The man pulled out a thick, heavy purse and began counting out silver. Soon a small pile sat on the table before us. "Will this do?"

"Yes, thank you." Her father returned one of the silver coins to him. "This much is fine."

Sir de Grecy's mouth quirked in a half smile as he took back the extra silver coin. "An honest baker. That's new. What's your name?"

"Alan Blakenhale." Her father gave a small bow.

"This your daughter?" He nodded at Bronwyn.

"Yes." Her father rested his hands on her shoulders. "She's a dab hand in the kitchen."

The man glanced at Bronwyn with dark eyes. "Deliver these to the kitchens by sunset and there'll be more orders where that came from." He walked off, whistling.

Her father let out a breath. "Well, what do you make of that, Bronwyn? Serving bread at the castle, eh? Margaret will be impressed."

"D'you think so, Papa?"

"I do." He paused. "I was going to go to Mass, but there's too much to be done. I'll have to buy the flour and then make the rolls in time for tonight. You mind the stall for a bit, all right? I'll be back soon."

She asked, "Papa, what did he mean by 'the French wench'? Is he talking about…?"

Papa's face clouded and he drew close. "Mind you don't go repeating what you've heard, Bronwyn. You know whom he means. The Countess of Anjou, the woman who calls herself 'Empress Maud.'"

He was right, she realized. She'd heard mention of her before in hushed tones, and more recently, she'd been spoken of as a nuisance, an interloper, French.

Since King Stephen had taken control of the castle, they had seen more armored men, more soldiers, and the streets had been busier, but she had noticed little beyond the comings and goings of people buying breads, and the daily happenings of the bakery. Her family's lives felt small by comparison, but she idly wondered if it would stay that way.

What she wanted more than anything was to travel, to see another part of England, even France, Wales, or Scotland or Ireland. To see what life was like beyond her fair city. People spoke differently, they dressed differently. She wished to see the world. She loved her father's bakery and the life she had in Lincoln, but something about the soldiers and men walking the streets hinted at something in the air; something was brewing, but she knew not what. She wasn't sure she wanted to find out, but all the same, she desired a change.

She watched the stall and sold more bread. A man tried to haggle and gave her a toothy, leering grin, refusing to pay the full amount, even though the loaf was only a few pennies.

She did her best impression of her stepmother and put her hands on her hips, glaring at him, when a deep voice said, "Is this man bothering you?"

She turned toward the voice. A pair of sharp, grey eyes met hers. She breathed in; the man's gaze was so intense, she imagined this was what looking into the eyes of a lion felt like, except so much more. He was young, perhaps not too much older than she, with tanned skin and shoulder-length, blond hair that shone gold in the sun. His smile was friendly, and she found herself unconsciously touching her hair, then she put her hand down, annoyed at herself. She had no time for men, not when there was an obnoxious customer to deal with.

She turned to the man who'd tried to cheat her. "No, he's going to pay what is owed. Aren't you?"

The older man leered some more and took the bread in his dirty hands. "What if I don't?"

"Then I'll call the watch," Bronwyn said.

The man guffawed. "You think they'll listen to you?"

In seconds, the young man had the older man's arm twisted behind his back and a short blade pricking his neck. The man dropped the loaf with a cry of pain. The lionlike young man growled, "Pay the baker."

Her heart beat in her throat. Would he really hurt, possibly *kill*, a man over an affront? To a woman he'd never met before?

The older man stiffened, spat, and with his free arm, reached for a small bag that hung at his waist and tossed a coin on the ground. He jerked from the lad and slunk away, picking up the now-dirty bread. He gave her a glowering stare as if to say, *This isn't over.*

She blinked as the young man sheathed his blade and picked up the coin the customer had thrown on the ground. He handed it to her as she thanked him.

"It's all right. Always happy to help a lady in need." He smiled again. "Although I've yet to meet such a pretty baker. Who are you?"

"She's my daughter," Bronwyn's father said, coming to her side. "And who might you be?"

The man stood to attention, his back straight, his chin up. "Rupert Bothwell, at your service. Squire to Sir Baldwin of Clare." He winked at her.

She ignored him. "He was helping me with a rude man, Papa."

"I saw. Thank you. We shouldn't keep you from your master," her father said.

The lad nodded and bid them both a bow before winking at her again. He left, his golden hair shining in the sun.

Her papa looked at her thoughtfully.

"What is it, Papa?"

"You turned eighteen last June. If you were a son, I'd have you apprenticed and at a journeyman's level by now. You know almost enough about baking to almost run your own shop, I daresay. Your mama will want us to think about marriage for you at some point soon. You could run a bakery near us."

Getting married to a man in Lincoln and never stepping outside the city seemed like a waste, and the last thing Bronwyn would want to do. Besides, the only other bakers in town either had sons she didn't like or daughters. "I don't think it's the right time, Papa."

"What makes you say that?"

She nodded at a pair of armed soldiers walking past.

He hefted a bag of precious white flour over his shoulder. "You about sold out?"

"Almost. We'll need to bring more rolls for the afternoon."

"Right. Let's go." They trundled the cart back to the bakery inside the city, where her stepmother and Wyot were doing a brisk trade. Papa eagerly shared the good news about the order and began preparing loaves. Once they were proofing, he took Wyot with him back to the market, with a serious look at Bronwyn before parting.

Bronwyn and her stepmother worked all afternoon, baking and selling to whoever entered the shop. By nightfall, they were glad to have sold the lot of what they'd baked, and they just had time to attend Mass in the evening when Papa and Wyot came back, the cart full of bags of flour for the next day.

Papa checked on the fine, white rolls and once they were ready, covered them with a cloth and brought her with him, walking up the steep hill to the castle. They were both out of breath by the time they'd reached the top—the road Steep Hill had earned its name for a reason. Her father was so tired, he had to rest. Just inside the castle gate, he gasped, his white breath puffing white clouds in the evening air. "You go on ahead, Bronwyn. I'll just rest a minute. Deliver the rolls to the kitchen and come back. I'll be here waiting for you."

At the gate, a pair of guards questioned her, but when she revealed the breads and gave the name of de Grecy, they parted and let her through. She swallowed and walked inside, wheeling the small cart with the lovely, white loaves through a very large courtyard lit with torches. Men in armor strolled by and directed her to the pathways and corridors to the kitchens. Once she'd reached them, she stepped into chaos.

Cooks, pages, and potboys ran about, plating dishes and turning spits, others stirring soup, bubbling broth, and pottage in various cauldrons. Servants arranged food and took dishes, returning others, all amidst the noise of clattering plates and utensils scraping against trenchers.

One middle-aged cook looked at her. "What do you want? You lost?"

"No, I have an order of white bread for Master de Grecy."

The burly man's eyebrows knit together. He crossed a pair of thick arms over his round stomach.

"He ordered them and paid," Bronwyn explained. "For tonight, he said. He'll be cross if he doesn't get them."

The man whistled and called over a fellow cook, a tall, stocky man whose apron was stained and whose sleeves were pushed back over burly arms. "Who's this?"

"I'm Bronwyn. My father is Alan Blakenhale. We run a bakery in town."

The man nodded. "You help him?"

"Yes."

"You help make these?"

"No. Not for something this nice. They were ordered by Hugh de Grecy. Is he here?"

The men laughed. "You won't find him here. He's at the table."

"Should I go to him?"

"No. Not unless you want a hiding. Give 'em here, we'll see to it," the stocky man said, pulling the cart toward him. He whipped off the cloth and surveyed the round buns. "Manchets?"

"Yes, sir."

"I'm no 'sir.' But these are good. No sand added?" He picked up one and felt it.

"No," Bronwyn said.

"De Grecy will be pleased. He's been talking about it to the good brother, those knight friends of his, and anyone who will listen. A little gift for the king."

She gulped. "King Stephen?"

"Is there any other?" the stocky man said with a shake of his head, rolling up his sleeves. "Mind yourself, girl. Help us unload these and then be off with you."

She helped the men unload the loaves and glanced around the kitchen. The stocky fellow said, "You look skinny. You can stay for a bite to eat if you want. There're scraps to be had from the head table, and the meat drippings."

If the kitchen were not already noisy, he would have heard her stomach growl.

He laughed. Apparently, he had heard it. "I'm Godfrey. This

is Odo. Take a seat and we'll save you a plate."

She sat but realized her father was waiting. She got to her feet. "Thank you, but I can't. I have to go. My papa is waiting on me outside."

"Off you go, then. Farewell, girl." Godfrey waved.

She turned to leave when she spied a servant leaning over the loaves. He was slim and moved quickly, but his manner disturbed her. A dark-green hood was pulled low over his face. He bent over the rolls, his arms moving as he did something, but she couldn't tell what. An uneasy feeling grew in her gut as she spied him hovering over the white loaves.

"What's he doing?" she asked.

The man in question glanced back, revealing a scruff of black hair. He tugged the green hood more over his face and sprinkled more of something atop the loaves.

"What'd you say? Speak up," Odo said, evidently distracted. He crossed his arms over his chest, frowning at two boys flicking soapy water at each other. "Oi, quit playing around!"

"That man. I think he's messing about with our rolls." She pointed, but no one paid any attention to her. And she spoke too quietly, she realized. Amidst the hustle and bustle of the kitchen, louder voices than hers were filling the space.

"Oi!" She darted over and grabbed his arm, but he shoved her back. She crashed against a potboy and they landed on the floor.

"Watch it," the boy complained. Her dress and hands now dirty, she helped the boy up, but the man had disappeared.

"That man. Did you see him? Where did he go?" she asked.

The boy shook his head and shot her a wary glance.

"What man? I didn't see anyone." Odo strode over to her. "You should go. We've got enough to do without you tripping over everyone."

"But that man—" she started, cut off by a scream.

A woman's shriek stopped everything. It was followed by a loud thump, like something heavy hitting the floor. All voices inside the kitchen quieted. The only sounds were the bubbling pots of sauces and soups, and the sizzling roasting meat on the spit as it turned. Bronwyn ran out into the castle corridor to see. There, a woman of middle age had crumpled to the floor.

Bronwyn went to her side. The woman wore a dress of fine-spun wool and a necklace that dangled at her throat. Her skin was pale and her eyes were closed, her mouth hung open.

"What happened?" a guard asked.

"I don't know. I heard a scream and found her. I think she's fainted."

Bronwyn gently shook her, but the woman didn't awaken. Tension seized Bronwyn's chest, and she gently peered down at the woman's body, leaning close.

"What are you doing?" the guard asked.

"Checking to see if she's breathing. Can you fetch someone?"

By this time, a few cooks and more guards had entered the corridor. "What's going on here?" one asked.

"This lady fainted."

"Fetch a physician. Where's Brother Bartholomew?"

A guard was dispatched to find him, and Bronwyn stayed there, trying to wake the woman, when she was conscious of a few boys standing close, watching. She turned to one. "You."

Five pairs of eyes glanced at her.

"Go bring me a spice. Or a bit of fish. Something smelly."

A boy in the group of about twelve years old, asked, "Cooked or not cooked?"

"It doesn't matter, as long as it stinks. Bring it here."

The boy left, and Bronwyn held the woman's hand. She didn't know who she was or why she'd fainted, but she didn't want to leave her side. Perhaps she felt as alone as Bronwyn did.

Odo came out of the kitchens. "What's happening here? Why are you all standing around like a bunch of sticks? If it's more work you need..."

"A lady's fainted. She might be dead," a boy said.

Odo's eyebrows rose, and he saw Bronwyn. "What are you doing?"

"Waiting for help. I can't wake her."

He pushed forward and shook the unconscious woman, then slapped her cheeks.

"Oi, stop that!" Bronwyn said. "You'll hurt her."

"She might already be dead. Did you see what happened?" Odo asked.

"No. I was in the kitchen when I heard her scream."

"Come on, girl, there's nothing for you here. Go home to your father. Where's Brother Bartholomew?"

"Someone's gone to get him," one of the boys said.

"All right, then, leave the good lady be. All of you, back to work."

"But—" Bronwyn paused. "I don't want to leave her."

"You're not her maidservant. There are guards enough to look after her." Muttering, Odo added, "Not that they did any good."

A boy came bustling up, holding a very stinky dead fish in his hands. "Will this do?"

"What foolishness is this? The lady needs a physician, not a fish. What are you thinking? Do you have wool for brains?" Odo turned on the boy, whose face grew pink.

"I asked him for it," Bronwyn said, motioning the boy forward. She took the fish and held it beneath the woman's nose.

In seconds, the woman's eyes fluttered, and she opened her eyes. "What? What? What happened? Where am I?" Then a moment later, she cried, "I saw him! I saw him with my own eyes. William de Roumare, here. He was walking the halls."

There were a few exchanged looks and smirks as people digested this. The woman's face turned pink and then red as she looked down. "None of you believe me. But it's true. I saw him!"

A heavyset middle-aged man entered the group. He had a head full of brown, greying hair; a round, surly expression; and an impressive mustache. He wore a knee-length tunic belted at the waist, over hose and shoes. But the small blade hanging at his belt marked him as a warrior, and one not to be trifled with.

"What's this? Mistress de la Haye, are you all right?"

"Sir Nicholas, I saw him," said the lady. "William de Roumare. He was here, walking clear as day. I recognized his black hair, dark as night."

Sir Nicholas turned to the other guards, who looked to him, awaiting instruction. "Send a man to the dungeons and check that de Roumare is there."

Bronwyn held the fish away as people surrounded the woman and helped her sit up. Seeing as maids and guards were present, Bronwyn rose and stepped back. As she followed Odo back to the kitchen, she asked, "What do you mean, the guards didn't do any good, Master Odo?"

"That woman who fainted, she's the chatelaine of the castle, Mistress de la Haye." He added in a hushed voice, "It was she and her husband, the castellan who let de Roumare and de Gernon inside the castle when it all went to hell. Now she's seeing things. Probably just wants attention."

Bronwyn went to check on the rolls that the green-cloaked man had been messing with. The rolls now bore little bits of crumbled-up mushroom on them, some pieces so tiny, there was no chance of brushing them all off. She frowned.

"What are you still doing here, girl?" Godfrey looked over her shoulder at the rolls. "They look good. You can eat one if you want. They'll never know."

She shook her head.

"Well, never mind. We'll serve these now."

"I don't think you should," she told him. "Did you see the man in the green hood?"

Godfrey gave her a look. "No. There are a lot of men who wear green hoods. What of it?"

"The girl thinks she saw someone," Odo said. "Could be trouble."

Godfrey glanced at him, then Bronwyn. "I didn't see anyone. I say serve them."

Odo ran a hand through his thinning hair. "You know we

can't take any chances. Remember last time, when we added a spice to the potatoes and it made the masters cough? They fretted it was poison and we had to deal with their tasters for a fortnight."

"We made the rolls plain. We didn't add anything," Bronwyn said. "You shouldn't serve them."

Odo and Godfrey's expressions hardened.

Odo said, "Girl, you don't make the decisions here." To Godfrey, he said, "She has a point, though. If the man didn't order any mushroom topping, we should brush it all off. He could raise a fuss, or accuse us of mistakes."

"Good idea," Bronwyn said, then she faltered at their dark looks.

Godfrey said, "And just what are we supposed to think? You bring in rolls and then you say you didn't add the mushrooms on top. How do we know this isn't a trick?"

"It's not. Why else would I bring rolls to the castle?" Bronwyn asked.

"Hoping to see the king and queen for yourself, maybe," Godfrey said, his eyes narrowing.

"I didn't. De Grecy ordered them."

Odo said, "You don't have a say in this kitchen. You delivered your rolls, now go. I'll handle this."

Godfrey put his hands on his hips, frowning at them both. "I make the decisions in this kitchen. If I say the rolls are fine, they're fine. I'll even try one and prove it."

Bronwyn swallowed. "But that man messed with them. De Grecy ordered these rolls plain. If he'd wanted a topping, he would've said so."

"D'you really think a man like de Grecy would know about toppings?" Godfrey said. "Or know what he wants? These knights are all the same. They eat, they fight, they sleep around, they die. That's it. And we only deal with safe mushrooms here. Trust me, de Grecy won't care about a bit of mushroom. He might even like it."

"I don't care. Those are my family's rolls we made. Let me take the mushroom toppings off. They should go to de Grecy like he asked." She looked up at Godfrey, taking in his annoyed expression, wishing she were taller.

"What's the problem here?" a familiar voice asked.

Bronwyn whirled around. The golden-haired youth from the market stood there, Rupert the squire. He looked surprised to see her.

"Someone was messing with the rolls I brought in," she said.

"Who?" Rupert asked.

"I don't know. A servant. Someone with black hair in a dark-green hood. I didn't see their face."

"Man or woman?" he asked.

"Man."

Godfrey cut in. "But Odo and I didn't see nobody, and now you're causing a fuss. You think anyone can just walk in here without my approval? Think again. I think you're making it all up. First Mistress de la Haye's seeing things and now you."

"But I wasn't the only one who saw him. The other cooks did too." She looked around, but people either weren't paying attention or were too busy with their own tasks.

"Master Godfrey, I believe her," Rupert said. "If she says she saw someone messing about with the food, I'd take her word."

Bronwyn looked at him, her lips pursed in displeasure. She didn't need nor want him to speak for her.

"Oh? And just what other cooks saw him?" Godfrey retorted.

"Well..." She looked around but didn't recognize the boy she fell over.

"Did any of you lot see a man in a green hood in here, touching the food?" Godfrey called out.

People stopped and looked over. A few shook their heads. Others looked at her blankly.

"See? No one saw this mysterious man but you. Now clear off," Godfrey said to her. To Odo, he said, "I've heard enough about these blasted rolls. Let's bring them in already before they grow stale." He turned to Rupert, his voice hard. "You know as well as I do, Rupert, that we don't want to keep de Grecy waiting."

"But someone's put some kind of mushroom on them. He didn't order that," Bronwyn said, her voice growing heated.

Rupert came to her side. "Hey, there. You say you saw someone in a green hood. I know a squire who got one recently." He turned to Godfrey. "Doesn't Roger come here to taste the food before his master?" He added as an aside to Bronwyn, "His master, Sir Bors, once got sick from eating bad fish. Since then, Roger often tastes his food before it comes out of the kitchen. But Sir Bors doesn't want to seem fearful in front of the other knights, so Roger comes here in secret. It might've been him you saw."

"But that doesn't make sense. Why would he add mushrooms to food not his?"

Rupert shrugged. "His master might've asked for them. He might be taking them specially for his health and not want anyone to know. Or… he might want to play a trick on de Grecy. They are not friends. De Grecy is not popular at court."

"But how would they even know the rolls are for de Grecy?"

Rupert smiled. "These knights often posture and try to one-up each other. If de Grecy ordered expensive rolls for dinner, he'd make sure the other knights knew about it."

"But De Grecy ordered those rolls plain. And the person ran off. If it was this Roger like you say, why wouldn't he have stayed?"

"You think it was someone suspicious?"

"Maybe," Bronwyn said.

"This girl is seeing suspects everywhere," Odo said. "If she did see someone, and I doubt it, it was likely Roger, on an errand for his master. There's nothing to worry about. Let her go home already so I can get these loaves upstairs. We can't keep them waiting."

"But we don't know what kind of mushrooms were sprinkled on there. At least let me take it off," she said.

"We'll sort this," Godfrey said. "Now be off with you."

Bronwyn watched unhappily as the men placed the rolls on a serving platter to be taken into the front room.

"Wait!" she said, gripping a worktable. "What if the mushrooms are poison?"

That stopped all sound into silence. Everyone froze, from the potboy scrubbing pots to the men turning meat on the spit. Even the cooks stopped what they were doing, sauce dripping off of their spoons.

"What are you talking about?" Godfrey asked. "You think Roger would try to poison his master?"

"I don't know this Roger," Bronwyn said. "But if it was him, why would he run away? What was he hiding? Would you let a stranger change your dish? Your sauce?"

"Of course not. But that's different," the cook said.

"How?"

"Well…."

"It seems to me the girl has a point," Rupert said. "We all know they'd be turning the spit for weeks if anyone so much as dared alter your cooking, Master Godfrey."

"That's right. But that's due to me, as the head cook. There's a way and proper order of things. Obviously, if Roger did put mushrooms on the rolls, he had good reason to. He should have come to me first, but I trust the lad. He's honest. Not so suspicious of others." He looked at Bronwyn with meaning.

She stood up to him. "And I'm telling you, de Grecy ordered those rolls plain. What if he doesn't like them and blames me and my father for adding mushrooms when he didn't want it?"

"Then that's on you for making shoddy rolls," Godfrey growled.

Bronwyn glared at him, hands on her hips.

"Oh, for heaven's sake." Godfrey tore a hunk off one of the mushroom rolls and stuffed it into his mouth, chewing furiously. He smiled, swallowed, and helped himself to a cup of wine. "Mmm. The mushrooms taste delicious. See? It's safe. You're worrying about nothing. It's a nice topping. Take the rolls in."

Bronwyn tensed and her shoulders slumped. She felt helpless as a servant carried the rolls out of the kitchen. "But…"

"Go home, girl. And next time, send your father in. You don't belong here. A kitchen's for working, not silly girls with poison in their heads. Next, you'll be thinking someone's trying to murder us all," Godfrey joked.

She picked her way out of the kitchen, stepping around serving boys and cooks, then dodging servants and scullery hands. Her stomach growled at the luxurious smells of fresh bread and beef dripping, but she kept walking, slipping into the shadows at the earliest opportunity until she reached the outside.

"Hey, wait." A hand touched her shoulder.

"What?"

Rupert stood before her. "Don't worry. Godfrey is a bear, but he's not that bad. And he's a good cook. He's just busy and you caught him at a bad time. Don't let him get to you. And he's right about Roger. He's often in here, but he is trustworthy."

She shrugged and kept walking. "He doesn't want me in his kitchen."

"Don't take that to heart. He throws one of the cooks out every day, sometimes every week. But he'd be nothing without all of us, and he knows it." The torch played shadows on his face, showing a friendly smile.

"Thanks for standing up for me back there."

"It's the least I could do for a pretty girl. I never did get your name," he said, keeping pace with her as they walked out into the castle courtyard and past the guards, through the gate, and back out onto the street.

"Do you say that to all the girls?" she asked.

"Only the pretty ones. Especially those who cause trouble in the kitchens." He grinned. "What's your name? Are you hiding it? Is it a bad name?"

"No." Bronwyn frowned. She hated her name. It sounded like a boy's name to her. Why she couldn't have an elegant or pretty name, like Rowena, or Agnes, she didn't know.

"Then why not tell me? Otherwise, I'll have to guess, or give you a new one. Aethelreda… or Marion, maybe."

Bronwyn rolled her eyes. "Keep guessing. Don't you have a knight to get back to?"

"I do, but I wanted to see you safely out first. Want me to walk you home?" Rupert asked.

"No, my father's just waiting for me." Bronwyn raised an arm in greeting at the welcome sight of her papa, who waved back.

All of a sudden, there was a commotion, and a pair of guards raced away. "What's going on?" Bronwyn asked.

"I don't know. You'd better go. G'night." Rupert hurried back toward the gate.

Her father clapped a hand on her shoulder. "There you are. I was beginning to worry. All is well inside there?"

"I think so." She told him the situation about the mushrooms.

He frowned, his expression lit up by the moonlight. "That's very odd. And you didn't see who did this?"

"No. I thought it suspicious, but the head cook, Godfrey, he tasted one of the rolls and said it was fine. They all think that it was likely a squire named Roger who did it, but they declare he's trustworthy, so there's nothing to worry about." She pursed her lips. "I don't like that someone sprinkled mushrooms on it and then ran away."

"Agreed. But it's done now and we were paid, so if they get indigestion, that's on them. Let's go back. Margaret will have pottage waiting for us." He rubbed his hands together.

Her stomach rumbling at the thought of a steaming plate of peas, cabbage, turnips, and carrots in a hearty stew, Bronwyn rolled the cart faster when a voice cried, "After them!"

"Don't let them escape!"

She turned to look and saw guards coming straight at them.

"Papa…." she started.

"What is it?" he asked, turning to see.

In another moment, they were surrounded by armed guards.

Her father stopped the cart and clasped her to his side.

One guard demanded, "Are you the baker? Who delivered the rolls to the king's table?"

"I delivered them to the kitchens. Why?" Bronwyn asked.

"What's this all about?" her father asked.

"Come with us," one guard said.

"What for?"

"On order of the king."

Bronwyn's eyes grew wide. "What?"

"The king has ordered you to an audience with him. Right now."

"But why?"

"He wishes to know why you attempted to poison him."

Chapter Two

B RONWYN BALKED IN disbelief. The mushrooms. They'd been bad, after all. And after all the suspicion she'd raised. But she had bigger problems, as she eyed the unfriendly looks and weapons the guards carried. "Poison? You're joking."

"Bronwyn…" Papa started. To the guards, he said, "This must be some mistake. We are humble bakers, not killers."

"Your rolls killed someone," a guard said.

Bronwyn's mouth dropped open and she tugged on her thick, blonde braid. "Somebody died?"

"Yes. You have to come with us," one of the guards said, hefting a spear in his hands.

"Papa?" she asked.

"Let's go with them," he said.

Surrounded by stern-faced guards, they returned to the castle gates.

"You said it was poison," Bronwyn said. "Was it mush-rooms?"

The guards exchanged a look. "The king has questions for you."

They marched Bronwyn and her father through the gate and into the courtyard, around the tradesmen's entrance, where they bypassed the main building and left the cart outside. They escorted the father and daughter through the buildings past more guards and some very well-dressed people into an antechamber, where her father drew a quick breath.

"Papa?" she asked.

"Just hold your tongue and stay by me," he said. "Nothing will happen to you. And pay attention to what they say. Don't just stand there with your head in the clouds."

They were penned in on all sides by armed guards. The men wore serious expressions and chainmail over their tunics and leggings and carried swords or spears at their sides. They spoke not a word.

Bronwyn swallowed and kept walking. She did not want to be at the end of those spears.

They were escorted into a chamber that gave the impression of grandeur. The room was richly decorated in wide tapestries that spanned twelve feet or more, proudly hanging on wooden walls with deep inset paneling. To her surprise, the room was largely empty, except for a handful of guards at the entrance, who announced them, a pair at their flank, and then a small number of people at the other end of the room.

It wasn't her first time looking upon a king, but it was her first-ever royal audience, and at spearpoint. When he had returned to Lincoln with his forces, King Stephen had ridden through the streets and once he'd retaken the castle, he had paraded through and even waved at the crowds. Bronwyn had seen him and the queen from a distance, as the streets had been packed with people. This was her first time seeing them up close. Now standing just feet away from them, she felt special, just being in their presence. But now she felt terrified—and lighthead-ed, as if she might faint. Would he kill her over some mushrooms? She trembled and realized she was literally shaking in her shoes. She put a hand to her thigh to stop shaking and bit her lip to distract herself.

King Stephen was older than she'd imagined. He was middle-aged, somewhere between mid-forties and fifty years, and had sharply-cut blond hair that curled above his shoulders. He wore a richly woven tunic of red over dark leggings, tied by a golden belt that caught the candlelight, and a heavy golden chain around his shoulders that hung to his chest. His skin was tanned and his eyes were kind, but his expression was serious. He had a look about him that suggested in other circumstances, he might have been friendly, but not tonight. A big man with a small crown on his head, he filled out a wooden throne with a tired demeanor as he surveyed Bronwyn and her father.

Beside him sat his lady, whom she guessed to be Queen Matilda. She was a pretty woman in her mid-thirties, with her dark hair parted at the center and hanging in two long braids interwoven with ribbons, whilst the rest of her hair was covered by a veil and a small headdress. She wore a pink dress of fine material, golden necklaces about her neck, and a thin, golden belt that pinned back her small waist. Her expression too was soft and kind, but as her gaze flicked to Bronwyn, she could sense a strength in her dainty form, and a quiet fury if provoked.

Behind them stood two armed guards who watched, and a youngish man dressed in a monk's habit and a tonsure, the telltale bald spot on his head. A wooden cross that had a piece of shined glass at its center that caught the light hung from his neck. Tall, thin, and lanky, he surveyed Bronwyn with suspicion, beside a heavyset man armed with a sword sheathed at his waist. There was no doubting these other people's expressions. Standing before them was also Odo, the cook, who glared at her.

"So you are the bakers," the queen's light, polite voice said with a heavy French accent.

"Yes, Your Grace," her father said. "I am Alan Blakenhale and this is my daughter, Bronwyn."

She met their eyes, then glanced back down at the floor.

"Do you know who I am?" the man on the throne asked.

"You are King Stephen, and that is your lady wife, Queen Matilda." Bronwyn eyed her delicate shoes.

"Yes," the king said. "We are joined by the good Brother Bartholomew and the head of my guard, Sir Nicholas de Aldenham. I believe you already met Master Odo. Young lady, mind you tell us what happened tonight."

Bronwyn relayed the story of how de Grecy had ordered the rolls and how she'd seen someone messing with them until the scream, then ending her tale by pointing out Godfrey had eaten a roll himself and dismissed her.

King Stephen said, "And Godfrey is now very ill. Brother Bartholomew examined him and says it appears the man was poisoned by deadly mushrooms, and it will be a miracle if the cook survives the night."

Bronwyn breathed in noisily. So it was poison. Just as she'd feared.

King Stephen asked, "And you, Master Odo. Did you see Roger?"

"No, Your Grace. But he is in the kitchen sometimes and we know him well."

The king raised an eyebrow. "But you didn't see him. And apparently, he ran away, rather than stay in the kitchen. Why would he run?"

"I do not know, Your Grace."

"You say he is a squire. Who is his master? Let us call them both here, at once."

Sir Nicholas spoke up. Bronwyn recognized him as the senior man-at-arms who'd ordered the guards around earlier. "Your Grace, the boy's master is Sir Bors."

"Bring him here."

In moments, a large man came in. He was a noble, that much was clear. He wore a knight's tunic with bold colors over hose and sensible boots, and he stood tall with broad shoulders. His voice held a deep, bass timbre. "Where is the boy? Have you found him?"

Bronwyn imagined if he chose to raise his voice, it could clear forests. Birds would fly out from the trees and the very ground would tremble.

"No, we thought you would know," King Stephen said. "It's thought he was in the kitchen tonight. We have reason to think he was behind the mushrooms on the rolls, which we have now determined were poisoned. What was he doing there?"

Sir Bors's eyes grew wide. "I do not know, Your Grace. The boy has been missing since this afternoon. He wasn't around to serve me dinner and I thought you'd found him drunk or whoring somewhere. You don't think he's behind this?"

King Stephen steepled his hands.

"I don't know where the boy is, but he wouldn't poison anyone. Neither of us would. I wouldn't. We're both loyal, Your Grace." Sir Bors tugged his tunic down from his throat.

"A poisoner *would* say that," Brother Bartholomew pointed out.

Sir Bors shot the monk a dirty look. "And where were you when all this happened, eh? Off kissing the feet of some nobleman?" He looked at King Stephen and swallowed. "I swear I'm no traitor, Your Grace. Honest. And I don't know where the boy is. But when he gets back, I'll wallop him into next Sunday."

"Please, Sir Bors." The king raised a hand. "It appears that either young Roger has disappeared, the girl is making up tales, or someone else was in your kitchen, Master Odo."

Bronwyn was about to defend herself but Sir Nicholas cut her off.

"Hush, girl. Do not speak until you are spoken to," he admonished.

The queen sniffed with derision.

"This is nonsense," Brother Bartholomew said, his upper lip curled back in a sneer. "The girl is clearly lying. She's probably a traitor, paid to kill you, Your Grace. Perhaps you both. Or even the entire household."

"And what reason would I have to do that? I don't know any of you." That earned Bronwyn some surprised looks. "Besides, we only made these rolls because de Grecy ordered them. Where is he? He can tell you the same thing."

"De Grecy is dead. Your rolls killed him," Brother Bartholomew said.

"What?" Bronwyn's eyes widened. Her mouth hung open.

"He ate one of the mushroom rolls and became ill," Sir Nicholas informed her.

Odo frowned and scratched his double chin. "I don't understand it. I never saw anyone. This girl came in and started causing a fuss. Godfrey tried the mushrooms and said they were delicious—"

"You let the rolls come out of the kitchen, knowing they were tampered with?" Sir Nicholas asked.

"No, of course not," Odo said. "But none of us saw anyone and we thought if anyone had messed about, it was just Roger, acting on orders from his lord to prepare his food."

The king and Sir Nicholas exchanged glances.

"But we know those rolls were ordered by de Grecy, so why would Sir Bors have asked his squire to touch them?" Sir Nicholas asked.

Odo's face turned red. "I don't know. It was just a thought, as we've seen some squires like Roger in the kitchen before."

"Then I was right. Whoever was wearing the green hood poisoned the rolls. Be it Roger, or someone else. I knew something was wrong about him." Bronwyn looked at King Stephen and Queen Matilda. "I'm sorry, I should have tried harder to make sure the rolls weren't taken out. I knew something was wrong and I did try to say—"

King Stephen held up a hand, his expression tired. "Enough. It is too late for apologies. A man is dead, and my head cook is sick. Guards, send out a search for Roger."

Sir Nicholas said, "You Grace, I can speak for the boy. He would not have done anything to hurt his king and queen. He is a good and loyal servant to the Crown."

Sir Bors gave a loud, "Aye!" but quieted at a stern look from the king.

King Stephen surveyed Sir Nicholas with a level gaze, then fixed his sight on the cook. "Master Odo. You understand the gravity of this situation we find ourselves in. You feed us, you prepare our food, and yet a man has died at my table. Your master is sick. If he lives, he will face punishment for this crime. But you, how can I trust anything you say, or safely eat the food you place before us? If you did not see anyone, then that is negligence, and if you did see someone but chose not to interfere, then that is an act against the Crown. Which is it? Are you a fool or a traitor?" King Stephen's voice was so calm and measured, yet it held a hint of danger about it. He sounded so reasonable, he might have been asking for a cup of wine.

Odo shook. For such a large man as he was, his voice was barely audible. "I couldn't say, Your Grace. But I am no traitor."

The king's expression darkened, and his gaze pinned Odo to the spot where he stood. "Leave us. Pray that Master Godfrey recovers."

Odo bowed his head gravely. "Yes, Your Grace."

"Excuse me," Bronwyn said. "But that's not fair." She bit her lip and thought furiously, *He's the head cook now—shouldn't he be to blame for letting rolls out that were poisoned? She'd tried to stop them going out and no one would listen. And he'd admitted to not having a proper watch over the food that leaves the kitchen.* But even to her ears, the protest sounded whiny.

The king glanced at her. His voice held a note of warning. "It is our decision."

The king stroked his beard. "Now that leaves us with a problem. Thanks to this unfortunate incident, I am now down a man, and a cook."

"I agree with Brother Bartholomew, Your Grace," Sir Nicholas said, eyeing Bronwyn and her father. "She's likely a spy or a trained killer, sent here to infiltrate the castle and cause trouble. They likely both are, Your Grace."

"I am not a spy," Bronwyn said.

"Prove it." His right hand edged toward his sword.

She swallowed. "How can I? I—"

Bronwyn's father put a hand on the back of her neck. It was a power move, and one meant to stopper her tongue. It worked.

He said, "Forgive us, Your Graces, but we are but simple bakers. The only thing Bronwyn is trained to do is bake pies. I should have checked the rolls before they went from the kitchen, and that is my fault. My daughter should not be blamed. If you wish to punish someone for this, punish me."

"No," Bronwyn said, her thick, blonde braid whipping around her shoulder and striking her chin. "No. You did nothing. This wasn't our fault. Someone messed about with our rolls."

Queen Matilda surveyed her thoughtfully, a dainty index finger tapping her lips. Her golden ring winked in the light. "My love, I wonder. Perhaps we might make use of them."

"My lady?" King Stephen asked.

"As you say, my lord, you are down a knight in your court and a cook. We could punish this baker and his daughter—"

"The good lady speaks sense," Sir Nicholas rumbled.

Queen Matilda frowned at the interruption. "But I think it would be better if we were to use them. I too, tasted one of the rolls, but mine had no mushrooms. I think the girl was clever to notice something amiss and meant to stop it but was overlooked. If the cooking staff did not see anything, that is inexcusable alone, but for her to notice a man interfering with the food to go to our table, and yet be ignored?" She shook her head. "We cannot dismiss these mistakes. Master Godfrey will account for this. One man has already died. Who's to say what could have happened if we had not thrown the rolls away?"

The men nodded.

Queen Matilda said in a sweet, kind voice, "I did not fall ill, and I found the roll to be delicious. I should like more. I would not wish to ruin this good baker's livelihood over such a matter, especially when he had no part in it. I would suggest we put the girl to work in our kitchens."

"But…" Odo started.

"She is smart and has a good heart," the queen said.

Bronwyn felt a wave of warmth come over her. A queen had just complimented her. Wait until she told her stepmother and

Wyot.

Queen Matilda added, "She is honest, I think. I believe she meant no harm. Let us have her work in the kitchens for a time. We will need the help until we can find a new cook. Say until the feast of Purification of St. Mary? By then, I trust we will no longer need her services."

"But what if she is the poisoner?" Sir Nicholas asked. "That would allow her to attempt to poison again."

"Not under Master Odo's watchful eye, I am sure." Queen Matilda eyed Bronwyn.

"No, Your Grace, I mean, yes. I mean…" Odo stammered.

"She will work in your kitchens as Master Godfrey regains his strength. I trust you can step into his shoes in the meantime, Master Odo."

Odo blinked and stood up taller. "Yes, Your Grace."

The queen waved him away. He ducked his head lower and hurried as fast as his squat legs could carry him.

"You speak wisely, my dear. That is a good decision." King Stephen looked at Bronwyn's father. "You will agree to this?"

As if there were any question. "Yes, Your Grace." Her father bowed his head, showing the beginning of a balding pate, but his hands were stiff against his tunic and leggings.

"Very good," King Stephen said. "That is all."

Bronwyn looked up at Queen Matilda, daring to meet her gaze.

"One more thing," Queen Matilda said, giving them a level look. She clasped her hands, almost as if in prayer. "We cannot allow this crime to go unpunished. Until we determine who it was who interfered with the bread rolls and killed de Grecy, we must hold someone accountable."

"Take the father," King Stephen ordered.

"No," Bronwyn breathed.

"Bronwyn," her father said, grasping her hand.

"Take him away," King Stephen said.

"Why?" Bronwyn said. "He's done nothing wrong. Take me

instead."

"Don't be daft, Bronwyn," her father said.

"We are not in the habit of imprisoning young women. We will take your father," Queen Matilda said.

Sir Nicholas addressed the king, "Your Grace, I respect your counsel. But what if she is the poisoner and tries to do it again?"

Queen Matilda frowned at him. "Then we will know it's her, and they both will pay for their crimes against us."

Seeing Bronwyn's look of protest, King Stephen said, "We must act. Until we find Roger, we will hold the baker in our prison. We cannot overlook the chance that they were working together, with the rolls being the delivery method for their attempted murder plot. To do nothing would be a sign of weakness, and would invite others to play their hand. My hands are tied. Guards."

Odo bowed low in apology.

Bronwyn hugged her father tightly as the guards tore them apart, their heavy gloved fingers digging into her arms and pulling her away. They gripped so hard, she knew she'd have bruises later but didn't care.

Tears came to her eyes as her father was pinned by two guards, his hands pressed behind his back and tied together with a bit of rope. A spear was jabbed into his back, and he bit back a noise of pain.

"You don't have to do that! He won't run away," Bronwyn said hotly.

One of the guards glared at her, but King Stephen bid them away with a hand.

Bronwyn watched, mute with anger as the guards marched her father away, her hands clenched into fists. She looked at the king and queen, her eyes wet and blazing. A tear rolled down her cheek, but she refused to acknowledge it.

King Stephen's hand stiffened and curled over the armrests of his wooden throne, his eyes darting around the room. He looked to be seeing would-be killers in every corner. Meanwhile, Queen

Matilda looked at her with interest. "Such spirit. Would that you were a man, I would make you a squire."

Bronwyn met her gaze, no longer caring if she were to be dismissed or struck dead. Her father was gone. Her family's livelihood was threatened, all in the space of an evening. What more could go wrong?

"I shall look forward to more of those rolls, girl," Queen Matilda said.

King Stephen clapped and the guards led Bronwyn away.

Once she stood outside the castle walls and the gate, she wheeled the empty cart away without a word, relieved at the harsh, cold air that chilled her face. Not until she stood back in the shop did her fierce courage disappear.

"What's taken you both so long? I expected you back ages ago," her stepmother said as Bronwyn walked in the door. "Why the long face? Where's your father gone?"

She began to cry. Her stepmother took Bronwyn in her arms, patting her back. "What's happened? Where's your father?"

Bronwyn told her the whole story.

Margaret collapsed in the nearest chair. "Alan's gone?" It took her a moment. "What were you thinking?"

"I…"

"Are you out of your senses? Involving yourself in castle business? And now someone is dead." She let out a sound of disgust and shook her head. "You've landed us in hot water now, Bronwyn. I've lost your father, and you are to work in the castle kitchens for the month." She frowned.

"I'm so sorry, Mama. It's all my fault."

She crossed her arms beneath her chest. "This is madness. Poison? And now you're to work in the castle?" She drummed her fingers on the worktable beside her. "I've got half a mind to speak to this Queen Matilda myself and make her see sense."

"Don't, Mama." The last thing Bronwyn wanted was for her to march up the hill and curse at the guards and king and queen. They all might end up in the castle dungeons together.

"Those cooks should have recognized the mushrooms as poisonous at once. My parents taught me when I was a child how to tell the safe mushrooms from the poisonous ones." Margaret's expression was stern. "I know your father must have taught you about mushrooms before."

Margaret clucked her tongue. "In any case, this isn't your fault. Your father should never have taken on that last-minute request from that nobleman. Thank the lord he paid first. You should have dropped off the rolls at the kitchen and returned home with your father. Then, none of this mess would be our problem. But it is what it is." She sniffed. "And those cooks shouldn't have ignored you when you pointed out the mysterious man. We would never sell food that wasn't prepared by us, and I don't see why the castle's cooks would let any food like that go out to the king and queen. And that queen, blaming your father for something that wasn't his doing. It's not right. Not right at all." Margaret wiped away a tear. "Your father in prison. What are we going to do?"

She didn't speak another word to Bronwyn that night.

The next day on her way to the castle, Bronwyn bumped into another apprentice baker, Alfred. They'd known each other since they'd been children, when he'd steal apples out of an orchard and share them with her, and she'd hidden the extras in her skirts.

He stood taller than Bronwyn and was older by two to three years. He had sandy hair that fell into his eyes and light-blue eyes. He'd changed from the scrawny boy who used to pull her braids. Now he was strong and his arms, used to long hours of baking, were muscular and filled out his sleeves. His mouth quirked in a smile when he saw her. "Bronwyn. Is it true? Your father tried to poison someone at the palace?"

"No." Her mouth instantly pulled into a frown.

His smile grew wider. "So you're not trying to kill the king and queen?"

"No."

He jabbed her side with his elbow. "Don't pretend like you

didn't want to. Half the city is happy they're here, and the other half wish the French wench were in power. Your pa never liked politics, but that doesn't matter a whit when you're stuck in the middle of it. What happened?"

She told him the story and he whistled. "You're deep in the muck now, eh?"

Bronwyn glared at him and started walking.

He put a hand on her arm, stopping her. "Hey, wait. Don't go. I was only teasing. I know your family would never. And don't worry. The time'll pass soon. I sometimes deliver bread and rolls to the palace, so I'll see you sometimes."

She brightened. At least there would be one friendly face there. "I'm nervous," she admitted.

"Why?"

"What if I don't know how to bake anything and they hate me?"

He laughed. "A person used your rolls to poison someone and you're worried about not baking well enough? Of course that's what you'd think about."

"I'd better go." Bronwyn left him with a wave and went on to the palace, where a new pair of guards demanded to know her name and what she was doing there. Once in the kitchens, Odo gave her orders.

It was clear that everyone in the kitchens knew her father was in prison for allegedly conspiring with a poisoner. From the darting, little looks and suspicious glances she received, Bronwyn knew she was persona non grata, meaning that she had no friends, and no one really to talk to.

Godfrey, for all of his bravado in swallowing a bite of the mushroom loaf, had fallen ill and was at death's door. One bite had been enough to knock a man of his stature off his feet. From the cooks prepping dough to the boys polishing cups, everyone treated her with suspicion. Some likely believed she was in cahoots with the alleged poisoner, and some wondered if she was trying to get the squire Roger in trouble. Either way, she was unpopular.

Her status became clear to her that morning, when she spotted a sauce bubbling over and went to take it off the heat and give it a stir. But as she reached for it, an older cook brushed her aside. "I'll get that."

"But I—" she started.

"It's fine. I've got it." His voice was pointed, sharp and unfriendly.

Bronwyn stood back as he attended to the sauce, feeling useless.

"But I can help. I was just trying to—"

"I said, *I've got it*. What are you going to do, accuse me of poisoning the sauce?" The cook's dark eyes were hard. "You've made a lot of fuss. How do we know you're not going to try and poison us all, eh?"

Her jaw dropped open. She wished she could think of a smart retort, but nothing came to mind. Her mind was blank. She stood by, her mouth fixed in a frown.

She soon realized that the people there either didn't believe she wouldn't try to poison them all or they didn't think she knew her way around a kitchen and therefore, she couldn't be trusted with any but the smallest of tasks.

For Bronwyn, that meant pot scrubbing. She'd never liked scrubbing pots or lugging buckets of water from the well but wasn't one to complain. Not now.

When she got home that day, her stepmother's initial kindness and patience had dried up. After a day of hard work, without her husband to lean on and share the load, Margaret was tired, sweaty and cross. Up before dawn and working past dusk, Margaret had dashed around trying to make breads and fulfill orders, as well as take payment and send Wyot out to deliver breads. In the next few days that passed, Bronwyn found her, more often than not, either dead on her feet and stumbling around or asleep in her chair at the dinner table, with a cold plate of pottage waiting for her for when Bronwyn returned home. Her father's presence was sorely missed.

Bronwyn ran into Alfred again one morning and grumbled when he pinched her elbow instead of saying *hello*. She aimed a kick at him and he dodged, laughing.

"What?" she demanded.

"Stop with the scowling."

"How can I when Papa is in prison? He could die. And Mama's so tired, she's barely awake long enough to talk to me."

His expression softened. "I know. She's trying to carry on the business herself, but it's too much for any one person alone. And she's worried about your pa." He gave her a warm smile. "I was hoping I'd bump into you today. I wanted to tell you. I've talked about it with Master Johann and it's fine for me to help out your family in the bakery while your pa's in prison."

Her sour expression disappeared. "You will? But how? You're a journeyman elsewhere so…"

He shrugged. "Master Johann's taken on another apprentice and that means too many of us working for him. He never was one to turn down money. Anyway, he's got two apprentices and another about to be made journeyman. He doesn't need me. I talked to him this morning and he can spare me."

"Oh, Alfred, that would be wonderful. Thank you." Bronwyn touched his arm.

He brightened. "No problem."

That evening, she found her stepmother in good spirits, having accepted Alfred's kind offer. "We're saved, no thanks to you," Margaret said with an even look and a yawn. "I always knew that boy was a good soul. Very Christian of him, to help out when we're in need."

Bronwyn said nothing. She didn't want to rile her further.

Margaret glared at her. "Here you are living it up at the castle, and I'm so busy I don't even have time to visit your father. Clean the bakery." She handed Bronwyn a broom.

"I've been visiting him every day. I'm bringing him food." It was true. The second day at the castle she'd started visiting him instead of attending church services. Her disappearance had so far gone unnoticed, she hoped.

"Well, it's not very good, is it? He shouldn't have to be relying on you for food at all, but then we've got you to thank, don't we? If you had just delivered the rolls and returned home, rather than mixing with those castle folk, we wouldn't be in this mess."

Seeing Bronwyn's look of protest, she said, "I know. It's not your fault what happened. But it's the devil's own luck that you got mixed up in all this. Bronwyn Sibyl Blakenhale…" Margaret used her full name, a sure sign of her anger. "I've been working and baking non-stop, and poor Wyot has been working at all hours. There's not enough of us to manage the shop and sell at the market, and…" Her chin gave a tremble. "It's just hard without your father. He did so much. We need help, especially now with winter upon us. The business doesn't stop just because your father is in prison."

Bronwyn stood there mutely, broom in hand. She couldn't rebut what Margaret had said.

"I just thank the Lord that young Alfred has come to help. He's doing that out of the goodness of heart, and Christian charity, mark my words." Margaret walked away, over to the stepladder, where she slowly climbed up to the upper floor, where the family slept. A day passed, then two. Bronwyn soon fell into a pattern: each morning, she would rise and take breakfast with Margaret and Wyot, then work in the castle kitchens, scrubbing, delivering platters of food or drink, washing, turning the spit, whatever was needed. She became no better than a dogsbody but didn't care. After a midday meal, some of the people went to Mass, but she slipped away down to the castle dungeons, where she gave the guard a bit of bread or a coin and went to see her father.

He looked dirty and despondent. He was a sorry sight, but she made sure to keep him fed and tell him the news of her working in the kitchens and how Margaret and Wyot were doing. For an hour each day, instead of attending Mass, she would tell him stories and try to amuse him. He seemed to like her visits, but when the church bells rang she knew it was time to return.

Each day at the end, he asked if she'd learnt anything about the poisoner, but she had nothing to tell. She'd learnt nothing. She would occasionally ask in the kitchen about Roger, but as soon as she mentioned his name, the cooks' eyes turned shifty and they refused to speak about it.

A feeling of dread came over her as she bid her father good-bye and clasped his hand through the iron bars of his cell. His hand was cold, and it chilled her. She had to do something.

On the third day, she was summoned. A page came to her, a boy of no older than eleven, and barely as high as her chest. He had short, blond hair cropped close to his head. "You are Miss Bronwyn?" he asked in a high-pitched voice.

"Yes," she said, scrubbing the inside of a pot, her hands wet.

"My lady wants to see you."

"If it's about the bread, she can ask the cook. Odo is just there." Bronwyn pointed.

"It's you she wants."

"What for?"

"She wants a white roll. With honey. She said you'd make it for her."

Bronwyn tensed. "Your lady is…"

"The queen," he said proudly. "You coming?"

She looked around the kitchen. "It's going to take time."

She didn't tell him she'd never made a white roll before. She didn't know how her father did it. She'd only watched him a few times, which wasn't the same as doing it herself.

The boy disappeared and she asked Odo, "How do I make a white roll?"

"You don't know this?"

"My father always did it."

"Ask him. I'm not telling you our secrets." The man turned his back on her.

Anger and indignation warred within her. She'd worked

steadily in this man's kitchen for the past week and no one had died. He wouldn't even help her now?

She ran to the dungeons, her thin shoes slapping the stone and wooden floors, not stopping until she'd dashed past the guard, who looked half-asleep, and hurried to her father.

"Bronwyn, what's wrong?" He stood at the front of the cell in an instant.

"Tell me how to make the white rolls. The queen wants them."

He blinked at her. "Will none of the cooks do it?"

"She's tasked me with it and they won't help me. Please," Bronwyn urged him.

His face set in a frown, he told her how, with strict instructions. Once he was confident she'd memorized those, he bid her run. It would take time to make and she'd wasted enough precious moments already.

Bronwyn returned to the kitchens, out of breath, and put aside the clean pot she'd been scrubbing.

"Oi, what are you doing?" one of the boys asked.

"Working. The queen wants a roll."

"So what? Give her one of those." He nodded to the growing pile over on one of the worktables.

"She wants a white roll with honey. A special one," she said, clearing a bit of workspace and starting to sift white flour.

He crossed his arms. "Not like the one that killed that man…"

"Yes. But without poison."

He stood in her way.

Bronwyn squared up to him, her blonde braid flashing angrily as a horse's tail. "The queen has asked for it. Are you going to tell her you stopped me when I was following her orders?"

His expression faltered, and he stepped back, glowering. "It's above your station."

"You think I don't know that?" She moved around him and set to work hastily, trying to remember her father's instructions. "Either help me or move. Just think, if she doesn't like it, she'll blame me, anyway, and throw me in the dungeons. So either way, it's no problem of yours." She spoke through gritted teeth and began scattering flour on the worktable.

Bronwyn could feel him watching but didn't care—she was just angry. Angrier than she'd been in a long time. It was as if rage had quietly burned inside her, hotter than any furnace, and the cook's snide refusal to help her had simply struck the tinder and set it alight. She mixed the dough, sifted and mixed again, then prepared it just like her father had instructed, adding in honey to make it sweet.

Other cooks watched, but once they'd heard who it was for, they kept their distance.

As she was just making a small number, it took less time than she'd expected. She made four, just in case one was wrong, and prepared a plate for them. In the meantime, she tidied up her workspace, wiped the worktable clean, and returned to scrubbing pots, keeping an eye on her rolls.

It was just as well, for Odo appeared at her shoulder as she removed them from the oven with a wooden peel and dumped them on a serving plate. He took the least attractive one and helped himself, biting into the soft, hot roll, hefting it from burly hand to burly hand. "Ha!" he said.

"What?" Bronwyn set aside the peel and looked at him, hands on her hips.

"Not bad. Not as good as what we would make, but not terrible. They may go." He waved his hand grandly.

The pageboy stood waiting. Bronwyn took the rolls and followed him up into the castle keep, through corridors, and into rooms, with more than one servant, courtier, and person watching and sniffing the air with interest as they walked past.

"Keep up and don't stop to talk to anyone," he said. "Otherwise, they'll nick your rolls and she'll get mad."

Bronwyn followed him to a private apartment, decorated richly with tapestries and intricately carved wooden furniture. Queen Matilda sat reading and lowered her book. "Thank you."

She watched as Bronwyn set the platter on a side table near her. The queen took up the roll, biting into it.

"Delicious. Thank you, Samuel. That will be all." She put the roll aside as he left. "Now. You can be at no loss to understand why I called you here."

Bronwyn shook her head.

"It might surprise you to know that I have since learnt a bit about you, Miss Blakenhale. No doubt you wish to prove your father's innocence, yes?"

Bronwyn nodded.

"I thought as much. I have also heard that when the good Mistress de la Haye fainted, you went to her side and were loath to leave her. That you had the good sense to try to wake her with… Is it true you tried to waken her from a faint with a fish?"

Bronwyn blushed. "I've seen ladies faint before, my lady. I thought that if she were near something smelly, it would awaken her senses. I did ask for a spice or a fish, something strong-smelling. It did work."

The queen smiled. "As I thought. You have a quick mind. I have been thinking over this, and I have made enquiries but have gotten nowhere. The boy in question is still nowhere to be found. So I have a little task for you. I understand that you tried to stop the rolls being sent out and were ignored. Perhaps we might make use of that. I want you to look into this matter and find out who the poisoner is. We do not know who poisoned those rolls, or if it was this missing squire the cooks speak of, but it is not enough that we have imprisoned your father for this. We need to find who did it and stop them before they try again. I have no doubt that whoever it was aimed to kill my husband or myself."

Bronwyn breathed in. Would she be imprisoned too?

"It is why I wanted you to start work in the kitchens. You can keep an eye on what goes out, as no doubt Master Odo will, and meanwhile, you can start looking into this. I also wish for you to learn more about the dead man, de Grecy. You should know he joined our court only recently, having turned from *that woman's* camp. He was keen to show support for my husband, but I wonder why would someone use his rolls to attempt to kill us? They would know that if we survived, his life would be forfeit." She looked at Bronwyn. "Find out. Next time I ask for a white roll from you, I want information with it."

Bronwyn nodded.

"Go."

Bronwyn found her way back to the kitchens, but not before being accosted by Sir Nicholas, who stood before her. "What are you doing out of the kitchens, young lady?" His breath stank like sour wine.

"I was delivering rolls to the queen," Bronwyn said.

"Why you and not a page? Are you looking to get close to her?"

"No," Bronwyn said hotly, realizing all too late that a mere slip of the tongue might land her in trouble. "The page led me to her, then she sent him away."

His burly eyebrows knit into a frown. "It's not wise to have a disobedient tongue in this place. Why were you really there?"

"She called for me."

Servants scurried past like squirrels, but a few saw Sir Nicholas questioning her and whispered amongst themselves. At a glare from Sir Nicholas, they scattered, shooting little looks behind them as they left, no doubt memorizing what they had seen.

He looked down his nose at her. "Do you know what I do, girl?"

Aside from getting in her way, no. Bronwyn wanted to remind him of her name, but something also told her it might be wise to be forgettable. "No."

"I am the head of Their Graces' personal guard. That means I have a care for their personal safety. Why would the queen ask for you when she could have a page deliver rolls?"

She looked up at him. She didn't know if he could be trusted.

"That is between me and her," Bronwyn said.

This reply evidently annoyed him further. His cheeks turned

pink and puffed up as he said, "May I remind you, I can make life difficult for you here. I have seen you visit the dungeons."

She tensed.

"Your father. I could make sure the guards don't allow you to see him."

She frowned up at him. "What do you want?"

"Information. What is it the queen bid you? Why you?"

"She has a hold over me." *As you well know*, she thought.

"Would that all girls were so devoted to their fathers. What did she ask you?"

Bronwyn gritted her teeth. "She bid me find out who the poisoner is. All I saw was he wore a green hood and had black hair."

He snorted. "A young woman with no training, no knowledge of the outside world aside from her own kitchen. And tell me, Mistress Baker, will you take on this little quest?"

Her temper rose. "I have no choice. I have to. For my papa's sake."

"Yes, I suppose you do." He stroked his bristly, dark beard. "Very well. I shall help you."

She blinked. "You? But why? The queen said she made enquiries already."

"Well, she was not thorough enough. She should have come to me first. There is no need for her to ask you. Especially since without me, your search will get nowhere. And this reflects upon both of us. That the queen asked you, a mere baker's daughter, to find a poisoner is laughable."

She met his frown head on—then realized he was jealous. And worried for his position. This poisoning had happened under his roof, his remit. He must have feared for his head.

She nodded. "I think she asked me to look into it because I'm a member of the kitchen staff, and so I might speak with people who would be intimidated by you." She thought to herself, *There, that was diplomatic.*

He blew out his moustache and loomed over her. "I'm not

intimidating."

Her eyebrows rose, and she began to smile. After she'd fully grinned, they shared a laugh. "She has told me a bit about de Grecy, and said I should start there. But I don't know anything about him. She's given me till the feast of Purification of St. Mary and then if the poisoner isn't found by then…"

"Then your father's life will be forfeit," he finished grimly.

She froze. "They would kill him? But he's innocent. He didn't do anything wrong."

"Doesn't matter. They need to show strength, not indecision. And punish the cooks for letting this happen right under their noses. If they were to let every man who only allegedly committed a crime go, the streets would be rife with criminals. That is why you need my help—so that he is proven innocent."

Bronwyn's shoulders slumped and she leaned against the wall, wary of the richly hanging tapestry that hung above. To be around such grandeur, and to feel her father's life at stake, was horrible. She blinked back tears.

"Shake with me, girl, and we'll call it a deal." Sir Nicholas held out his hand. She clasped his arm, with him gripping her arm for longer than necessary.

"Looking for weapons?" she asked.

"Old habit. Can't imagine a baker's daughter would carry a knife, but you never know." The left corner of his mouth almost crinkled into a smile.

Bronwyn returned to the kitchens. Odo berated her for taking her time, but she shrugged and returned to scrubbing pots as if she'd never left.

Her mind wandered as she thought madly about de Grecy. Who was he? Why had he defected from Empress Maud's camp, and why had he thrown his lot in with King Stephen instead? Had he been a poisoner or a victim? Would he have knowingly plotted to have the rolls poisoned and meant to take a plain one for himself? And if de Grecy had just joined the court, why would he go to such lengths to kill the king and queen? Unless this had been a plot all along to worm his way into their good graces and be above suspicion.

If he was innocent, why would someone be willing to kill him in an attempt to get to the king and queen?

At the mid-afternoon meal with the cooks and pages, she gratefully sat at the end of a long, wooden table and joined in as they passed around trenchers of meat, bread, and pottage. She shared a hard, stale bread trencher with one of the potboys at the low end of the table, reserved for the lowest of the staff. The boy informed her his name was Abel, and together, they made short work of the bread and meat drippings on offer.

Bronwyn looked up to find some of the cooks eyeing her. Whilst there were some women amongst the servants, there weren't too many girls in the kitchen, and she listened to the conversation.

"What do you make of this death? De Grecy?" one of the journeyman cooks asked Odo.

"Dunno." The man glanced at Bronwyn and chewed his meat.

"He was a traitor, wasn't it? He was one of Maud's men," the journeyman said.

"So what if he was? He's dead now and that's all that matters." Odo set his drink down with enough force that it slopped over the sides of the cup. "Don't see what business it is of yours to be digging this up."

"I agree," another cook said. "The man is dead. Let's forget about it."

"Isn't it odd? The man comes here from Empress Maud's court and then later he's dead? Doesn't that seem strange to you?" the young man asked.

"The only thing that seems strange is you asking so many questions. Now finish your food, unless you're keen to get back to that lord of yours," Odo said, shooting the youth a look.

The young man tucked into his food and Bronwyn got a closer look at him. It was Rupert, the squire of one of the knights in Stephen's court. She'd been so busy eating that she'd been oblivious to the familiar voice, and to whom it belonged.

Conversation switched topics, and it wasn't until she'd finished her meal and begun stacking the used trenchers that she sensed a presence at her side. The scent of horse, hay, and sweat hit her nose.

"Rupert," Bronwyn said.

"Mistress," he said, giving her a courtly bow. He grinned as if pleased with himself, and she looked away haughtily. She felt like a joke in front of the boys.

"Is she your lady?" one of the potboys asked.

Bronwyn cursed, flinging suds at the boy. He grinned and dashed away.

"What do you want?" she asked. It was rude, but she felt heat on her cheeks, and the boys' grins and smirks only added to this. Not to mention Rupert's own smile. He looked very satisfied with himself.

"To ask you some questions." He leaned against the worktable and got his sleeves wet, then stood, brushing at his damp elbows. "Can I walk you home tonight?"

She shrugged, tossing her blonde braid over her shoulder. "I don't need an escort."

"For your protection. The streets aren't safe at night, especially for a young woman."

That riled her further. As if she needed his protection to walk down the road.

But she thought on the matter and knew that Margaret would have something to say about her walking alone with a young man. But maybe that would get them talking again. Since Bronwyn's father had been imprisoned, Margaret had been exhausted on her feet when Bronwyn came home, and even with Alfred's help, she was usually tired and not open to conversation.

Rupert waited a bit. "Mistress…"

She glanced at him, her clearly mind elsewhere. "All right."

He grinned. "I'll call for you at Compline, after the nobles have their dinner."

"Don't you have to attend your lord?" she asked.

"Once he's had his meal, he'll settle down for a game of chess or a night by the fire. I won't be gone long." He gave her a confident smile.

"You're so sure of yourself," Bronwyn said.

"'Course I am. There's no reason not to be."

She rolled her eyes, earning a laugh from him.

"Till tonight, then, my lady," he said, giving her a courtly bow.

She turned her back on him and scrubbed the pot harder, sinking her hands into the water. His laughter echoed behind him as he left.

That afternoon, she wandered up to Odo as he was preparing cuts of meat for the main table, watching until he handed her a knife and said, "Chop those carrots."

She began chopping, staying silent as he barked orders and gave instructions for the platters to be brought out, when he asked her, "What do you want?"

She waited until they were mostly alone to respond. "The night that de Grecy died, you said it was Muriel de la Haye, the chatelaine of the castle, who fainted."

"So? What do you care about her for?" he asked.

"I just wondered what made her faint."

He shrugged. "Women faint."

"She said she saw someone."

"Aye, but the old woman's telling tales. She's getting on in years, isn't she? She and Robert de la Haye, it's no surprise after what happened."

"What do you mean?"

He looked up at her. "Well, she and Robert are chatelains of the castle. You could say it was through their ineptitude that the empress's men were able to come in here and overwhelm the forces. Either that, or some people think they *welcomed* Maud's men in. So either they're traitors or inept. And now she's saying she's seeing things. It's no wonder no one believes her."

Bronwyn cocked her head.

"William de Roumare is in the dungeon with your pa, girl. Did you not know?"

She blinked. "She thought she saw him?"

"Aye. But everyone knows he's locked up tight under lock and key, along with the rest of the knights King Stephen captured." He looked around the kitchen. "Enough talk. I've got enough to worry about without you stirring up trouble. Keep your questions to yourself. Oi, you! Pay attention to that sauce!" he shouted at a cook who had let a sauce burn.

That evening at Compline, Bronwyn found herself tarrying and finding reasons to wait after her main duties were done.

"You waiting for that squire of yours? Rupert?" one of the cooks asked.

"No," she said, her face warm.

"Could've fooled me."

"'Course she is. He's always popular with the girls, that one," another said.

"He is?" she asked.

The older cook looked at her confidently, mischief in his eyes. "Yeah, he usually flirts with all the girls, then he moves on. Admit it. You're waiting for him."

"I am not," she said hotly.

"Then why are you still here?" he asked.

"No reason." But almost an hour later, there was still no sign of Rupert. She had no other reason to stay, so she got her thin coat and cap and left, shrugging into it and tying the strings up tight to keep warm.

After working all day in the warm kitchen, the icy cold was waiting. She stepped out into the castle courtyard and shivered. Her breath blew white, steaming clouds into the cold night, and she could see it clearly against the bright light of the moon. She hurried by the guards, muttered a goodnight, crossed through the gate and out onto the main street, her shoes sliding against the dark uneven cobblestones.

She trudged down Steep Hill, watching her steps, when a hand slipped over her mouth and pulled her backward. She slipped and flew back, her hands splaying out, then fell to the ground, crashing into someone. She backed into the person, their knee jamming against her rear. She yelled in pain, and the man jerked her coat around, choking her.

Chapter Three

BRONWYN COUGHED AND scrabbled, scraping her hands on the slick and dirty cobblestones as the person let out a foul expletive and tugged harder at her sheepskin coat, pulling her by the neck. "Do you want to die tonight?" A low voice growled in her ear. Steel flashed in the moonlight and she tensed. The scent of sour wine, meat, and refuse hit her nose. The tip of a small blade pricked her side.

"Asking questions, Miss Baker? Maybe you need a lesson in manners. Keep your mouth shut if you know what's good for you."

She squeaked, which made the person laugh. She froze completely, the wetness from the cobblestones soaking the bottom of her dress. Her hands felt numb and pain shot through them where she'd fallen to the ground. The man jerked her around to face him, but he was bathed in darkness, and she couldn't see his face.

"L-Let me go," Bronwyn said shakily.

The man laughed, spraying her face with spittle. He sliced the strings of her coat. The coat flew open and she emitted a *meep*, like a terrified mouse. He laughed again and she swallowed, her face dripping with his spit.

A male voice said, "Oi, back off."

Bronwyn's eyes widened as the man stiffened and lowered his blade.

"Take your hands off her," the voice said.

The man shoved her away.

"One move and I'll skewer you like a fish," the new voice said. It sounded familiar.

Bronwyn scrabbled backward, scraping her hands further. Rocks and pebbles cut into her skin, but she didn't care, she wanted to put as much space between her and these men as possible.

She got to her feet.

"Are you all right?" her rescuer asked. It was hard to see in the darkness.

"Yes."

"Get out of here."

She ran.

A light rain started to fall, misting against her face. She slid down the hill, skidding on the stones. Once at the bottom of the hill, she slipped and fell on her hands and knees, the damp biting into her dress. She got up, warm tears streaming down her face, when the echo of hurried footsteps hit her ears and a hand touched her back.

She shrieked and whirled around, when a voice said, "Halt! Mistress Baker, stop. It's me."

She stopped and stared. "Rupert?"

"It's me." He came toward her. "Are you all right?"

She stepped back, her shoes almost slipping again. "Stay back."

"It's me." He held his hands up in the darkness. "I'm the one who scared off that man. Trust me. I know better than to attack a kitchen maid."

He stepped closer.

"Stop there," she said, "Don't move."

He stopped. She walked toward him, leaned in close, and sniffed. He smelled like horses and hay, but nothing like the sour wine and body odor of which her attacker had stunk.

"You're smelling me?" he asked.

"I had to be sure." Her shoulders slumped and she gave a little laugh that sounded almost hysterical. All the emotion rushed out of her. "Where were you? That man…"

Rupert took off his coat and put it around her shoulders, pulling it tight. He looked her in the eyes. "It's all right. You're safe now. You are unhurt?"

She let out a shaky breath. "I think so."

Together, they walked, and he touched her elbow, helping her navigate the slippery stones. Misting rain came down, wetting their faces. "I was detained by my lord, who wanted me to lay out his clothes and deliver a message to a lady."

She could hear the regret in his voice.

"By the time I got to the kitchens, you had gone, but the boys said I'd just missed you, so I ran after. Then I saw the man attack you and you fall. From there, it was easy to put my blade against the back of his neck."

She stiffened. "You were prepared to kill him?"

He murmured into her ear, "I wasn't joking when I said the streets weren't safe."

"But were you going to *kill* him?"

"He could have hurt you. I'm just grateful I found you and scared him off. What did he want?"

Could she trust him? "He…" She hesitated.

"Come off it, I know you're looking into the poisoning. The pageboy who had you deliver the rolls to the queen is also a page to some of the ladies in court, and they pay him to tell them everything. He was listening outside the door when the queen spoke to you."

Her eyes widened. "So then he heard."

"Almost the entire court knows. One of the maids was gossiping about it and told her lord, and now it's what everyone is talking about—the queen ordering a kitchen maid to solve a murder. It's ridiculous."

"Why is that? I'm smart." She rounded on him.

"It's not that. It's that you're a nobody, when everyone

knows it should be Sir Nicholas who would investigate this sort of thing. You're the daughter of a baker. There's no sensible reason why you should be solving crimes instead of baking cakes and rolls."

She kicked at a pebble, then her shoe almost slid out from under her. He grabbed her arm, steadying her. "Try to stay upright, at least until I see you home." He laughed.

She yanked her arm free.

"Why are you angry?"

"No reason."

"Tell me," he said. "You're annoyed you slipped, or that I helped you up? I was only teasing."

"I'm angry I have poor shoes."

"I'd be more bothered that you don't have a sense of balance." He held up a hand in defense. "All right, all right. I'll stop teasing."

Bronwyn mentally cursed her thin shoes. They were damp and her feet felt numb. She wouldn't have been surprised if icicles had formed on her toes. They walked until they came across her family's shop, the rain making the smell of bread and pastry dissipate in the night air.

It was then she caught a familiar face. "Bronwyn!"

"So that's your name. Pretty," he said.

"It's like a boy's name."

"I like it."

"I hate it."

"It's much prettier than Gertrude, or Griselda."

She made a noise of frustration and stopped as a familiar face approached. "Alfred?"

"There you are. I was looking for you. We waited for you at dinner and when you didn't come home… your ma is worried. Where have you been? I told her I would find you." He stopped and glanced at Rupert as if seeing him for the first time. "Who is this?"

"Rupert Bothwell. Squire to Sir Baldwin of Clare," Rupert

said.

Alfred's eyes traveled up the sight of him and was unimpressed. He ignored him and said, "Bronwyn, let's get you home. Your mother and Wyot are worried sick."

"You know this man, Bronwyn?" Rupert asked.

She nodded. "This is Alfred Dale, a journeyman. He's helping out at the bakery whilst my papa is…"

She didn't want to say it aloud. Almost as if speaking the truth in the night air would somehow make magic happen, and none of it good.

She shrugged out of Rupert's coat and handed it back to him. "Thanks. I'm all right."

He surveyed her. "Are you sure?"

"She'll be fine. I've got her. Thanks, mate." Alfred put an arm around her shoulders and steered her away from Rupert, in the direction of home.

She glanced back and saw Rupert watching. For some reason, that sight warmed her soul, but she quickly shivered in the cold night.

Alfred asked, "Who was that?"

"He's a squire at court. He was going to walk me back, but we missed each other and…" She paused. "A man attacked me on the road."

"What?" Alfred whirled her around to face him. "What happened?"

"He heard I was looking into the murder from the poisoning and wanted to give me a warning. Rupert surprised him and scared him off before he could do anything." She shivered.

"Are you all right?" he asked.

She nodded. "I ran and he caught up with me and then you found us."

"I'm glad I did. Your ma was getting worried. Come on." He led the way down the street. "Wait a minute. You said you were looking into the murder? Like a man-at-arms or something?"

"Yes."

Alfred guffawed, his laughter ringing out in the air. "That's the funniest thing I've heard in ages. How do you expect to find a murderer?"

"Well, I don't know. But Queen Matilda asked me to, so I'm going to," she said, her temper rising.

"Wait, she *asked* you to? Why? Doesn't she have a man for that?"

"Yes, he's looking into it too."

"Then why does she need you? What can *you* do? You're just a baker's daughter."

Her temper rose more. "I don't know. She ordered me and I said *yes*. I was afraid I'd lose my head. Pa is in prison and now I'm working in the kitchens and have to report to the queen. If you think this is funny, then go ahead and laugh, but I don't think it's funny at all." She glared at him and stomped away, her shoes sloshing into the wet muck that covered the road.

"Bronwyn, wait." He caught up to her easily, him and his long legs. "I didn't mean to laugh. You must admit, it is funny. But… it's almost like she set you up to fail."

She looked at him. "She's given me till the feast of Purification of St. Mary. That's only a few weeks away. Then if I haven't found who did it… Papa will die. Do you think…."

"She's played her cards well, I'll give her that. Just think. She arrests your father, puts him in the dungeon, then tasks you and her man-at-arms to find out whoever tried to kill her and her husband." Alfred's face turned grim. "Then when you fail, because who wouldn't in your shoes, she kills your pa and sees justice done in the eyes of the people, or at least until they find the real killer."

"And if the poisoner strikes again—"

"Then she'll either be dead, a widow, which she might prefer, or she'll find someone else to blame." He gritted his teeth. He didn't think it was so funny anymore. "And now someone has attacked you in the street. Someone's been spreading the word that you're on the hunt. These noble ladies, they always fill their heads with gossip, don't they? Let's get you home. I don't like this." He steered her home and didn't stop until they knocked and the door to the bakery flew open, revealing her stepmother and Wyot.

"Bronwyn, where have you been?" Margaret pulled her inside and shut the door behind Alfred. "Thank goodness Alfred found you. What were you doing out so late? I expected you an hour ago at least." She stared, looking her up and down. "What on Earth happened? You're filthy."

Alfred opened his mouth when Bronwyn stepped on his foot. "It started to rain as I was going down Steep Hill and I slipped and fell."

Margaret gave her a suspicious look. "Your dress is soaked through and what happened to your coat? Your hands…" She took them and turned them over, revealing the scratches and dirt. "That's it. You need a bath, immediately. Wyot, fetch some water. You can use the old water leftover."

Bronwyn snorted softly. Margaret cared for her, but not so much as to order their apprentice to fetch fresh water. She'd be washing in water leftover from the workday, with the remnants of dough floating in it.

"With soap," Margaret said.

Bronwyn groaned. Weeks ago, her stepmother had purchased soap at the market, a block of soap made from ashes and tallow. It smelled, but she'd stuck leaves and flowers in it to smell nicer and was sure of its curative properties.

Once Margaret had bidden Alfred goodnight and ordered Wyot to prepare a bath, Bronwyn stripped, sat in the wooden washtub, and scrubbed her face, hair and skin with the smelly soap. The water wasn't the cleanest, but she felt relieved to scrub the rain off her face and the sweat of the day from her skin.

After her bath, she found Margaret waiting for her. "Bronwyn, what happened to you tonight? Why were you home so late? I had to send Alfred to look for you."

"I got held up."

Margaret inspected Bronwyn's hands. They were indeed scraped and the flesh was tender. "That's it. I'm wrapping these up."

Bronwyn sat by in a fresh dress as Margaret dried and braided her hair and wrapped it in a kerchief. Together, they sat on a bench as Margaret wrapped Bronwyn's hands in stiff rags and tied the ends.

"It was raining and I slipped and fell," Bronwyn reiterated.

"That Steep Hill is dangerous, especially at night. You're lucky Alfred went to look for you. He was afraid something had happened. He's very thoughtful, that boy."

Bronwyn shrugged. "I'm fine. A friend was walking me home, anyway." But the memory of the man who had accosted her, his stinking breath and blade that glinted in the moonlight, sent a shiver down her spine.

She'd frozen like a rabbit, and she felt ashamed. She should have acted. She should have shouted for help, shoved him back, or fought him. Anything but just sit there on the slippery stones like a statue.

"Nonsense, you're lucky you didn't catch a chill. Go to bed and we'll talk in the morning."

As Bronwyn climbed down the stairs to her pallet and snuggled beneath the coverlet, she was soon sleepy. "I'll bake him a roll tomorrow at the castle to say thank you."

"That's a nice idea. I'm sure Alfred would appreciate that."

The next day, Bronwyn took some of the extra flour—the grain deemed too ill to be used to make bread and rolls for the nobles—and made two rolls. One she filled with rosemary, the other she dusted with flour, a simple roll. In both, she cut three slices across the top for effect. Once they were done, she waved over the nearest page and bid him take the rosemary one to Rupert.

He looked at it hungrily.

"Take it to him and say thank you. If he doesn't get it, I'll know."

He grumbled. "Who from?"

"He'll know who. Go on." She shooed him away and he scattered.

That afternoon, Bronwyn was sent off into the nearby woods to collect herbs. Her basket soon full of rosemary and sage, she pulled her coat around her and looked around. The sun was out, but she couldn't shake the feeling that someone was watching.

She turned. "Who's there?"

A bird sang and trilled nearby, but of another person, there was no sign. She walked back, her basket full, but it was hard, considering the ground was wet and in some places brittle and cracked from the winter.

Her thoughts railed at her, again and again, as she spotted lone mushrooms in the wood. What if she was thinking about this all wrong? What if the king and queen hadn't been the intended targets of the poisoning, but de Grecy had been? If so, who would have wanted to kill de Grecy and why? What had he done? Had he ordered the rolls as a gift and been the victim of an unfortunate accident, or had he just wanted some with his own dinner? And who would have had knowledge of mushrooms enough to be able to tell which ones were safe versus poisonous? But considering that whoever had messed with the mushrooms had now disappeared, it was clear that this was no accident.

She thought back to the day they had met, however briefly. De Grecy had placed an order for fifteen of the sweet white rolls with honey, a favorite amongst the nobility. To her, that meant he'd meant to share them with others, for it was too much for one person. And then he'd want a servant to bring them out.

She stopped. He was a knight. Of course he'd have his own squire to look after his needs. Could de Grecy's own squire have been the one who'd poisoned him? No, that didn't make sense. Even if the squire had intended him harm, he'd easily have been identified by the cooks and questioned, and when the man had died, the squire would have been punished. She needed to speak with his squire, whoever he was. She hurried back to the castle and unloaded the basket of herbs in the kitchen. After the midday meal, she spent an hour or so scrubbing pots, and then asked one of the potboys, "Who was de Grecy's squire, do you know?"

The boy she addressed looked about ten. He shrugged and went back to scrubbing. He looked pale and downcast.

"Oi, what's wrong?" she asked.

He sniffed. "Godfrey's dead. He died last night. It was the rolls that killed him, they say."

"Oh."

The boy shrugged and scratched at a flea on his leg. "He's probably lucky. The king would have killed him, anyway, so maybe it's for the best." He left her, still scratching.

That explained why there was a subdued air in the kitchen that day. People went about their chores, and Odo kept a watchful eye on everything, but it wasn't the same. Godfrey's presence was missed.

Bronwyn wiped her hands and walked out of the kitchen, down the corridor to the garderobe, where she might find the privy. She waited, for this one only held space for one, thank goodness, and once it was her turn, she held her nose as she entered the narrow room. She used hay and moss scattered on one side to wipe herself clean and walked out, wiping her hands on her work skirt as she left, when she bumped into a page.

"Oi, watch where you're going," he said.

"Sorry. Um, do you know where I could find de Grecy's page, or squire?"

The boy stopped. "What do you want with him?"

"I want to talk to him."

"You can't," he said simply.

"Why not?"

"He didn't have one." The boy went inside the privy and closed the door.

She took a step after him and stopped. No one would appreciate her waiting for them, so she called, "Why didn't he have a squire or page of his own?"

"Dunno. Not all knights do. Why all the questions?"

"I want to know."

"Are you sweet on him?" the boy called from the privy.

She cursed at him.

Chuckles came from the queue behind her. She turned and saw several cooks and servants waiting their turns for the privy. She called one last time, "But—"

"I don't know nothing. Can I have a wee now?"

More laughter. Bronwyn rearranged her dress, straightened her headwrap, a kerchief that kept her blonde hair out of her face and coiled atop her head, and left in search of Sir Nicholas. She walked down the corridor and through the courtyard, to the castle green.

It was a grand sight. Part of the castle sat on a hill, a "motte" they called it, and from there, it served as a lookout for invaders who might attack.

On the castle green, the air was filled with the loud grunts and thwacks of squires training with wooden swords and spears, whilst knights pounded across the muddy ground with their horses, training with lances or spears. Some knights fought with wooden swords as well, whilst others stood by talking, gambling, or practicing their archery skills. Friendly chatter and banter sounded amidst the noise of arrows hitting their marks, followed by applause and laughter. Squires and pages ran to and fro, bringing drinks and food.

She loitered by the entrance to the courtyard and watched the men train and compete until a man came up to her. "What are you doing out of the kitchens?" Sir Nicholas looked down his nose at her.

"I was looking for you."

His bushy, black eyebrows knit into a frown. "Well, you've found me. Now, what is it?"

"Did you know that de Grecy didn't have a squire or a page?"

"That's not important. Many knights don't. Not all can afford to keep one."

"Then who would have served him the poisoned rolls?"

"Any of the pages. They set the platters on the table for the guests to eat from. In case you haven't noticed, there's a war going on. We need to learn more about who would want to kill the king and queen, not who served a wayward knight."

She blushed at his implication, then paused. "What do you mean, 'wayward'?"

He glanced around. "The night de Grecy died, he had made a big fuss about ordering white rolls for the king and queen. A token of his fondness for Their Graces."

Bronwyn cocked her head. "That afternoon, he came to our stall and ordered the rolls. It was an expensive order. Like I told the king and queen, that night, I spied a man in a green hood adding the mushrooms, but the cooks didn't see anyone and assumed it must have been the squire Roger."

"And then it was too late. Did you get a good look at the man?"

"No. He wore leggings and a green hooded tunic over his head. I couldn't see his face." She hesitated. "Do you think Muriel de la Haye was right, and that she saw William de Roumare walking the halls?"

Sir Nicholas shook his head. "The men went down to inspect the dungeons and found him there. The woman was mistaken."

He turned, clearly ready to leave, when Bronwyn said, "What about de Grecy's room? His belongings?"

"What about them?"

"Have you looked into them?"

"His things? No. Once the man died, I ordered his room locked." He spoke with the confidence of a man used to being obeyed.

She raised an eyebrow. "Can you let me in there?"

"Into his room so you can rifle through his clothing? What and look for something you can steal?"

Bronwyn's temper rose. "No, so I might find some reason as to why he died."

"The mushrooms, girl. It's obvious."

"That was *how* he died, not why. I bet there's something in his things that would tell us. Let me in?"

"So you can cause trouble?"

"You can watch me. If I don't make any headway in this search, my papa's life is over. Please."

He gave her a hard stare. "You promise you won't steal anything? You'll just look?"

"Yes."

"I don't like members of the court knowing about your task."

She shrugged. "Apparently, a page overheard Her Grace and the rumors spread from there."

He gave her a grim nod. "Very well." He led her up the circular, stone staircase and through a series of corridors, past pages, servants, maids and more than one lord and lady. No one dared question him about his business, and he had a ready glare for anyone who looked his way for a second too long.

He led her away from the main rooms, the bedrooms, and farther from the main activity of the castle center. Wherever de Grecy's rooms were, he'd been far from the main reach of his fellow knights and nobles. Bronwyn wondered, *Was this a slight or a sign of distrust?*

Sir Nicholas stood by the door to a room and held his arm out first before she could enter. "How did you know the mushrooms were poison?"

"I didn't know for sure. I just thought it was odd for a man to be adding them to my father's rolls at the last minute, when that's not what de Grecy ordered. Odo thought so too," she said. "My parents taught me about mushrooms before, but I can't always remember which are safe to eat. I know people have gotten sick from them so when I saw the man adding them, I didn't trust it."

"But you're a maid. You've worked in the bakery all your life. Surely, you would know the difference between mushrooms which are safe and which are not. Don't all cooks know these things?"

She shook her head. "I haven't finished my learning yet. That's something a journeyman would know."

"Then you've got a lot to learn," he said sourly. He pushed open the wooden door, his burly, black eyebrows furrowing as it slid open easily. He walked inside and gave a start. "Who are you?"

Chapter Four

BRONWYN FOLLOWED SIR Nicholas inside the room. There was a noise and a crash, as a woman's voice cried, "Stay back!"

Bronwyn looked past Sir Nicholas's bulk to see a young woman standing by the small hearth, a small scrap of paper at her feet. She wore a dirty, brown woolen peasant's dress, her hair covered by a low-hanging kerchief. Yet she wore no apron and did not move with the subservience or meekness that Bronwyn would have expected in a fellow servant.

She held part of her kerchief over her face, as if she were hiding herself. But the small dagger she held out carried a warning. "Who are you? I demand to know."

"Give us your name, girl," Sir Nicholas ordered.

"You first."

"Sir Nicholas, it's just a girl. She's not doing anything," Bronwyn said, wanting to appear calm. She had experienced nervous customers before at the market, including those who were so poor, they needed to beg, or planned to steal. The trick was to remain clam. She held up a hand. "You can put the knife away. We won't hurt you."

The young woman snorted softly.

Bronwyn stepped toward her like she would approach a wild animal. The girl shoved past, knocking her hard to the floor, and flung her knife at Sir Nicholas.

The knife thwacked into the wood by his head with a jarring

sound. He lunged for her but was too late—the young woman slipped past him and ran down the hall. Sir Nicholas tripped and fell, crashing into Bronwyn. He cursed and they helped each other up. He dashed out of the room. "Guards! Find that girl."

Bronwyn heard a guard approach. "Sir Nicholas?" a man asked. "What girl?"

"The one who just ran out of here. The girl in the brown dress."

The guard's footsteps retreated down the corridor.

Sir Nicholas returned to the room. "Stupid girl! You shouldn't have let her escape."

"You scared her. If you hadn't frightened her, we might have found out what she was doing here."

"We know what she was doing. Stealing," he said.

"Are you so sure?" Bronwyn walked over to the knife stuck in the wooden doorframe. The blade was slim and pretty, and it bore an ornate handle. She tugged it out of the wood. It fit well in her hand but was uncomfortable. She'd never held a knife like that before. It was different from the knives used in the bakery. This was light and measured. Perhaps it was meant for throwing.

"Let me see." He took the knife from her. "A woman's weapon. Fancy, too."

"Did you recognize her?" Bronwyn asked. "I mean, I know she covered her face, but…"

"Would I have asked her name if I did? No, I've never seen her before. I don't often see servants carrying weapons. You?"

"No," Bronwyn replied. The girl had been dressed like a peasant, yet her air had been haughty for one caught nosing about someone else's room. And her instant reaction had not been to show fear, but to throw a knife at them. "She must be a noblewoman."

"What makes you say that? Did you *see* the state of her clothes?"

"Her boldness. She demanded to know your name. And she threw a knife at you rather than make excuses for her being here.

She's no servant and she didn't smell."

"You're saying *I* do?"

Bronwyn raised an eyebrow. Surely, he knew he smelled. So much time outdoors had left him with a lingering scent of rust, iron, and dampness from sweaty clothes that needed washing. "Only that most of the servants smell like hay, or the kitchens, you know." She looked around the room. "So de Grecy stayed here."

"Yes. I wonder if she was his wench," he said.

Bronwyn's eyebrows knit together. "I don't think so."

"Why not?"

"Her expression was angry. We'd interrupted her, in whatever she was looking for. If she was his… companion, then she might have been sad or tearful. Instead, she threw a knife at you. What sort of woman does that?"

"There's a few I could name…" He turned pink.

"Sir Nicholas?"

"What?" He cleared his throat. "Look around. See if you can find out what she was looking for."

Bronwyn took a quick glance of the room. It was small, not very grand. There was a small, raised pallet on the right side of the room, wood-paneled walls, a chamber pot beside the bed, and a small table and chair, along with a chest. She peered inside the chest but found nothing but guest linens. The room's walls bore no decoration; it was decidedly spartan.

The bed bore a few clothes, a doublet, a spare shirt and trousers, and a set of hose. Nothing that couldn't be stuffed into a small travel bag at a moment's notice. She glanced over at the small hearth in the room and saw it had had a fire very recently, as the coals were still hot. She walked to the small pit.

"Leave it, girl. There's a servant who will rake out the ashes. If you're needing work, the kitchens will want you," Sir Nicholas said.

"The girl was burning a fire here."

"So? What of it? It is winter."

"You said after de Grecy died, you had his room locked up. That was days ago. So who would have been in here? Look, there's a bit of paper." Bronwyn looked at the scrap of paper on the floor. It had escaped the flames but was so small, she could barely make out what it read. She handed it to him. "What does it say?"

He peered at it, blinked hard, and held it away from him and then close to his eyes. "I can almost make out a name, but... No. I cannot tell. It is too faded to see." He put the scrap in his leather pouch that hung at his waist. "But this fire is too recent. Who would be burning parchment?"

Bronwyn shrugged. "Maybe the girl we found was looking for it."

He crossed his arms over his round chest. "I do not like this, Bronwyn. This stinks of mischief."

The bell for Mass rang, and she met his eyes. "I have to go."

"Go on. Keep an eye out for any young woman bearing knives."

Bronwyn went to the kitchens and snuck a bit of food out, hurrying to her father in the underground prison. He smiled at her and tucked into the food. "We are fed, but this is better." He bit into a roll. "Did you make this?"

She shook her head.

"It's good. Not bad. Better than what we'd see in town."

Bronwyn told him about the girl they'd run into, and the scrap of paper in the hearth.

"No doubt the man had some questionable papers he didn't want getting out. Servants will go through everything and know all their masters' secrets," he said thoughtfully.

"If only we could see de Grecy's body, there might be some clue as to why someone would poison those rolls."

"That would be easy enough."

Bronwyn met her father's gaze. "What do you mean?"

"We're in the middle of winter. The ground will be too hard and cold to bury him. The man's body is likely in a cold storage."

"You think his personal things will be there with him?"

"Maybe. I don't know anyone who would want to touch a dead body, but… you might find something." His eyebrows rose and he blinked. Something like hope dashed across his face, then he schooled his features. "Bronwyn, I don't want you looking at him. This is a bad enough business without you getting involved."

"But, Papa, if I don't, they're going to blame you for this."

"King Stephen is said to be a just king. I trust justice will find a way," he said. "I shall pray."

His stomach rumbled.

"And I shall bring you more bread," she said.

Bronwyn was sent out to gather herbs and to see what she could forage for the castle kitchens for the next day. There were the grain stores, of course, and the larder so the castle's inhabitants would not go hungry, but fresh food was favored over anything else. She didn't mind, though, and relished the fresh air.

Bronwyn pulled on her sheepskin coat and retied the strings her assailant had sliced through so easily. It made for a looser fit, but it still fit. She trudged out with a basket and left through the castle courtyard, departing through one of the side gates. Once down the hill and out of the city proper, she walked through the woods and surrounding fields, whistling an off-key tune.

But as she dug and knelt by some fresh rosemary, just like before, a chill shivered down her back. Someone was watching. She took a small paring knife in hand as she bent over the bush, just subtly hearing the noise of steps crunching against the hard, frozen earth.

She hummed, then felt the air grow still and the birds quiet. She whirled around, paring knife in hand.

The girl in brown from de Grecy's room froze and stepped back. "Ah!"

Bronwyn said, "You? What do you want?"

Her face not completely hidden by the kerchief, her expression grew haughty. "I want my knife back. But first, do you have it?"

"What?" Bronwyn cocked her head.

"The message, dimwit."

Bronwyn looked at her in confusion.

She let out a noisy sigh. "Are you really this dumb?"

Bronwyn slipped the knife up her sleeve and put her hands on her hips.

"The message de Grecy had. Did you speak to him before he died?"

Bronwyn shook her head.

The young woman's face screwed up in a frown. "Well, that's done it. Now he's dead and we'll never know. I don't suppose you know who his person was."

"His 'person'?"

"The turncoat. Who he was working with inside the castle. The little parchment I burned mentioned me but not the other person he was working with. Did he tell you?"

"No." A shiver ran through her.

"What is it?"

"We're not alone."

The young woman fled, faster than Bronwyn would have expected. She wore a smart, grey cloak and held up the kerchief to cover her face as she ran, hurrying through the trees.

Bronwyn turned, looking for the shadowy figure she'd seen lurking nearby, watching. She slipped the paring knife out of her sleeve and held it ready. "Who's there?"

Rupert stepped out of the trees. His face was a picture of disgust.

"Rupert," Bronwyn said with relief. She slid the knife back up in her sleeve. "I thought you were someone else. I—"

He gripped her wrists painfully and pinned them behind her back, faster than she could blink. She gasped and he said in her face, "Mind telling me why you're speaking with a spy from Empress Maud's camp? Are you a traitor to the king?"

Chapter Five

"LET ME GO," Bronwyn said.

"Not until you tell me what you were doing with that woman," Rupert said. His handsome face was serious, his blond eyebrows furrowed. In that moment, his blue eyes looked beautiful.

"You're hurting me."

He lessened the pressure on her wrists. "Talk."

Bronwyn glared and kneed him in the groin. He jumped and shuddered with pain. She shoved and stumbled away from him, her shoes sliding on the damp ground.

"Bronwyn, wait," he called.

She almost reached the tree line, when he called, "What I saw could be considered treason. I could report you to the king. Do you want to end up in jail with your pa?"

She froze. Without her to look into this matter, her father would never be freed. And if she were accused of treason and put in jail with him, that would leave no one to investigate.

She turned and waited for him to catch up. He picked up her basket and moved gingerly, picking his way through the rocks and uneven ground. He handed her basket over.

She took it and shot him a frown. "Are you going to report me? Why would you hurt me like that?"

He shot her a dirty look. "I could ask you the same thing."

"I'm a loyal subject of King Stephen."

"Are you? Then why were you talking with that woman about de Grecy?" he asked.

"*She* came to *me*. But now that you suspect me of treason, I don't see why I should tell you anything."

He frowned in return. "Why should I believe you? I heard you two talking. Who was that person she was talking about, someone of de Grecy's?"

"I don't know. I would have learnt more if you hadn't come crashing through the woods like a boar."

His mouth thinned into a hard line. "You weren't so quiet yourself. What if I'd been an enemy? I could have murdered you both."

"Thank goodness you aren't," Bronwyn said hotly, matching his steely gaze.

Their faces were close, she realized. Glaring at each other. She could smell him. Sweat and evergreen and woodsmoke, mixed with hay.

His eyes darted to her mouth. His lips parted as if to say something more, then he stepped back, ran a hand through his red-blond hair, and shook his head. "You're playing a dangerous game, do you know that?"

She jutted her chin upward. "I have to. My papa's life is at stake."

"But there's more to it than that, isn't there? You could have refused this mission of Queen Matilda's. You're just a girl. You didn't have to accept."

"You're joking. I can't refuse a request from the queen. I'd lose my head. Besides, what would you have me do? Just let my father die in prison, or wait for him to die when no culprit is found?"

"I'm just saying, you didn't have to take up her cause. You could have asked someone more knowledgeable about the ways of court to look into this for you. What if you fail?"

Her chest hurt at the thought. "I can't fail. I mustn't."

"Someone else could do it."

"Like who? We're just a family of bakers. We're nobody to anyone. No one would care."

Rupert looked at the ground and shifted his feet. He mumbled something.

"What was that?"

"*I* would." He looked at her. "I mean, if you asked me to. I'd do it."

"Why?"

He shrugged.

She didn't know what to say to that. Instead, she held out her palm.

"What are you doing?" he asked.

"Offering you my palm and arm. So you can see I'm not hiding a weapon. Would a traitor offer to shake hands?"

He took her palm and shook it, grasping her arm. "You still could be a traitor."

Bronwyn smiled. "I didn't tell you that my weapon is in my other sleeve."

His eyes widened and he dropped her hand. He laughed. "Let me walk you back to the castle."

The afternoon sun was already fading, and the trees looked black against the blue-grey sky, with clouds stretching across the horizon like tufts of wool.

Bronwyn didn't realize how long she'd been outside gathering herbs. Her basket was full of rosemary, sage, and even some thyme. The castle didn't hurt for bread, and the preserved meat was for the aristocrats and rulers, so the rest of the staff had pottage most days.

She and Rupert bid the guards *hello* as they walked back through one of the gates, then cut across the castle courtyard and to the kitchens, where he stood by from the doorway. "I'll come by for you later to walk you home."

"Thanks, but I don't need an escort," Bronwyn said. He'd attacked her and accused her of being a traitor. They might have been at peace again, but she didn't feel too friendly toward him at that moment.

"I'll be by in an hour. Wait for me." He left.

She looked after him curiously. *What was all that about? First he tries to attack me and then he's keen to walk me home. Boys are odd,* she decided.

She returned the basket and herbs to the cooks, who put the herbs to good use. The smell of roasting meat on the spit hung in the air and her mouth watered. Odo tossed a bread roll in her direction. "Catch."

She fumbled and barely caught it, then tore into it. He smirked at her clumsy catch and came up to her. "Mind you don't get too close to that lad, girl. He's got an eye for the ladies."

Bronwyn raised an eyebrow, her mouth full of day-old bread.

"Takes an interest and then once the girl falls for him, he's off chasing another one. I've seen it happen. It'll only end in tears. If you're smart, you'll stay on your guard. That's all I'm saying."

She thanked him for the bread roll and helped stir soups and pottages. Here in the castle, nothing went to waste. Even the dogs were given scraps to eat.

Bronwyn finished for the day and went to collect her coat at the kitchen entrance, where she found Rupert waiting.

"Ready?" he asked.

She nodded and they walked in companionable silence, through the main gate to the castle, past the guards, and slowly down Steep Hill.

Torches lit part of the way, but much of the hill and the houses around were in darkness, so there wasn't a lot of light for the pair to see. At one point, she stumbled, and Rupert caught her arm. "Here, you can hold on to me if you like."

"I'm okay." She rubbed her hands on her thighs as they walked, trying to keep her fingers warm.

Rupert walked her to the main part of town, where they were met by Alfred, who stood solidly in the road.

"Bronwyn, I was just coming to look for you." Alfred's easy smile fell when he saw she was not alone.

"Why? Is everything okay?" she asked.

"Sure, sure. Just wanted to see you back home all right is all. It's been a long day." He gave Rupert an unfriendly look. "Thanks, mate. I'll see her home from here."

Rupert turned to Bronwyn. "Shall I see you the rest of the way home?"

"Oi, mate, I told you, I've got it," Alfred said.

"I was talking to Bronwyn." Rupert's eyes flicked to Alfred and were equally unfriendly. "Bronwyn?"

"I'll be fine. G'night," she said.

Rupert bowed his head and watched as she walked away with Alfred, who shot him a dirty look.

"Come on," Bronwyn said, tugging on his sleeve. She walked on ahead, conscious of Rupert's watchful gaze.

They walked on into the night. Alfred caught up to her in seconds. She could smell him. He carried the familiar smells of bread and stale ale, and she knew if she saw him better in the light, he'd have a dusting of flour on him.

"I don't like that squire," Alfred said sourly. "He acts like he thinks he's better than us. You shouldn't walk with him anymore."

"He was making sure I got here okay. He was doing me a kindness."

"You don't want him to get the wrong idea."

"What do you mean?"

"You go around walking alone with a lot of men, people will think you're wanton. Loose. Like a strumpet."

Bronwyn laughed out loud. "Me? Anyone who sees me will know that's not the case. Besides, I don't have time for boys."

"Why not?"

"I'm too busy trying to find out who killed de Grecy."

"You're wasting your time. You should be baking, not chasing after ghosts. What if you never find anyone? Why not tell the queen you want someone else take over? There must be men out there who are better at finding a traitor than you."

She fumed quietly. "Because I *am* doing this. Why should I back down? A stranger won't care for my papa."

"It's just… You don't want people to talk, Bronwyn," he said.

"People talk as often as they breathe, Al. What do I care?"

"You'll care when it means the boys don't want you. They'll think you're a bit funny. Touched in the head. Or worse, that you're a girl trying to do a man's job."

She faced him and put her hands on her hips. "Alfred, I don't know what to make of you. Women and men share jobs all the time, so how is this any different?"

"It's just…"

"First you don't want me walking about with boys and then you don't want me to help my papa, for fear the boys won't like me. Which is it? My head is spinning from all your talk."

Even in the darkness, she could sense his face turning red. "I mean, Bronwyn, that you should beg the queen's mercy and see if she'll release you from this silly quest. Ask her to let you return from working in the castle kitchens. Or better yet, see if she'll let you help your ma in the bakery. She needs the help. And you need to stop running around to the castle."

"You make it sound like I'm having a lark. If I don't do this, no one will find out who killed de Grecy and my papa might as well be dead."

Alfred cleared his throat. "The rulers won't let that happen. They're just. They'll look after you. Your family won't starve."

"Oh, really," she said hotly, "and you're so close to them, you can speak for the king and queen? What are you, their personal servant? Funny, I didn't see you there when they imprisoned my papa for something he didn't do."

They stood in the shadows and torchlight from houses and shops shut for the night, but she could still see Alfred's face in the flickering lights. Bronwyn glared up at him, cursing that she was mere average height for a woman, and shorter than him. It gave Alfred the advantage to look down his nose at her.

His eyes burned brightly and reflected the torchlights in the darkness from the homes and shops. "One of these days, Bronwyn, you'll say too much, and that tongue of yours will get you into trouble."

She crossed her arms over her chest. "Alfred, I'm getting pretty sick of you telling me what to do. You're not my papa or my mama. You sound like a gossipy, old woman."

He laughed, and she turned her back on him.

"Would a gossipy, old woman do this?" He pulled her arm back to face him and planted a kiss on her lips.

She stopped, stunned. *My first kiss.*

He held his lips against hers as if he expected a reaction. When she didn't respond, he grasped her shoulders and pulled her closer, kissing her again.

Bronwyn pushed his hands away and stepped out of his embrace. She glared at him, her cheeks warm.

He smiled. "There. That ought to do it."

"Do what?"

"Shut you up for a minute. You need reminding that you're a woman." He looked so pleased with himself, he grinned from ear to ear.

Bronwyn stepped on his foot. Hard.

"Oi, what was that for?" he asked, hopping on one foot.

"I don't need reminding. And I never asked you to kiss me." Her feet felt shaky.

"You never have to ask." He grinned. "I'll do it again if you like."

"Don't." She stomped away.

"I'll just wait, Bronwyn," he called. "You'll come asking for it again."

She stomped all the way back to the main road. With every stomp, she grew madder. She thought angrily, *Who does he think he is, kissing me like that? He just did it, as if I were a possession to be had, a toy to be played with or in this case, a doll to be kissed. He never even asked my permission, and just made free with my body. These were my lips, not his.* She had more angry thoughts, but they had to wait, for she found herself standing in front of the bakery.

She knocked on the bakery door and was let in by Wyot. He slid the wooden bolt and looped the lock back over the door.

"Bronwyn?" Margaret called.

"I'm back."

"Good, I've just put dinner on."

The three of them sat over a quiet meal of pottage consisting of onions, stewed cabbage, peas and with day-old rolls to mop it up with.

They sipped cups of stale ale and exchanged the day's news. Margaret and Wyot had made rolls and Alfred had taken Wyot to sell them in the market, whilst Bronwyn's stepmother had done a brisk trade from the shop. They were surviving, but word had gotten around that her father had been imprisoned, and it was starting to show. Fewer people had come back to purchase rolls that day, and fewer had come to the bakery. Mama with her ear for gossip knew it was because of the rumors.

"What are people saying?" Wyot asked.

"Oh, this isn't for your ears. I need to talk with Bronwyn about some things. If you're finished, go wash your hands with soap and get ready for bed," Mama told him.

Wyot grumbled, stole another roll from the table, and cleared his trencher away, setting it aside for the next day. He climbed the pull-down ladder into the upstairs room, where the family slept, as the heat from the oven rose and kept the room warm in the evenings, and Margaret waited for him to disappear before she leaned in close.

"The women are talking. The rumor is that Alan is in prison for trying to kill the king and queen," she said.

"He's not guilty, though. Did you tell them that I've been tasked by the queen to look into this and prove his innocence?" Bronwyn asked.

"Ha, no one cares about that. They'll think it's just an excuse. No one believes a queen asked you to find a murderer."

Bronwyn looked down at her ale. "But it's true."

"Don't lose heart, poppet. You find whoever did this and then they'll see. Make them eat their words."

Bronwyn nodded.

"I thought Alfred was coming back with you. Where's he gone?"

Her expression darkened at the thought of him, and against her better judgement, her cheeks warmed.

"What is it?"

"He kissed me."

Margaret's eyes widened. "He did?" A smile lit up her face. "Tell me."

Bronwyn didn't like the excited look in her eye. "We argued, and he kissed me."

"That's it?"

"He said it was one way to shut me up." She frowned at the memory of his words, feeling her anger rise again. He'd looked so pleased with himself, like he'd stolen a prized cake, or like a cat that had eaten a mouse. She wanted to punch him in the nose and wipe that smile off his face. See how he liked kissing with a mouthful of broken teeth.

"Well, I can't say the boy talks a lot of sense, but his heart is in the right place. And at least he's shown you what he wants," Margaret said with a smile.

"What's that?"

"*You*, you silly girl. He wants you. I suppose he should have asked your father's permission or me first before he started courting you, but—"

"Mama, we're not courting. We aren't anything. It was just a kiss."

She gave Bronwyn a shrewd look. "You say that now, but that's how it starts. One kiss will lead to another, and then I'll hear word of you two holding hands and him leading you behind the hay bales, and then I'll be a grandmother before you're twenty. We'll have to plan the wedding soon."

"Wedding? Mama, no. That's too much. We're not anything."

Her stepmother hardly listened to a word she said.

"Mama," Bronwyn said. She repeated her name twice before she looked at me. "I'm not getting married."

"But, Bronwyn, you're eighteen. You're in your prime childbearing years. Any older and your womb will shrivel."

Bronwyn burst out laughing. "Where did you hear that?"

She turned pink. "Women talk. Heloise the midwife told me. And I believe her."

"Well, I'm not ready to bear children yet. And I'm not ready to get married, either. I don't want either of those things."

She looked scandalized. "Bronwyn, you don't know what you're saying. Of course you want children. Marrying and bearing children is the natural way of things."

Bronwyn shrugged. "What if my womb shrivels? Will I die?"

"It's possible."

Bronwyn tried not to roll her eyes. "I'll take my chances. I am not going to marry Alfred. Just because he kissed me doesn't mean we're engaged."

"But that's how it starts, don't you see? One good kiss is all it takes."

"Well, then he needs practice because it wasn't good at all." Bronwyn turned her back, her blonde braid flying around her shoulder.

"Just you wait, Bronwyn. One of these days, a man will catch your eye and you'll be wishing he'd want to kiss you."

"That'll be the day." Bronwyn harrumphed and went to bed.

The next day, Bronwyn slipped out early, darting through the darkness in the streets. Her feet moved of their own accord and she was at the castle in no time. It felt like her family home had become stifling, but not from any physical heat. She wanted to hear no more of Margaret's talk about marrying, and she most definitely did not want to chance running into Alfred.

He was cute and all and she liked him, but she disliked him pulling her arm and kissing her, as if she were nothing but a prize to be had, or a busybody, gossipy woman to be shut up with a kiss. He had offended her somehow, but she hardly knew how to put that into words.

If Odo the cook was surprised to see her that early, he did not say so. He just nodded *hello*. As Bronwyn hung up her coat on a peg and walked over to the pots and the pail of water, he stood in her way.

"What?" She looked up at him.

"What are you doing?"

"I'm about to start cleaning pots."

"No, you're not. Get over there and start prepping the dough."

Bronwyn blinked in surprise. "But—"

"You're a baker's daughter, aren't you?" He scratched his double chin and tapped his fingers on the nearest worktable. "Let's see what you can do. I want to see twelve rolls before the others come in. Get to work."

Bronwyn blinked, tied on an apron, and pinned her hair back beneath a kerchief and set to work. As she began prepping the dough, she couldn't hide the growing smile on her face. She'd been moved up from potboy, which was promising. She'd long felt that scrubbing pots was the least of what she could do—all that was needed was a pair of hands—but she hadn't been about to protest. This was a sign she might be trustworthy. It was a start.

The day began well; she presented twelve rolls within the next hour or so. Odo bit into one and declared it passable, then bid her to make a loaf this time. Bronwyn set to work with gusto, but then an order came down from the queen for three soft white rolls with honey. She exchanged a look with the page who'd delivered the message; they both knew what that meant. Queen Matilda wanted information.

Bronwyn prepared the rolls and made four this time. She split the fourth in half and gave half to Odo, then the other half to the pageboy. When Bronwyn walked into the queen's chamber with the plate, Queen Matilda lowered her embroidery and watched as Bronwyn set down the plate on a table by her right side. She delicately took a roll, bit into it and said, "I heard there was a strange girl in de Grecy's room. Sir Nicholas had the guards looking for her all day, yet they didn't find anyone. You were there, yes?"

Bronwyn told her what Sir Nicholas and she had encountered in de Grecy's room.

"This girl. Who is she?"

Bronwyn described her. "I've never seen her before." But she relayed what had happened in the woods.

The queen's eyes widened. "She thought you were working with him?" Her petite hand drifted to her mouth. "Then he *was* a traitor. Even more important that we find this girl. How she got into this court without being seen is shocking."

Bronwyn bowed. "My lady."

Her eyes were hard. "Do not bow to me—you're not a boy. You're a young woman with a smart head on your shoulders. I expect you to act like one."

"Milady?"

"Curtsey. You are the in the presence of a queen. Don't make me tell you again. And never turn your back on a ruler."

"So how do I..." Bronwyn backed up a step and tripped on her skirts.

Queen Matilda shook her head in distaste. "Learn to curtsey, then rise and back up. When you are far enough away you may turn and exit. Go." She waved her hand in a dismissal.

Bronwyn curtseyed awkwardly and backed toward the exit. Once outside her chamber, she had not gone a few steps when she was accosted by Brother Bartholomew.

"Oh! Sorry," she said.

"Ha, you should be. But of course, you are running around this castle without any help, so it's no wonder you're bumping into people," he said gravely.

"Excuse me?" Bronwyn looked at the man, her mouth twisting in displeasure.

He stood tall and thin, humbly clasping his hands over his thin stomach. He bowed, and much like his demeanor, this was short and stiff. His expression was slightly mocking. She didn't trust it.

He rose with a smile. She tried not to show her dislike.

"Our meeting is fortuitous. I can help you. I heard about your little plan. I know all about it."

She raised an eyebrow. She suspected he wanted her to ask what the word *fortuitous* meant, but she refused to give him the satisfaction. She'd ask Sir Nicholas later.

"There's no need to play coy with me, girl. People were talking about it. You're the queen's little spy." He smirked.

"No, I'm not."

"Of course you are. Don't try to deny it. You're just lucky I heard about your little scheme first. I told them all they were misinformed."

"He has not been found guilty."

"Hasn't he? It is only out of good grace and mercy that our king and queen have decided to delay his punishment and offer you a chance to prove his innocence, because they haven't the heart to kill a man in front of his child. Never mind that he is suspected of working with a lowly squire to attempt to poison Their Graces. Their little mission for you is a mere formality."

"But they've given me until the feast of Purification of St. Mary."

"It is because they are kind, and want to appear just. They know, just like everyone else, that you will find nothing because there is nothing to find. Your father planned to kill the king with his poison and killed a good man instead. He was caught and soon, he will die. The best you could hope for is a swift death, and not to be killed yourself."

Such words, from a Christian monk. "My father did not try to kill anyone. He is innocent. We both are." Her chin trembled, and her mouth began to curl into an ugly sneer, when she saw the excited light in his blue eyes. He was hoping to get a rise out of her. Bronwyn cocked her head at him.

"You think I am cruel, but I'm doing you a favor. Do you really think anyone in their right mind would answer questions from a baker's daughter?" He snorted.

"But they'll answer you?"

"Why, yes. *I* am popular at court. I come from a distinguished and wealthy family and have many lands, which I have donated to the church." He bowed his head as if in prayer. "I know my place, and I know my business at court."

"Your 'business'?" She scratched her head.

"This is a great game you have entered into, baker's daughter, but you do not know how to play. Allow me to play for you."

Her temper rose. "Why is it that men want to do this task for me? Why does no one believe I can find out who killed de Grecy?"

Brother Bartholomew spoke as if it were obvious. "There are queens, there are princesses, and then there are merchants, peasants, and humble bakers."

His self-satisfied smile made her want to punch his face in. "What does that have to do with anything?"

Brother Bartholomew looked at her oddly. "It is the way of things. You are a mere baker, so you should stay in the kitchen and bake. Leave solving crimes to the men who are best suited to the task. It could be… dangerous for one like you."

"But not you."

He sniffed. "I know how to maneuver my way around court, and how to be seen without being detected."

"What does that even mean?" She was losing her patience.

His mouth lit up with a smile. "That is how I play."

"But you're a monk. You shouldn't be mixing with court politics."

"I never said I did. But I am a member of this court and you would do well to respect my position." His smirk grew. "I, of course, will help you solve this matter. You will obviously need my help, for you have no hope of finding out anything that will answer the call of justice."

Bronwyn gritted her teeth. "I'm smarter than you think."

"Of course you are. And it's so preposterous, the idea of a maid like you investigating. I told everyone the very idea was nonsense. Now, come. Tell me what you've found out so far. We are on the same side, after all."

She gazed at him with her best impression of Margaret when she was unimpressed. He had been so quick to accuse her and her father of being traitors, when they had their first audience with the king. And now he was offering to help her? "Why should I tell you anything? From what you've said, I know nothing."

"Don't be sour. I told them that to throw them off the trail. You may have that busybody look about you, but there is intelligence too, possibly. Now come, tell me what you know."

Bronwyn did not trust the man one bit. "Why would I share information with a man I've only met once before? I do not know you. You were in the throne room when my father and I were interrogated by the king and queen. You had nothing nice to say then, and my papa was put in prison."

He weighed this in his mind. "That is true, but not my fault. Very well. I shall prove it to you. I shall find out a little nugget about this dead de Grecy of yours and tell you. Then you will have to believe me. I am a man of my word, after all." He shuffled away.

Bronwyn shook her head and returned to the kitchens. At this point, hours of baking and pot scrubbing seemed like a welcome break.

At the midday meal, she ate quickly and slipped away to visit her father. He scratched at himself, likely from fleas, and his face was a bit drawn. He needed a shave and a bath, but he seemed happy to see her. "Bronwyn," he said with affection. He reached through the rough and jagged bars to grasp her hand.

She fretted. "Your hand is cold." She quickly looked at his stone cell. It was not a big space, but it had straw, a chamber pot, and an empty trencher on the floor. "You need a blanket."

"I need more than that. The air down here is…"

She knew what he meant. The air was thick and dank. The jail smelled of mold, damp water leaking, and urine, but her nose always got used to it. She passed over two rolls she'd made earlier that day.

He took them and munched eagerly. "How goes the hunt for the killer?"

She tried to brighten but faltered. She couldn't give him false hope. Not when he depended so much upon her. Walking home with Rupert and Alfred felt like she'd been wasting time, dallying with boys when she should have been investigating.

Bronwyn looked at him. "I'm investigating with Sir Nicholas and a new man is helping me, Brother Bartholomew."

Her father looked at her with earnestness and saw her mouth twisted in a frown. "I know during our first meeting with him, he was suspicious, but he is not so bad as you think. He often comes down to lead us in prayer."

"He said he would find some information for me."

"Mayhap he will. But I'd be careful who you trust. You don't want to get in trouble or give the queen any wrong information," he warned. "How is your mama?"

"Well enough." Her face darkened.

"What's wrong?" her father asked.

"It's about Alfred."

"He's a good lad."

"He kissed me." Bronwyn kicked at a loose rock, sending it flying down the corridor. It scared a rat that went scurrying away.

"Did he?" Her father's face was serious. "What did your mother say?"

"She's ready to start planning a wedding," Bronwyn said sourly.

Her father nodded. "She does like a wedding."

"I don't love him. I'm not even sure I *like* him."

He glanced at her. "In our world, dear poppet, that doesn't

matter. Girls younger than you have been married off for far less. Love doesn't play into relationships, only commerce."

"What do you mean? I always thought when a man and woman fell in love they married and… That's it."

He smiled. "A lot of times that is what happens. But if the families don't approve, then there's trouble. Seems like your mother already approves of young Alfred."

Bronwyn leaned a hand against the rough bars of the cell, then jerked away, as the uneven edge caught at her sleeve. "I don't. He kissed me and didn't ask first. He just grabbed my arm and did it."

Her father's eyes narrowed a fraction. "What did you do?"

"I stepped on his foot. Hard."

He smiled. "That's my girl. Good on you. If a man kisses you, you don't have to take it." His face fell. "If I weren't in here, I'd have a word with him. I'm sorry, Bronwyn."

"No, Papa, it's not your fault. That's on me." Her spirits sank. She hadn't solved the crime yet, and the days were passing. If she didn't find the real culprit soon, her father would hang. She could practically hear the rope creak and swing in her mind. "I'll get you out of here. I promise."

They clasped hands again, and she left, more determined than ever. She worked hard in the kitchens, and that night slipped out early so as not to have any more run-ins with Rupert or Alfred. She stuck to the shadows. As she scurried down Steep Hill, she tried to make as little noise as possible.

The next day, she took a blanket to her father and paid the guards a coin to allow it. They didn't much care, fortunately. Her father accepted it gratefully, along with a roll she'd snuck in her sleeve. His hands were still cold, and he shivered in the dampness of his cell. He looked dirty and unwashed, and her heart went out to him. She had to find out who de Grecy's killer was—she had to. She just wanted her father to see sunlight again, and for him to feel the sun's warm rays on his face, even if they were cold in January.

At this point, she was wary about accepting his aid, but she decided to accept all the help she could get and sought out Brother Bartholomew the following afternoon on her way back from the privy. He was chatting and laughing with some of the nobles, and she caught his eye from passing by in the corridor. In two minutes she hung by the circular stairwell and waited. A minute more and he stood at the top of the stairs. "Bronwyn," he said.

She nodded in greeting. "Have you found anything?"

"I have indeed, baker's daughter. Come with me." He motioned her to follow downstairs and they walked one behind the other down the stone, circular staircase, their hands trailing against the hard, chilled walls.

In a small room that was empty but for a small fire in the hearth, he pulled her aside and said, "I've learnt something about that night de Grecy died."

"Tell me," she breathed.

"I was there at dinner the night he choked on the poisoned roll. He'd made a big fuss about them, how he'd paid so much money to procure these fine, sweet white rolls with honey. But with any dinner like this, you need to consider the players."

This again. "Living at court isn't a game, Brother Bartholomew. A man died."

"Exactly," he said. "We all assume the rolls were an attempt to poison the king and queen. Unless… It was an attempt to kill de Grecy? He was new to court, and in that short time, had proven himself proud and overbearing. He did not have any friends here."

Her eyes widened. "You think the green-hooded man attempted to kill him, instead of the king and queen?"

"It is possible. And of course, he was unaware of a rather important detail."

"What's that?"

"I have just learnt that Their Graces did not trust mushrooms and would rarely eat them. One of their men told me. Had de

Grecy bothered to learn their tastes and habits, he might not have placed them in such danger, or fallen prey to it himself."

She breathed in. That just made it clearer that this had been no ordinary mistake of mistaking mushrooms. This had been a clear attack. The question was, upon whom?

Brother Bartholomew said, "Out of the group of knights and nobility present the night de Grecy died, there were just five you need to be aware of."

"Why five? Why not any of the servants here?"

He shook his head. "A servant would not risk their place, or their head, by involving themselves in a plot. The king and queen traveled here with their company, but they did not send out the servants already working here out into the cold. Some servants are loyal to them, while others may only pretend to be. But in all honesty, I think most servants have their own work to do, and get to it. They are kept too busy to be partaking in little schemes, and life at the castle is fairly regimented. If any servant acted out of turn, the others would notice. It would cause comment. The knights however, do what they please."

"What do you mean?"

"The men hold the money, and most women cannot read. Some can, as a better way to read their little prayer books, but it is a rare gift to know much beyond your own name."

She disagreed with his assessment of the women but nodded, her face warming. *I wish I could read*, she thought.

"In any case, there are five men you should know about. They are Gilbert, Bors, Gabriel, Grossetete, and Clarke. You should also suspect Sir Nicholas."

"Sir Nicholas? Why him?"

He shrugged. "All I know is he had a bone to pick with de Grecy and made no hide of his dislike of him. Didn't trust him. He came here only lately, you know."

"When?"

"A few weeks past."

"Why?" she asked.

"Yes, Brother, tell us why. How do you know so much about de Grecy?" Sir Nicholas came from around the corner and stood behind Bronwyn.

She jumped.

Brother Bartholomew tensed. "Nothing, I know nothing. Excuse me, I've got somewhere else to be." The monk hustled down the stairs.

"Mind telling me what you were doing talking to that self-righteous prick?" Sir Nicholas asked with a raised eyebrow.

"I was getting information. He'd found out something about the night of de Grecy's death and was telling me when you interrupted."

Sir Nicholas lifted one shoulder in a half-shrug. "That man does like the sound of his own voice. Don't pay attention to anything he says."

"Why shouldn't I?" she asked, frowning. Her eyebrows knit together in a little line. This man was not her father, so why did he get to tell her whom she should and shouldn't speak with? "Or is it because he named you as a man who didn't like de Grecy?"

He stared down at her, his piggish eyes turning hard. "Mind your tongue, girl. Don't be talking to your betters like that unless you want a stripe on your hide."

She glared at him. "Then tell me why you and de Grecy didn't get on."

His mouth broke into a smile. "You're relentless. You're just like my old charger, Fleur. Good beast, that."

She tried not to roll her eyes. Just what she needed, to be compared to a horse. "So why didn't you like him?"

He walked over to one of the windows, looking out through the thin-paned glass.

She followed him and stood at his side, waiting.

"You look out there, and you see the town, you see the houses and shops, you see the city, the people of Lincoln."

"Yes," she agreed.

"I see roads that need better defenses. Gates that need more men. Places where archers are needed, and where we need more spikes, more blades, more soldiers. This war between Maud and Stephen, it is at our throats, and most of the people working below are too blind to see it. The war will be at our doorstep, and it is only a matter of time before Maud's forces come here for a fight."

"What will happen when they do?" She took a deep breath at the thought, and dark visions of burning fires, smoke, and chaos in the streets filled her mind.

"Then you will need to run, and God help you," he said simply. "War's no place for a girl. A battlefield has no room to spare for girls, or small children. De Grecy came to us a few weeks ago, begging to parley. I didn't like him from the start, I make no bones about that. He came begging to be taken in, for sanctuary."

She waited for him to continue. He was deep within the memory.

"That was the first time we'd laid eyes on each other, and right from the start, I could tell something wasn't right. A man begging for sanctuary would be humble, honest. He'd come here with his cap in his hands, so to speak. But not de Grecy. He was too cocksure, too full of himself. Too proud." He shook his head. "Here he was begging sanctuary, saying he'd fled from Maud's camp and couldn't bring himself to serve her anymore, but he had no good reason to say why. Just that he'd come to see the light and wanted to throw his lot in with King Stephen. I told him sanctuary could be claimed at church, not here, and he ignored me. Me, the right hand of the Crown."

"That was rude of him."

"To say the least," Sir Nicholas said. "King Stephen took him in; we need all the blades we can get. But I did not trust him. A former sympathizer of the enemy, coming here? Too easy. I counseled Their Graces against it, but they didn't listen."

"So when he died?"

"It created confusion, but I thought it was justice. It would be God's own work if he was poisoned by his own roll."

"Do you think that's what happened?" she asked.

"I think he deserved what he got," he said. "But he wouldn't have eaten rolls he knew were poison. No man is stupid enough to do that. Someone poisoned those rolls."

"Perhaps they meant to kill de Grecy, rather than the king and queen. We've been so focused on the idea of the poison being intended for Their Graces, but what if it wasn't?"

He pondered this, playing with his impressive mustache. "You may have a point. What we need to find out is who would have wanted to do it, and who had the means, and the opportunity."

"You were present at the dinner, and you're aware of the goings-on at court. Who do you think could have done it?" Bronwyn wondered.

"Anyone. But I can tell you that out of those names the good Brother gave you, I'm innocent."

She smiled. "Why should I believe that?"

He straightened and squared his shoulders. "I'd never stoop so low as to poison a man. I'm a man of honor. If I'm going to kill a man, I'll challenge him to a duel or run him through."

"I believe you."

"So that leaves just five men for you to investigate."

"What about their ladies?"

He shrugged. "If Gilbert was seeing someone, he was keeping it quiet. Bors and Grossetete are confirmed bachelors, Clarke does nothing without his wife's approval, and Gabriel… I'm not sure. He could have done it. I'll ask around."

"What happened at the dinner, exactly?" she asked.

"We were dining and drinking as usual, when de Grecy announced he had a little treat for us. He called for the rolls and there was some delay, then they were brought out. He announced they were for the king and queen and took one, passing the plate down. The queen took a plain one, but the king refrained, for he's never cared much for mushrooms. De Grecy bit into his first and stuffed it all in his mouth, not realizing of course, he should have waited for Their Graces to eat first. The queen ate some of hers and all seemed well enough, but after a minute or so, de Grecy began to cough, then he turned red, then white, and he fell out of his chair. No one knew what to do, and he died."

"No one did anything?"

He shook his head. "We are knights, not medical men. We lead armies, fight battles, walk and ride in formation. We do not care for the sick."

"What happened then?"

"There was an uproar. The king demanded everyone put down their rolls and people threw them to the floor. Servants picked them up before the dogs could get them and tossed them into the fire. The king ordered that the head cook and the baker who baked the rolls be brought forward immediately, and you know the rest."

Bronwyn nodded and turned to go, when he said, "Oh, and of course, there's Sir Baldwin of Clare."

"I know that name."

"You should. It's his squire you've been walking around with."

"What? I haven't been walking with anyone."

He chuckled. "You expect me to believe that, when I see you two walking down Steep Hill every night?"

She paused. "You mean…"

"You know the lad. Rupert. He's the squire to Sir Baldwin of Clare. A fine knight, to be sure, but… he seemed altogether too calm when de Grecy began to cough and die. I wonder if he suspected or knew what was to happen before anyone else did."

"You think he could be behind this?" she asked.

"I didn't say that. But when the man died, I got out of my seat and was ordering the guards to help, and Sir Baldwin sat there peacefully, almost like he was at church. He looked at his bread roll and tossed it to the floor like the others. I wonder about him. But he is a fine knight, and a good rider. Dependable in a fight."

Or a killer, she thought. Was Rupert squire to a murderer?

Chapter Six

THE NEXT DAY when Bronwyn stepped outside her family's shop it was busier than usual, and noisier for Lincoln's streets. She'd wondered if it was a parade of sorts, or some knights riding into town, but this was different. The mood was more melancholy. Dozens of people, soiled, unwashed and dirty, trudged past. Old men, too old to fight, women and children. Many looked tired and hungry, as if they'd spent hours on the run. A few eyed her family's bakery, their noses lifting at the smell of freshly baked bread in the air. Bronwyn quickly shut the door closed behind her. As dawn's early light edged up through the black trees and buildings of the city of Lincoln, showing great bars of orange and dark blue sky, Bronwyn wondered what had happened. She did not know these people.

Once at the castle kitchens, she hung up her coat and stamped her feet to rid herself of the slush and dirt that had clung to her boots as she'd walked up Steep Hill. The cooks, pages, servants, and potboys were in an uproar. People hurried about their chores, faces downturned, and more than one man looked harried and nervous, their eyes darting around as if seeing enemies around every corner.

"What's going on?" she asked the nearest cook, a youth in his teens.

"Didn't you hear?" he said. "There was an attack last night."

Her stomach sank. So those had been the people outside her

family's shop. "No. Where? Here?"

He shook his head. "Outside the castle. I'm surprised you didn't hear of it."

"Was it Maud?" Bronwyn asked.

He nodded. "Who else would it have been?"

She went about her chores. Odo had her join the other bakers and make bread, as well as rolls with diced-up meat in them. Her favorite was making sweet treats with pastry—she loved rubbing the butter into the dough to make a mouthwatering pastry that would later be filled with something scrumptious.

But outside the kitchen, the corridor was full of people. Men, mostly. Knights and lords barked orders and shouted as servants dashed to and fro. Bronwyn went to one of the men who stood by the entrance and asked, "What is happening?"

"People are coming in from the attack. The French wench's army is getting closer and testing her strength. But when she can't get past our own fighters, she takes it out on the villagers living outside the city. These are people whose homes she destroyed." They stood back as men, women and some children walked by, while soldiers hastily erected tents and set up shelter in the castle courtyard. It was nowhere to put those who had come seeking shelter, but it was better than the bare outdoors.

"What do you need from us?" Bronwyn asked.

"You speak for the kitchen, do you?" he asked with a smile.

"No, she does not." Odo came up behind them. "Get back to work, Bronwyn."

She ducked her head meekly and returned, hearing the men chuckle behind her. Red-faced, Bronwyn did her best to ignore them and began making rolls, filling pies, turning the roast spit and serving up pottage for luncheon, and then passing through trenchers of extra for the people huddling outside in the tents. They were cold and hungry and had lost everything. Her heart went out to them.

She thought little that morning, dwelling on her own luck, in that her family was warm, safe, to a point, and had a roof over their heads. They had not been touched by war, not yet. She felt lucky and gave a private prayer to the Lord for thanks.

As the bell tolled for Mass, Bronwyn joined the others and slipped out early, taking a few rolls to visit her father.

He accepted them and ate hungrily, stuffing one in his trousers for later. He looked thin, cold, and wistful. His facial hair had grown and he no longer had a light beard that her mama had once declared was velvety soft and barely there. This now appeared bristly, unkempt, and long. He needed a shave, but of course, prisoners weren't allowed weapons.

Bronwyn told him of the attack, and how the castle was now feeding more than the regular inhabitants. As they clasped hands goodbye he said, "It will get worse before it gets better, I fear."

She went back to the kitchens, when a request came from the queen for four white rolls with honey. Bronwyn set to making them and when they were done was met by the page, who escorted her up to the queen.

But when he knocked and opened the door, she stepped inside. Bronwyn's eyes widened and her mouth dropped open. She lost her grasp on the plate and almost dropped the rolls, saving them just in time.

"Good heavens, girl, whatever is the matter with you?" the queen asked.

"Forgive me, my lady," Bronwyn said, still staring. "I slipped on my skirts."

"Well, never mind. You see, Alice, this is the girl I was talking about. You must try the white rolls with honey."

Bronwyn bowed her head and glanced at the newcomer, Alice, who was the reason she'd almost dropped the rolls. For there, sat next to the queen, was none other than the girl she'd found in de Grecy's bed chamber, the girl from Maud's court. Did she warn the queen that she had a spy from a rival court sat beside her?

Bronwyn began, "Your Grace, I must tell you, I know—"

"Oh, it's you." Alice set down her drink, rose to her feet, and cut her off, crossing the small space to her. "So you are the baker I've heard so much about. What a pleasure to meet you. But you were about to say something. You recognize me, perhaps? I do have that sort of face, I've been told." Her dark eyes narrowed, a warning to Bronwyn not to try her luck.

Alice shot her a little triumphant smile. From her even gaze and wide grin, Bronwyn knew that whatever story she wished to tell, Alice would spin one far greater and more trustworthy than hers.

Alice's eyes widened a fraction and were replaced with a knowing smile. Her dark gaze took on a wicked air, and she smiled prettily at Bronwyn, as if meeting her for the first time. No longer dressed in a dirty, brown woolen peasant dress with a kerchief to hide her hair and shield her face, she now wore a deep-blue dress and displayed her fine, silken-black hair. Alice shone in the warm candlelight like a fashionable crow or raven, so sleek were her tresses. Her skin was white and fair, and she looked a little tired. She said, "What a delight. I never thought I would try a white roll again in my life."

"Oh, hush, it's not that bad," Queen Matilda said, motioning Bronwyn forward.

Bronwyn brought the plate and held it out as the ladies both took a sweet roll. Queen Matilda bit into it and smiled. "Delicious. Such a clever young cook."

"When she's not tripping over her own skirts," Alice simpered.

Bronwyn's cheeks turned pink as she set the plate on a side table beside the queen. She looked from Alice to the queen.

"Will that be all, milady?" Bronwyn asked.

"Yes, yes. Go on." She bid her away with a wave.

Bronwyn curtseyed awkwardly, earning a snort from Alice. Blushing harder, the young baker kept her gaze to the floor and walked out, followed by the page.

As he closed the door, Bronwyn overheard Alice giggle. "Wherever did you find that girl? She's practically straight off the farm. Did you see her curtsey? It's no wonder she tripped. She moves like a bird."

Bronwyn walked away, followed by the page, who kept pace beside her. "Don't worry about them. That new girl doesn't have a nice word to say about anyone."

"Who is she?" she asked.

"Lady Alice Duncombe. She's a refugee who came to us after the attack."

"I didn't think the queen took refugees into her private chambers."

The boy shrugged. "She does if they're noble, like Alice."

"She's a noblewoman?"

He nodded. "When Queen Matilda heard a girl from a noble family had come seeking shelter and wished to pay her respects, she agreed to meet the girl straightaway. Took her in and said she can join her retinue."

The girl worked fast. "Amazing," Bronwyn said. "The queen is very generous."

"Aye." The boy gave her a funny look, then paused. "Bronwyn…"

"What?" She glanced at him.

He fidgeted, shifting his weight from foot to foot. "I… know you're investigating the death of de Grecy."

"Let me guess. You want to help me too."

"What? No. I… No." He fidgeted more.

"Then what?" she asked.

"Um…"

She gave him a hard glance. She'd just been made fun of by Alice to the queen, almost tripped on her face and dropped the rolls, and was no closer to solving the crime to save her father. She had little time for this.

"What if I knew something, about what happened that night? The night de Grecy died," he said.

"Tell me. What do you know?"

He tugged at his shirt collar and loosened one of the tied

strings. The page scratched the right side of his head and said, "I know who killed him. De Grecy, I mean."

"Who?" she asked, practically jumping.

"It was Roger. He's the only one of us with a green cloak like that. And he was showing it off to everyone, acting like he was so brave. But it was stolen. He was mad because his master gave it to him and then he had to ride out and he didn't get to take it. He was that mad. That was before the rolls were poisoned. But… I thought you should know." He stopped, seeing someone behind her.

"Wait, you said he was riding out? Where did he go? When was this?"

He bowed. "I have to go. Bye." He turned and left, as fast as his feet could carry him.

She turned and met Sir Bors. The way he carried himself, he practically filled the corridor, and he looked down on her with a slight interest in his eyes. "What is a kitchen maid doing wasting time with a page?" he boomed.

"He was escorting me back to the kitchens," Bronwyn said.

"You're that maid, aren't you? The one with her nose in de Grecy's business," the man asked, towering over her.

Bronwyn said nothing. The man could overpower her in an instant, and she hated that fact. He was built like a solid wall. Nothing could get past him.

"You should know that I had nothing to do with that business. I love His Grace," he said, his voice slightly slurred. He'd been drinking.

She raised her chin. "I have to get back." She turned, but he grabbed her. His entire hand encircled her upper arm like an iron glove.

"Don't turn your back on me, girl. You should respect your betters. D'you know who I am?" he boomed.

She glared, her temper rising. "Let go of me."

"I am Sir Bors. Don't you forget it."

Odo stood in the entrance to the kitchen. "Sir Bors, mind you don't pull my kitchen maid's arm off, I need her to bake rolls for His Grace. If you please?" His bulk filled the doorway of the kitchen, and he raised an expectant eyebrow.

Sir Bors shoved her away, and she stumbled at the force of it, tripping.

Odo frowned and said, "Back to work, girl."

She stood, smoothed down her skirts, and walked past Bors, who shot her a nasty smile and said, "Don't get in my way again, baker. I don't like women who nose around in people's business. Makes them smell worse than a whore after Easter."

Bronwyn tried not to shiver and held her held high as she slipped back into the kitchens. Odo soon followed and stood by as she woodenly went to the spit and began turning.

"You all right, Bronwyn?" he asked.

She nodded.

"That's Sir Bors, but I expect you knew that. Could hear the man across the kitchens. Built like an ox, that one."

The ghost of a smile drifted across her face. She tried to ignore the fact that his words had sent a shiver down her spine and made the hair on the back of her neck stand up.

"You should stay away from him. He's trouble."

She cocked her head at him.

"Oh, for heaven's sake. Just keep your distance from him. He's not one to be around. Cut from a coarser cloth, isn't he?" He scratched his chest idly. "Stay down in the kitchen the rest of today. If the queen wants more rolls, the page can bring them. Give 'em something to do, anyway."

She kept turning the spit, and Odo kept an eye on her, not letting her go anywhere outside the kitchens. Odo spent time teaching her and the other cooks how best to preserve pork, and the best way to season fish in a way that the king liked.

She slipped out to use the privy and once she'd finished, wandered to where she'd seen Brother Bartholomew socializing, waiting until she'd caught his eye.

He excused himself and wandered over.

"Well? Have you found out anything?" she asked.

"Oh, yes. So many things," he said with a knowing smile. He fingered the wooden cross that hung from his neck, the shined piece of glass at its center catching the light.

"Are you going to tell me?" Bronwyn asked.

"Is this man bothering you?" a knight asked.

"Sir Gilbert." The monk swept a stiff bow. "I must be off. I have places to be." Brother Bartholomew left in a huff, but shot a look over his shoulder as he left.

The knight stood in a loose, belted tunic and trousers but held himself with an air of being ready to fight at a moment's notice. He carried himself with strength, and his eyes surveyed the room, seeming to miss no detail, however small. But as he turned his gaze to Bronwyn, his blue eyes crinkled as he smiled.

The knight smirked as Brother Bartholomew left, then turned to Bronwyn. "What is a servant girl doing out of the kitchens?"

"How did you know I work there?" she asked.

"I've not seen you around here before, and I never forget a pretty face. Also, your apron is covered with flour. It's not hard to surmise." He smiled. "What's your name?"

"Bronwyn Blakenhale."

His eyes lit up in recognition. "You're that girl, aren't you? The one asking questions about de Grecy."

She returned his smile with one of her own. He was so friendly, it was hard not to want to repay his kindness.

"I am Sir Gilbert. One of the king's men." He gave a small bow.

She curtsied and rose. He was one of the men Brother Bartholomew had warned her about, so she took in the sight of him. Tall, blond hair, cropped short with a trimmed, straw-blond mustache and beard. He wore a thick, padded jerkin over a long, belted tunic and trousers, and a sheathed blade hung at his side. He moved like a man who knew his business, and that business was war.

"Well met, Bronwyn. Tell me, what is it you're doing out of

the kitchens? Did you mean to ask the monk for information? He's made no secret of the fact he's investigating this death of de Grecy."

She shrugged. "He offered to help. I thought men might talk more easily to him than me."

"You would be right. And yet, you choose your comrades poorly. He is no better than a fool," Sir Gilbert said.

"Why do you say that?"

"He is never there when you need him, and always around when you don't. He reminds me of a weasel. I was there that night when de Grecy died. What is it you wish to know? Ask me."

She peered up at him. "Do you think someone wanted the king dead? Or de Grecy?"

He threw his head back and laughed uproariously, slapping his knee. People glanced over, causing her to blush. Sir Gilbert grinned and laughed again, motioning for a servant to bring a cup of wine.

He accepted a cup and drank, wiping his blond beard with his sleeve. "You make me laugh, Mistress Blakenhale. I haven't heard anything so funny in days. De Grecy is one thing, but I, want the king dead? No. He has saved my life in battle too many times, and I his. We look out for each other. But that does not mean that there are others who would overlook their love for their king."

"Like who? And why?"

He snorted softly. "I would not give away the names of inno-cent men." He paused. "But if you do find reason to suspect someone, ask me and I will tell you what I know. I will not lie to you."

She raised an eyebrow.

"I am a man of God. I believe lying to be sinful." He offered her a fraction of a bow and stood back as the doors to the dining hall opened. In walked Queen Matilda, followed by a series of ladies.

"Who are those women with the queen?" Bronwyn asked.

"Her ladies," he said. "The important ones are the Countess

of Chester; the constable's wife; and the Countess of Cambridge, the wife of William de Roumare. That girl with the raven hair, I do not know. She is new, like you."

Bronwyn watched as the ladies filed into the room, chatting quietly amongst themselves. Queen Matilda looked very well as she became the center of attention, nodding to some nobles and giving a polite smile to others. Her manner was soft and demure as she navigated the room in a dark-blue dress, trimmed with a gold-tooled belt, and a circlet around her hair. She had her hair pinned back in a loose, thick braid, but even without the golden circlet, Bronwyn surmised that it would be clear to any who did not already know this was a queen, that this was no ordinary woman.

"Never an unkind word for anyone, our queen," Sir Gilbert said. "Even those whom she could have imprisoned, she keeps them by her side. Too kind if you ask me, but then women are soft-hearted creatures."

"What do you mean, those she could have imprisoned?" she asked. "You mean that because their husbands are in prison, they should be as well? And so it is through the queen's mercy that she keeps them at her side?"

He glanced at her with a nod of approval. "You *are* new. And clever. Well done. There's more to it than just that, however, so I'll tell you. But only so that you do not go spreading rumors like some girls do." He added, much louder, "All right, girl, you've seen the queen. Now it's back to the kitchens with you." He made to take her arm and she let him steer her away, under the watchful eyes of the ladies present, including Lady Alice, who eyed her keenly.

Once out in the corridors, he released Bronwyn's arm and said quietly, "This castle was under the protection of King Stephen, when before Christmas, the constable and his wife entertained the Countess of Chester and her friend, the wife of the Earl of Chester's half-brother, William de Roumare."

She nodded for him to continue. "I've heard about this. So

those are the wives in question."

"Exactly. When the earl and his half-brother came to collect their wives, they came unarmed and peaceful, then once they were behind the castle gates, they took over the castle."

"I know this story. The citizens of Lincoln wrote to the king asking for his help and he came," she said.

"He did. Reclaimed the castle around Christmas time. But what you may not know is that of the men who fought against his forces—those who did not escape, swear allegiance, or die—a handful were imprisoned in the jail cells below. Seventeen, to be exact, the Earl of Chester's half-brother, William de Roumare, among them."

Bronwyn breathed in. To hear it spoken of so lightly almost gave her a shock. Mentally, she knew they were down there, but it still sent a shiver down her spine. Those men were with her father. Traitors to the Crown, men allied with the empress.

"Aye," Sir Gilbert said. "We know that the Earl of Chester escaped and has likely gone to beg the imposter queen for help. This latest attack on the townspeople is a bad move. And that's just outside the castle walls. To keep the men imprisoned below from rebelling or causing trouble, the queen has kept their wives here, under her protection. And armed guard. She calls them her guests."

"So they are prisoners too, the wives," she said.

"A very easy sort of prison. They can walk around and talk and eat with the other nobles. But it is not without some measure of shame for what their husbands did. And some of these women were present at table when de Grecy died. So if you are looking for culprits, or someone who might have questionable allegiance to the king and queen, you might look toward them."

That meant the pool of suspects had just grown. "Why are you telling me all this?"

"I told you, Mistress Blakenhale, I would not lie to you. Not like some here. And besides, if we do have a poisoner here at court, they must be found. You should have seen them all the day after he died. Everyone was too fearful to eat a bite but not wanting to seem too afraid. If it weren't for the king taking the first bite, I think we'd all still be starving out of fear."

"Thank you."

"My pleasure. I do hope you'll catch the man." He offered her a slight bow, and she curtsied, or tried to. He smirked and said, "If you want to stay at court, you'll want to work on that."

Chapter Seven

BRONWYN RETURNED TO the kitchens and wondered as she prepared dough for baking, *What if I'm going about this the wrong way? What if I should not be solely asking the men, but also speaking with the women? If some of these women were essentially prisoners, then they must have something to hide,* she thought. *Did some of the women know what was going to happen when the Earl of Chester and his half-brother took the castle, or were they innocent?*

She pondered this as she pounded the dough, slapping it on the hard, wooden worktable, until a boy whistled, making her turn at the sound. There stood a well-dressed, middle-aged woman at the kitchen entrance, looking around.

"What's she doing here?" she asked.

"It's Mistress de la Haye." A boy glanced at her.

"So where is Master Odo?"

"He's out supervising the hunters. They're saying the men brought down a stag, pheasants, and ducks."

"So who is in charge whilst he's gone?"

The boy shrugged. "Dunno. He'll be back soon, anyway."

At that moment, Bronwyn felt a kinship to the chatelaine. Seeing as the boys were happy to stare, even though no one spoke to her, Mistress de la Haye looked around as if she wished to speak, then began to turn away.

Bronwyn set down her dough, brushed her hands on her simple cloth apron, and came up to her. "Milady?"

Mistress de la Haye turned back. She wore a long dress of grey wool, cut to her figure. Her silver-brown hair was braided too like Queen Matilda's, and she wore a plain strand necklace around her neck. She stood short, with a petite, round figure, and looked up at Bronwyn with wary, grey eyes. She must have been fifty or older.

"Did you want something?" Bronwyn asked.

"A roll. I am hungry." Mistress de la Haye paused. "A few of the ladies wanted something to nibble on, but there were no servants about, so they sent me." She colored with embarrassment and looked down at the floor.

"It is no trouble, my lady. I'll get some rolls for you and the others."

Bronwyn took a fresh loaf from the baking racks and cut it into slices with a knife, spreading churned butter on each one. She brought the plate to Mistress de la Haye and as the lady reached for it, Bronwyn shook her head. "It is beneath you to serve. I'll bring it."

Her eyes widened, her smile bittersweet. "Thank you. This way." She turned and led Bronwyn out of the kitchens. As they walked, she said quietly, "They wish to humiliate me, by treating me like a servant. My husband is castellan of this castle." She brushed away a tear. "I'm sorry, I…"

Bronwyn had no handkerchief to offer. "I'm sorry."

The woman wiped her eyes on her sleeve.

"Are you feeling well?"

"Well enough. Why?" Mistress de la Haye peered at Bronwyn. "You. You were there, when I fainted. You had a fish?"

Bronwyn smiled and nodded. "I'm glad you're feeling better."

The chatelaine wiped her eyes. "I've been such a fool. I had no idea."

"What do you mean?"

She looked away, patting her side braid. "I… do not have many lady friends. Passing acquaintances, and when my husband was made castellan of the castle, it was a great rise in status for us both. I was touched when the wives of de Gernon and de Roumare came for a visit. I stupidly thought they came in the interest of friendship." Her hands trembled and she smoothed down her grey skirts.

"Instead, they waited for their husbands to come, and then stood by as the men stormed the castle. They killed servants, people we had known and trusted. Good people. They beat my husband and threatened to kill me if we did not comply with their wishes. Those... *women* stood back and watched from safety as the men took the castle." She snorted bitterly. "I am a fool."

"You are not," Bronwyn said, keeping pace with her. "I think you are... kind-hearted."

"And look where it got me."

"You are alive. Is your husband...?" Bronwyn asked.

"He is alive, but shaken by the turn of events. He is happy to be back under King Stephen's protection—we both are. But we came under suspicion when they reclaimed the castle. It was thought we had welcomed de Gernon and de Roumare with open arms, when all I did was welcome them in for food and drink. I was so stupid." She shook her head.

"You are not," Bronwyn repeated. "You were taken in. Do you think the ladies knew what their husbands were up to when they came to see you?"

"How could they not? I mean, a man tells his wife most things, or a wife can overhear things. But... I don't know. All I know is since the king and queen returned, Queen Matilda is keeping all us ladies close, but at arm's length. She does not know who to trust, and so she quietly watches us all but asks none for counsel." She looked at Bronwyn. "I'm sorry. I do not mean to speak out of turn. It's just... I have no one to talk to but my husband, and even he is loath to speak at all. He fears the walls have ears, or eyes, or something."

Bronwyn smiled at her, and the chatelaine's eyes watered at the sight. "And then I saw him. I saw him, the night that foul knight died. But no one believed me. But I have proof." Her chin trembled and she dabbed at her eyes with the handkerchief. She plucked a long strand of black ribbon from her sleeve and wound it around her fingers again and again, then unwound it. She seemed unaware of the nervous habit.

"What is that?" Bronwyn asked.

"My proof. You recall the night that de Roumare surprised me. I knew it was him, even though no one believed me. I tried to grab hold of him, but my hand only came back with this. I have his hair, you see. This is it." She handed it to Bronwyn.

"How odd." Bronwyn looked at the hair. It was long and silky. "It's almost like horsehair."

"I suppose." She took the hair back and wound it around her fingers again.

"We could tell the king and queen, or Sir Nicholas. With this, they would listen to you."

Mistress de la Haye shook her head. "No one trusts us anymore. Not after we lost the castle and Their Graces had to come and take it back. They wouldn't believe me."

"Are you all right?" Bronwyn asked.

"Yes, yes, I'm fine. This is going to sound silly, but you are the first person to say a nice word to me that wasn't false, or rude. You speak honestly, plainly. I haven't had anyone say anything kind to me in a while." She gave Bronwyn a watery smile.

It pained her to see it. Being the wife of the castellan of the castle of such a grand size, it must have been a lot of responsibility. To have no one in whom to confide or with whom to chat on top of that sounded like a miserable, lonely existence. Bronwyn felt so bad for her.

"That's very kind. I thought I knew everyone who worked here, but I suppose not. Especially not now when we're accepting all these people into the castle and courtyard. What is your name?"

"Bronwyn Blakenhale. My father is a baker in town. He—"

A voice called out for her, and Mistress de la Haye looked harried. "I'd better go. Well met, Bronwyn Blakenhale. Perhaps we might speak again soon." She took the plate of bread.

"I'd like that. Mistress." Bronwyn curtsied, and the lady cracked a strained smile.

"I'll teach you how to curtsey too."

Bronwyn gritted her teeth slightly and harrumphed and stomped all the way back to the kitchens. What exactly was wrong with her curtsey?

She grumbled as she entered the doorway to the kitchen, when a voice whispered from the corridor. "Baker. Girl."

Bronwyn looked toward the source of the sound.

Lady Alice stepped from the shadows. "Hello again. What have you learnt?"

Bronwyn promptly crossed her arms over her chest. "What do you want?"

"You need to have a civil tongue when you talk to me," Lady Alice said with a frown. "I have the queen's ear. It would be a pity for you to lose the queen's trust over something so small as a bit of rudeness. You would be wise to befriend me, baker's daughter."

"What for? From what I can see, *you* are suspect. What were you doing poking about in de Grecy's room? I could tell the queen you're the woman everyone was looking for earlier."

Her eyes narrowed and Bronwyn was reminded of a raven, as the dim light shone on Lady Alice's jet-black hair, picking up highlights that looked like silk. "I could make life difficult for you. Tell me what you know."

"You first." Bronwyn put her hands on her hips.

They stared at each other, both refusing to back down.

"Do you know who I am?" Lady Alice asked.

A snot-nosed uppity aristocrat, Bronwyn thought, *who probably paid someone less fortunate to wipe her own arse.*

"I am Lady Alice Duncombe. My father owns one of the largest estates in Somerset," she said. "Do you even know where that is?"

Bronwyn's cheeks burned. She didn't. "You're a long way

from home, my lady."

With a light smile, Alice nodded, no doubt pleased at being called "my lady." "So I am. I was supposed to hear from de Grecy, but when he didn't make our meeting, we thought it best I come, so here I am."

"What were you supposed to speak with him about?"

"Why, the plan for a reb—" She paused. "You don't know. But I thought that you—" She clapped a hand to her mouth. "I'm wrong. Never mind."

She turned to go when Bronwyn caught her sleeve. Lady Alice whipped around, her mouth twisted. "Don't say a word of this to anyone, you hear? I *will* make life hard for you if you do. Do you understand me?"

"Wait, my lady. You thought I knew de Grecy?"

"Well, yes. When your family made those rolls for such a sum, apparently, he seemed far too pleased with himself, as if he'd made a new connection of his own. Although why he would consider a family of bakers worth associating with, I don't know. And then when I heard you were looking into his death, I thought it was a great joke. All of us did. I thought it simply a blind, to lure people away from the fact that you were working with him. And then when you covered for me in his room and didn't report me to the queen when you had the chance, well…"

"I felt bad for you when we found you in de Grecy's room," Bronwyn said.

"What?"

"I thought Sir Nicholas had scared you and so didn't want you to feel frightened. I didn't think you'd throw a knife at him."

She sulked. "It served him right."

"Bronwyn!" Odo called. "Where is that blasted girl?"

"I'd better go."

"Do not speak of this to anyone." Alice turned on her heel and left.

Bronwyn spent the early evening scrubbing the inside of pots as two of the potboys had gotten into the ale the night before and spent the whole day sick with sore heads. Odo had little sympathy for them and bade them to scrub pots and turn the spit until they fell over from fatigue, or puked their guts out, whichever came first.

The boys were the butt of many jokes and laughs, until one after another ran to the privy. Bronwyn gave them cups of ale to soothe their stomachs and went about her chores. As she stirred a pot of soup, adding in diced carrots and parsnips, she pondered what she knew. She wanted to talk it over with someone, but whom could she trust? She wasn't sure.

Bronwyn stirred and thought. When Sir Nicholas and she had entered de Grecy's room, the room had been disturbed, and they'd found Lady Alice inside, searching for something. When they'd met in the woods later, Alice had thought Bronwyn had somehow been connected to de Grecy and wondered if she'd been involved with him.

Bronwyn knew this much: de Grecy had not been honest. Her father and she had willingly taken an order for sweet rolls from a dishonest man. That did not matter so much, for she suspected many customers were liars on occasion, but they'd never had one use their rolls for murder before. And who was the green-hooded man who'd poisoned their rolls? The page had mentioned the cloak belonged to Roger the squire.

She turned to one of the potboys. "Do you know Roger? I heard he was given a green hood, but that it was stolen. Do you know anything about that?"

"No. I didn't take it."

"That night the man died. There was a man in a green hood who was messing about with the rolls. I bet it was whoever stole Roger's cloak. Did you see him?"

The boy shrugged. "Dunno."

One of the older boys looked at her with interest. "A lot of the squires come in here. Their masters send them to eat a midday meal sometimes, or when they want something and the pages have forgotten." He looked at her. "I know why you're asking about this, but Roger didn't do it. Like you say, someone stole his cloak. I saw the man push you, but I didn't see who he was. I didn't recognize him. But I don't think he was a servant here, or one of the squires."

"Why is that?" she asked.

The young cook scratched his head. "When he pushed you, the man moved fast, like he was running out of time. We don't go pushing each other 'round 'ere and definitely not women. He's not one of us."

She put her hands on her hips. "Why didn't you say anything when we were looking for anyone who'd seen him?"

The youth shrugged. "Don't see how it would help now. For all we know, it might've been your pa who's done it. We all know each other, but you're new here. We don't know where your loyalties lie."

She gave a noise of exasperation and tugged on her blonde braid. "Why don't you care about this? Of course it's not my father who's done it."

"They caught him, didn't they? Besides, do you have any idea how much work we've got on now that Godfrey is dead? Master Odo's finding his feet, and I've got five ducks to pluck, butcher, and roast before the next meal." He walked away, back to his a worktable, where five dead ducks awaited him.

She frowned and was no closer. She felt thwarted. As much as she disliked the youth for suspecting her father, she appreciated him talking to her. Many of the cooks were still tightlipped when she came near. But what now? She had seen proof of the hair, but Mistress de la Haye didn't think she would be believed. Still, this was evidence that a man had been there. Unless of course, Mistress de la Haye had fabricated what she'd seen, but Bronwyn didn't believe that. The woman seemed too unhappy at her situation to want to gain attention by adding false stories. She needed to tell someone.

Master Odo called Bronwyn over to join the cooks for a bite to eat. She would normally have gone home, but this might offer a chance to get to know them better. Besides, her stomach growled loudly. She joined the others for a bite at the long tables and absently picked at her pottage, stirring the chunks of peas mixed with other vegetables in a dull slop. Her stepmother's was better, but she spooned it into her mouth all the same.

A familiar face sat across from her. "Cat got your tongue, Lady Bronwyn?"

She narrowed her eyes at Rupert's teasing tone. "I am no lady."

"Saw you talking with them earlier. What do you want with Mistress de la Haye? And who was that dark-haired one you were chatting to in the corridor? She's a pretty one."

Her lips pursed. Perhaps the rumors were true, and he did only get taken by a pretty face one day, only to be distracted by another the following day.

"Her hair reminds me of a crow," Bronwyn said sourly. Was he being deliberately obtuse? Did he really not recognize Lady Alice from her flight in the woods?

"Never seen a crow so pretty as that," he said with a smile.

She ignored him and stirred her pottage.

The boys chatted, largely ignoring her. As Odo led the discussion at the head of the table, Rupert eyed her with curiosity. "Something on your mind, Bronwyn?"

She shrugged.

Once the meal had finished, Rupert took her wooden trencher away. She'd given most of the pottage to the potboy with whom she'd shared the trencher, anyway, so she was still a bit peckish. "Something is going on. I can tell. What troubles you?"

"Were you there the night de Grecy died? In the dining hall?"

He nodded. "Saw the whole thing. Why?"

"Can you tell me what happened?" she asked.

"Sure." He leaned his elbows on the worktable and watched the others work. "I was serving my lord at the time and all the lords and ladies were there. I served my lord food and stood by when de Grecy pounded the table and said he'd arranged for a surprise for Their Graces, a gift of soft, white rolls sweetened with honey.

"He arranged for them to be brought in, and took the first roll from the platter and stuffed the whole thing into his mouth. It was a sort of slight to the king, since they should have taken the first bite. The queen was nibbling hers and the king seemed disinterested in the rolls altogether. I think the queen only took one to be kind. But it all happened so fast. De Grecy took sick and began to cough and tremble. He clutched at his throat and then fell to the floor.

"Everyone stopped what they were doing and stood back, but when he coughed and collapsed, then all was still. I saw it all. Then the knight next to him looked at him and declared him dead, and that was it. Everyone dropped the rolls and threw them into the fire. Someone called for the kitchen hands, and the bakers, and the king demanded to know where the rolls had come from. They called for the physician to examine the queen, in case she felt ill, but she declared she was fine. Guards went to the kitchen and brought back Godfrey and Odo, but Godfrey was ill by that point and puking his guts out, until he fell unconscious. Odo said a baker's girl made them. The king and queen left, and my lord bid me attend him. The rest you know."

She nodded. "Yes. They said that the man wearing the green hood could have been Roger the squire, but I've heard that his hood was stolen. Did Roger have any enemies?"

He shrugged. "He wasn't popular, but I don't know if anyone would frame him for murder. Besides, men have their own clothes. No one is starving here. But when we serve at table we don't see what the others are wearing. I don't remember any green hood and don't know who it might have been. Sometimes our lords present us with gifts for good service, or for when they are at tournament."

At least now she knew his version of the events, and she noted it did not contradict what she'd heard from Brother Bartholomew or Sir Gilbert's accounts of the night. "Who were the other pages and squires serving that night?"

He stood up and scratched his chin. A golden fuzz was beginning to grow there. "There's Geoffrey, Matthew, Alan, John, and me. It was a small table that night. Most of the other fighting men ate in the main dining hall. What do you want to know the pages for?"

"Was anyone not there that night?"

He rolled his eyes at her questions. "You're so obvious. Why do you think it was a page who did it?"

"'Cause the knights are all big men, and this man was tall and slim. He was more likely a page, a squire, or a servant. And he wore a green hood. But now I'm not so sure anymore."

Rupert pondered this. "That's a fair point. A knight wouldn't have bothered to come into the kitchens. A lot of these fighting men just want their food and ale and women. Beyond that..." He shrugged. "And you probably heard already, Roger was in a foul mood earlier about his stolen cloak. Sir Bors had gifted him with a new green jerkin and hood, and he was going to show it to us, but someone had stolen it. He was raging mad and said if he caught whoever took it, he was going to thump him so hard, he'd want to jump in the lake. Then he disappeared. But that was the afternoon before de Grecy died."

"Then he couldn't have done it. If he was camped away from the city, there's no way he would have heard about de Grecy's order of the rolls, or get back in time to mess about with them." Her shoulders slumped.

They shared a smile.

"Don't worry. You'll find out who did this. Most people would have given up by now, even if they *had* been tasked by the queen. My master always says to use your mind in situations like this."

She gave him a sidelong glance. "What about Sir Baldwin? I heard he was acting strangely the night de Grecy died. Someone mentioned he seemed very calm when it happened."

Rupert raised an eyebrow at her. "Yes, he was. But that's just his way. Some people think he's slow to act, but they're wrong. He just takes his time to think things through. I like him. He's honest, and when he makes a decision, he stands by it."

"So the night de Grecy died…" she started.

"He took a roll, all right, but when the chaos started I think he spat out his mouthful and looked at it. Probably wanted to see how or why it was poisoned. Then when the king ordered everyone to throw their rolls away, he did. If you think he had something to do with this, you're wrong. I looked after him all evening. There's no way he could or would have gone into the kitchen without me knowing."

She nodded. "I believe you." And she really did. It wasn't just his kind eyes or the earnest look on his face. For the brief time she'd known Rupert, he hadn't lied to her. She trusted him. If he said his master was innocent, she believed his word.

An hour later, Bronwyn bumped into Sir Nicholas on her way back from the privy and told him what she'd learnt. He stroked his beard thoughtfully. "So that means a tall servant likely stole young Roger's new jerkin and hood, and whoever we see wearing it is likely the killer."

"But would a page have wanted to kill de Grecy? Why would a servant want to kill a knight?"

He looked at her evenly. "Not all masters are kind. Some rule with gifts, others with beatings. A few earn respect, but most pages lead a life of servitude and their families are happy to pay for the privilege."

"Why?"

"A lord will look after them. Provide them with food, lodgings, clothing, a healer when they are sick, and wine and ale in times of celebration. It can be a good life."

"Is that how you started? As a page?"

"At first, then a squire, before I became a knight. You will see the world, but it is not for everyone." His eyes took on a serious note, and he looked over Bronwyn's shoulder. "Brother Bartholomew."

"Sir Nicholas," a reedy voice said behind Bronwyn. "I would have a word with your baker."

She turned. Facing her stood Brother Bartholomew, whose light-blue eyes were unfriendly. "Walk with me, Bronwyn Blakenhale."

Sir Nicholas crossed his arms over his chest, eyeing the monk. "Remember what I told you, Bronwyn." He leaned down and whispered in her ear, "Be on your guard. He may be a man of God, but he is not kind."

Her eyes widened and she gave a slight nod.

Bronwyn and the monk walked. "Brother," she began.

"What are you doing out of the kitchens?" he asked.

"I was coming back from the privy."

"I see. And do you always speak first with your betters? I do not doubt that Sir Nicholas was on an errand when you likely accosted him."

"I did not—" She stopped. Had she?

He smirked.

"I apologize if I have given offense."

"It is not me you should apologize to, but God. And have you learnt anything about the poisoner?"

She shook her head, her eyes on the ground as she gripped the right side of her skirt, crumpling the dull, grey wool cloth.

"I thought as much. You are a Christian, are you not?"

"Yes," she said.

"Then if you have so much free time, I bid you go to church. I had thought that perhaps you might have taken my advice and looked into this matter to prove your father's innocence, but I can see that was too hard a task for you."

"But I am. I'm doing it," she said, "And how am I to learn anything when I'm baking? Won't God understand if I miss church?"

His eyes blazed in fury. "Do not take the Lord's name in vain, girl. As I suspected, you have found nothing. No, the best thing you can do now is pray to God for forgiveness and maybe he will have mercy on you and your father."

"Mercy?" Her spirits lifted, but they were dashed at his cruel smile.

"Yes. Pray that once he is found guilty, your father's death may be painful but swift. That is the best outcome you could hope for."

She glared at him, furious. Her face grew red.

She stopped, exhaled, and smoothed down her skirts. When she looked back up, Brother Bartholomew was smirking again, his dull-blond hair around his tonsure looking greasy in the light.

"Mind you keep a civil tongue, girl. It wouldn't do for you to be tossed into jail alongside your father." His smile was cold. "But then it wouldn't surprise me. You seem to have a knack for putting people's backs up."

"What do you mean?"

"Do you think the entire court hasn't noticed your little errand for the queen? Nosing around and accosting lords and ladies, demanding to know if one of them poisoned your precious rolls? It's a running joke amongst the court." He shook his head and *tsked*. "And whilst you're running around in circles, you're no closer to finding out who did it."

"That's not true. I'm talking to people and learning more about what happened that night."

"Like what?"

She decided to speak a falsehood, and if the Lord God struck her down for lying to a monk, then so be it. "Like the fact that it was probably Roger, Sir Bors's squire, who messed with my father's rolls. He hasn't yet been found. He'd been bragging about a green cloak he received as a gift. The man who messed with the rolls was wearing one."

He pursed his lips. "That's your great evidence? Do you have any idea how many men wear green cloaks around the castle? It is common. Your memory must be as shoddy as your investigative skills, for did we not address that very matter at your audience with the king, when your father was imprisoned? If you had any sense in that head of yours, you wouldn't be asking who did it, but *why*. Who would want to harm de Grecy, or the king and queen?"

She scratched her head. "Do you know who?"

"If I did, I wouldn't be talking to you, now would I? But if I were to consider it, a few names come to mind," he said. "Have you not looked into the men who were there that evening at table with the king? His trusted knights." He spoke almost mockingly.

"A little. But surely if de Grecy was new to court, the men would accept him," she said. "They would want all the able-bodied men who could fight."

"Now you're starting to think properly. De Grecy wouldn't have just come with nothing."

"You think he would have brought something to smooth his entry into the court."

Brother Bartholomew tapped his nose.

"What could it be? Money? Information?" she asked.

"I don't know. But once you find that out, you'll be a step closer to finding out who wanted to kill him." He blinked as if realizing who he was talking to and snapped, "Go to church. I shall pray for your soul."

At this point, she was glad somebody would.

Chapter Eight

BRONWYN SPENT THE next day in the kitchen, rolling out dough, making sweet pastries and rolls for the lords and ladies, and gladly taking her turn at rotating the spit of a large haunch of beef slowly roasting over the fire all day. She liked it as the hot grease and fat dripped and spat from the fire, perfuming the air. It was hot, sweaty work, and the delicious smells made her mouth water. But best of all, it served as a distraction, and at that moment, was better than running around after possible murderers. She wanted the time to do a dull task that kept her busy and let her mind wander.

And then she saw him lounging by the kitchen entrance: a man wearing the exact same green cloak she'd seen the day de Grecy had been killed. Was it the murderer, come back for more? She dropped the bit of dough she was rolling with a pin. "Hey!"

Boys stopped and looked at her. She waved the rolling pin and ran toward the green-cloaked man. "Oi!"

The green-cloaked person stood leaning against a worktable, chatting with one of the boys when he saw her walk up. "What are you doing—hey!"

She took him by his cloak. "You messed with my rolls. You killed de Grecy!"

The man brushed her hands away, patting down his green cloak and pulling down the hood to reveal his face. He didn't have black hair at all. He stood tall and thin, with a medium build and broad shoulders. In another setting, he might've been handsome, but his fair skin was pinched with anger and his blond hair had a rakish wave, his eyes narrowed with annoyance. "Who are you and why are you touching me with your dirty hands? Clear off, wench."

"All right, what's the problem here?" The baker Odo came up. "Who started it?"

"This was the cloak the poisoner wore in the kitchen the night de Grecy was killed," Bronwyn said. "It was him. I'd recognize this cloak anywhere."

The youth balked. "Are you joking? This is my cloak. What poison? I don't know what you're talking about. Odo, talk some sense into her."

She glared at him, and realized, this wasn't the same man who had pushed her, or had messed with the bread rolls that night. "I'm sorry. I… Where did you get that cloak? I thought you were the one who messed with my family's bread rolls that night."

The young man grimaced. "You don't know what you're talking about. I didn't kill anyone." He backed away. "Odo, who is she?"

Odo frowned. "Haven't seen you around much lately, Roger."

Roger shrugged. "I've been busy." He leaned in close. "I've been on a secret mission for the king." To Odo, he asked, "What's she wittering about?"

Odo scratched his double chin. "A man was killed a little over a week ago. De Grecy."

"And what is that to me?" Roger asked.

"A man wearing a green cloak like yours was seen poisoning his bread rolls and killed him."

Roger's eyes widened. "You don't think I did it?"

"The girl here and another cook saw a man wearing your green cloak do it. Whoever he was scared Mistress de la Haye half to death."

Bronwyn met Roger's eyes. "Well?"

"Look, I don't know what you're playing at here, but I didn't kill anyone. I wouldn't. And besides, my cloak was stolen. I've been wearing my old, grey one for days now." He touched the green folds. "I just got back. I've been out riding for days. I just got back a few minutes ago and came here to find something to eat. When I got back from my errand I found the cloak stuffed in a corner in my room, all dirty. It stinks like horse and I had to wash it twice to get out the smell. Whoever stole it's in trouble." His voice carried.

"What was the errand?" Bronwyn asked.

"None of your business," Roger said.

"Why should we believe you?"

He snorted. "Because I almost got a whipping for losing the blasted thing. My lord was in a foul mood that day. It's cold and he thought I was careless to lose his gift. It's not my fault it got stolen, but he thought I didn't like it or wasn't paying attention to my things. Anyway, I've been riding around the towns and villages for days looking to get more men to fight for King Stephen."

Rupert said from one of the kitchen entrances, "It's true. I saw Roger arrive at the stables half an hour ago."

Roger glanced behind at him and said, "See? I had nothing to do with de Grecy's death. I wasn't even here when it happened. I was outside the city. You're wasting your time. What's a girl like you doing asking questions, anyway? You shouldn't point fingers at your betters."

Bronwyn raised her chin. "I'm on a mission for Queen Matilda."

Roger burst out laughing. His laughter was loud, raucous, and made her cheeks turn red. "You? What's the queen want with a kitchen maid? Is she really that desperate or are you telling lies?" He slapped his knee.

"It's true." She huffed.

He mimicked her and stood up straight. "What a joke. I'm

hungry. Fetch me a roll."

"Fetch it yourself."

He peered into her face. "Fetch it for me now like a good maid, or I'll show you what happens when others cross me."

She glared up at him, her eyes burning into his. She breathed in his sour breath beneath his hot glare.

"Whoa there, Roger, you can't get enough of the ladies, you have to chat up kitchen maids? Come on." Rupert lightly cuffed Roger on the arm and got his attention. "There're some pretty girls amongst the queen's ladies now. Come see."

Roger looked at him with interest, then back at Bronwyn, the spell broken. His thick eyebrows narrowed. "If I see your ugly face again asking stupid questions, I'll make it the worse for you. You hear me?"

Bronwyn said nothing. She refused to give him the satisfaction of a response.

"I'm gonna tell Brother Bartholomew about this," Roger said. "See if he doesn't give you a hundred Hail Marys and Our Fathers for telling lies about me. You should go confess."

She narrowed her eyes. Anything she did would simply provoke him further. She knew she'd lose a fight if one began. He looked about twice her size.

His mouth withered. Instead, he knocked her dough off the table along with a spare plate, sending it clattering to the floor. Roger smirked as the sudden noise made her tense. He pulled his green cloak closer around him and walked off.

Rupert shot Bronwyn a look and went after him.

She cleaned up the mess, getting rid of the now-filthy dough and washing the plate. As she worked, a boy said at her shoulder, "You should stay away from Roger."

She looked at the youth, a potboy of around ten years old. Young enough to hear things, old enough to know when he shouldn't. "What'd he do?"

He said, "My friend Henry tripped him by accident and he stole his clothes when he was washing and he had to go out naked to ask for some, right when the queen was walking by."

For anyone that would've been humiliating, but for a young boy? Bronwyn could only imagine it would be worse. "So he torments people."

The boy nodded.

"Do you know what happened the night de Grecy died? I don't know if you were here in the kitchen, but…" He rubbed the side of his face, smearing a speck of dirt on his cheek. "Roger didn't have the cloak then."

"You stole it?" she asked.

"No, it weren't me. I didn't take it." He looked around to see if others had heard. "He threw mud at us that day, so we were going to rub it in his fancy cloak, but when we went to his room, someone was there so we left. Then he came in saying someone had taken his cloak and blamed us, but we didn't know where it was. Odo and Godfrey told him to leave unless he could prove it." He smiled and walked away.

She worked the dough, making rolls and loaves for hours in frustration. All these questions and yet she was no closer to finding out who was behind de Grecy's death. The next morning, she slipped away and visited her father in the dungeon. She gave him a bit of bread and asked how he was. He accepted it and ate it quickly, swallowing.

"Papa? Are you all right?"

He had a harried look in his eye. He leaned close and whispered, "There are knights in here."

"Oh?" She glanced around at the other cells. There were men in there, dressed in tunics and dirty chainmail.

He said in a hushed tone, "They are Maud's men."

"Maud?" Bronwyn whispered back.

"Loyal to the empress."

She nodded in understanding. Her father had never spoken openly of his feelings toward King Stephen or Empress Maud, but his shifting gaze told her he was uncomfortable in the presence of the knights. "How many?"

"When the king retook the castle, I heard his men captured seventeen knights and imprisoned them here. He gave them the chance to swear allegiance to him or stay in jail, and six accepted his offer."

"Who?" she asked.

"Gilbert, Bors, Clarke, Gabriel, Grossetete, and Clare."

Bronwyn tensed, her shoulders stiffening. Just the men Brother Bartholomew had warned her about. Were they all traitors to the Crown? And if de Grecy was one of their number, why would they dislike him so? Why would they single him out for such animosity?

He swallowed. "Their leader is here."

"Who's that?"

"William de Roumare, the Earl of Cambridge." Her father glanced to his left. "He's in one of the next two cells over. He's the empress's man." He paused. "Bronwyn... There's something you should know. There's talk of a rebellion. Did you hear anything of that in your hunt?"

"No."

"It might just be talk, but... one of the men said something about de Grecy working with a traitor in the castle. That means that whomever de Grecy was working with is still around. If he knows you're looking for him, he might try to hurt you." Her father's face clouded. "I think... I think you should stop looking for this killer." His eyes darted left and right. "Leave it be."

"What are you talking about? I can't do that.

"You must." He said louder, "Leave off, girl. You're chasing after something that doesn't exist. Go back to the kitchens, where you belong."

"But, Papa..." Bronwyn started.

"I mean it. Go on, before I smack your behind. Don't think I won't do it from behind these bars," he said, his voice carrying.

Snickers and laughter could be heard from the neighboring cells.

She backed away. "Papa?"

"Go. Say a prayer for your soul." He turned his back on her, shivering in the damp.

Bronwyn fled. She ran up the stone steps and up the curved staircase, bumping into a lady. "Oh, I'm sorry." She curtsied, badly.

Bronwyn vaguely recognized the woman from Queen Matilda's retinue. She wore a veil over her hair and her pale face was pinched with annoyance as she lifted her chain and gave an indignant sniff. The woman tutted, then looked her up and down and said with a French accent, "What are you doing in the jail?"

"Visiting my papa."

She blinked. "What did he do?"

"He is being blamed for a poisoning attempt on the king and queen." Bronwyn swallowed. The lady's grey eyes pierced her like an arrow and she could not look away, nor allow a lie to cross her tongue.

"Then he is either dumb or a fool. Which are you, girl?"

Bronwyn held her tongue and stared at the stone steps.

The woman let out a small noise. "Move aside. You are in my way."

"I'm sorry, my lady."

"Countess. I am the Countess of Cambridge, Lady Hawise. My husband languishes in those dirty cells you come from." She looked down her nose at Bronwyn.

The staircase was so narrow, Bronwyn couldn't move past without the lady letting her by, so she shuffled down the steps and stepped aside to let her pass. Lady Hawise gave a little huff and held her head high as she swept past in a long, navy-blue woolen dress, closely followed by an armed guard.

Bronwyn watched as the guard kept by the countess, a sheathed sword at his waist as he marched loudly in heavy boots, chainmail, and a tunic that smelled as they passed by. They moved to one of the cells as she inclined her head. "My lord."

"Wife."

Bronwyn left them, feeling eyes on her. She passed the main

dining room and saw Lady Alice laughing and talking with some of the other nobles. Bronwyn loitered in the entrance until she caught Lady's Alice's eye and the lady came over.

"Oh, good, you're here. I'll be wanting some sweet rolls, girl." She spoke loudly then steered Bronwyn into the corridor, away from prying eyes. "Tell me what you know."

"Is it true they're planning a rebellion?" Bronwyn asked.

Lady Alice breathed in. "Yes. That is what I heard was going to happen." She looked at Bronwyn shrewdly. "I was to meet de Grecy and make contact with him and his person here inside the court. But I was delayed and then found out he was dead."

"So you haven't been able to find out who he was meeting with," Bronwyn said.

"No. But it's no business of yours in any case."

"It is. Someone killed de Grecy and I need to find out who, or else my papa will be killed for it."

"Then help me, and I will help you," Lady Alice said.

"How?"

"There is something I want. Help me and I'll try to make it so that your father is released."

"What is it? Name it," Bronwyn said.

"There is a young man who is… attractive. Arrange an introduction."

"Who is it?"

"If I knew that, would I be asking you for help? No," Lady Alice said.

"What does he look like?"

"He is a young knight, I think. No more than twenty years of age, I would guess. Handsome, a pleasing face. Sharp eyes. I like it when he laughs. He has hair that touches his shoulders and looks like gold in the light, like a lion's mane. You know him. He almost caught me in the woods that time we were speaking together."

Bronwyn knew at once whom she meant. The boy who liked to tease her with a cheeky grin and who had saved her more than once. The young man whose hair shone in the sun and who unlike Alfred, hadn't tried to kiss her. So why did her chest tighten at Alice's request?

"Help me and I'll help you, if I can," Lady Alice said. "If you care about your father, that is."

"Of course I do."

They agreed and parted ways. That evening, as she finished in the kitchens and prepared to walk home, a familiar face greeted her at the entrance. "Hullo, mistress," Rupert said with a teasing smile. "Ready for your escort home?"

A ghost of a smile crossed Bronwyn's face. "Rupert, I wonder, have you met Lady Alice Duncombe?"

Chapter Nine

THAT EVENING, RUPERT escorted Bronwyn home, their shoes slipping and sliding on the wet cobblestones as they trudged through the gate and down the hill. It was slippery, muddy, wet going, and he held her arm more than once to steady her. Bronwyn told herself that was all he was doing, simply being friendly. Rupert was good like that.

"You're quiet. That's not like you," he said.

"Maybe I've got a lot on my mind. You know you asked me about the raven-haired woman I was talking to before. Her name is Lady Alice Duncombe and she…" She gave a tiny sigh. "She would like to meet you.

He grinned. "And why is that?"

Bronwyn raised an eyebrow. He was enjoying this, she could tell.

"Rupert?"

"So what does she like about me? I didn't think a lady would notice a squire. Maybe it's my dashing good looks or rapier-sharp wit."

Bronwyn rolled her eyes. "More like someone she can order around," she muttered.

"What?"

"Nothing." She swallowed.

"Lady Alice likes your smile."

"What?"

She glanced at him. He seemed utterly confused. His eyes were wide, and if he smiled any wider, it'd split his face. He was enjoying too much her having to tell him this. "She likes your smile, all right? The way you look. She thinks you're... handsome." Bronwyn looked away, grateful for the dark evening sky. She blushed even to say the words. "I'm only telling what you already know, I'm sure. You both like each other, so you can talk to her. You'll find a way."

He laughed. "I suppose I'll have to meet her, then."

Bronwyn gave a little chuckle, then felt sad. Was he won over so easily by the prospect of a pretty face?

But that night, Bronwyn opened the door to find Margaret setting down a table of dinner for their family and... Alfred.

"Mama?" she asked.

"Come in, come in, Bronwyn. Don't let in the cold." Margaret *tsked* and came toward her, closing the door in Rupert's face. She brushed down Bronwyn's coat. "Fix your hair and wipe your face. Alfred's stayed for dinner."

"Why?" Bronwyn whispered.

"Why not? He's worked here helping out for days now, no thanks to you. Now wash up and join us. The pottage is getting cold."

Bronwyn ignored Alfred's gaze, hung up her coat, and washed her hands, drying them on a spare cloth. She joined the others at the table, sitting on the left hand of Margaret, across from Alfred. Wyot sat across from her.

"Well, this is a very merry party," Margaret said, pouring a bit of wine into their cups. She spooned hot pottage into the dry bread trenchers and encouraged them to eat up. As Bronwyn spooned the pottage into her mouth, Margaret asked, "How was your work at Master Dale's bakery, Alfred? Before you came here?"

"All right, I guess," Alfred said. "He doesn't need me so much anymore, and honestly, I was getting tired of him. He's old and often forgets things. To be fair, I'm looking for a new place. I'm thinking of setting up my own shop in town."

"Oh?" Margaret said.

"But of course, I'd need someone to help me run it." His gaze drifted to Bronwyn. "I'll be looking to marry soon. A wife who knows baking would suit me down to the ground." He coughed.

Bronwyn would have said all the curse words she knew if she didn't think her mother would cast her in a nunnery. Maybe that would have been preferable, considering the circumstances.

Bronwyn shot to her feet. "Mama, I just realized. I have to go back to the castle."

"What? Why? At this hour?" she said.

"Let me go with you," Alfred said, rising. "You shouldn't be going out alone."

"No, no, it's fine. I was so busy today I didn't bring Papa some bread, and they're barely feeding them in the jail," Bronwyn lied. "He'll be hungry."

Margaret's expression softened. "All right. Go. But I cannot believe you would forget about him. Take him some bread." She hurriedly wrapped a small loaf of bread in a cloth and handed it over. "Are you sure you can't stay?"

"He looked hungry last time I saw him. I think he's worried about his safety," Bronwyn said.

"And no wonder, considering. Go, go. Alfred, would you go with her?"

"Sure." He'd eaten fast, and he scraped the last of his pottage from the bread trencher and wiped his mouth on his sleeve. He looked at Bronwyn with bright-blue eyes. "I'll just get my coat."

Once they had coats on and were outside in the cold night air, Bronwyn started a quick walk toward the castle.

"Bronwyn, wait." Alfred touched her arm. "Hold up. There's no hurry."

"There's every hurry. He's hungry and he'll be waiting on me," she lied.

"Wait." His grip tightened and she stopped.

"What?"

"I want to talk to you," he said.

"About what?" She pulled her arm free and kept walking. "Talk to me while we walk."

She mentally cursed his long legs as he easily kept pace with her.

He said, "I wanted to talk to you about us."

She swallowed. Of all the things on her mind, she did not want to talk about this. "There's nothing to say. We're friends."

"We could be more than that. I've known you since you were a child."

"I think of you like a brother." She could practically see him wince.

"I'm not," he said flatly.

She glanced at him and kept walking.

"Honestly, Bronwyn, will you stop and look at me." He grabbed her arm and spun her around to face him. "I'm not your brother." He took her chin in his hands and kissed her.

His kiss was light, but pressured. She felt the intensity of it, the push and pull of his want. He wanted her. He desired her.

But she didn't feel the same way.

His bristly beard and mustache needed a trim and it tickled her face, almost making her laugh. She stepped back. "I'm sorry, Alfred. I just don't feel that way about you." She looked down at the ground. It had been a sloppy kiss, and it took all her willpower not to wipe her mouth dry.

"Is there someone else?" he asked. "That boy who was walking you home?"

"No. He's just a friend."

The moon lit up the angry planes and shadows on his face. He retorted, "We're all just friends to you, is that it? Well, one of these days, Bronwyn, I'm going to be a head baker and successful and you're going to wish you'd kissed me back. You'll be begging for my kisses then."

She shifted her weight from one foot to the other.

He turned to go. "Find your own way to the castle. See if I

care. Your pa's a traitor, anyhow."

She glared at him. "My pa is no traitor."

"Then why is that word is flying around town that whilst he's cooling his heels in the castle dungeon, he's part of a plot to take over when the king isn't looking?"

"Who said that?" Bronwyn asked.

"It's common knowledge."

"Where'd you hear it?"

"Nowhere. Everywhere. It's just what I heard." He rubbed the side of his face, his big hand rubbing his bristly, blond beard.

"Don't believe everything you hear," she said.

"Anyone can tell when something's not right. But maybe you need a man to tell you these things. You're not a journeyman baker like I am." Alfred puffed up with pride.

Bronwyn rolled her eyes and began to walk. "Goodnight, Alfred."

He shouted something, but she didn't stay to hear it. Instead, she wiped her mouth thoroughly and hurried away, disappearing into the night. She was met by the guards and let in through the gates, and she slipped the dungeon guards a coin to let her pass.

Her father was surprised to see her. "What are you doing here? It's late. Did something happen?"

"Alfred happened. Mama invited him to stay for dinner and I didn't like what they were saying."

"What do you mean?"

She gave her father the bread from Margaret. "Mama is being not very subtle about marriage, and how she thinks I'd be a good wife to Alfred."

"She's got a good eye for these things and we've known Alfred for years. You probably *would* be good for him."

"What if that's not what I want?"

He looked at her fondly.

They shared a moment of silence, then she asked, "How are you?"

"Cold." He shivered and shrugged his blanket around himself

tighter, but the cell was cold and damp. He coughed, a wet, hacking noise. He'd caught a chill.

"Oh, Papa." Her shoulders slumped, and some of the tension she'd felt loosened.

"Two visits in one day? I feel honored," he said, coughing.

"I have to get you out of here."

"Never you mind," he said. "I just want you and your mama safe. And Wyot, too. Don't worry about me."

"Papa?"

"You should leave the city. Don't come back to the castle," he said. "You shouldn't be here. It's not safe. You should go."

"Why?" She came closer to the cell's bars. "Have you heard something?"

"It's certain now—there's to be a rebellion. Once Lady Hawise came to talk with her husband, the men were talking about it after. When the time is right, they plan to break out and take over the castle." He swallowed and coughed again.

"Did they say when?" she asked.

"Soon. They mentioned a day, but I didn't hear when. A feast day, I think. But it might have been a martyr's day too. Go home. Tell your mama I love her. Take care of Wyot. And don't think too harshly of Alfred. You might need someone to look after you."

His words sent a chill through her. They clasped hands, and his was cold.

She left the jail and slipped back up the spiral stone stairs into the main body of the castle, when she ran into a heavyset man. "Ooh!" she said, stepping back.

It was Sir Clarke, one of the king's knights she'd been warned about. What was he doing here? He looked surprised to see her.

"Watch where you're going, girl. Oh, you're a servant. What are you doing down in the jail at this hour?" the man asked, his gaze hardening.

"I… was delivering bread."

"Did Brother Bartholomew send you?"

"I—"

"Never mind. Tell de Roumare he's not coming tonight."

Bronwyn's eyebrows rose. The monk's kindness to the prisoners made her feel guilty about speaking back to him. She hung her head.

"What is it?" he asked.

"I missed prayer."

The man's face grew firm. "I'm sure he'll forgive you. Tell de Roumare what I said." He cast a snide look at the jail entrance, turned, and left.

Bronwyn paused. If she didn't relay the message, she might get in trouble. If she did pass on the message, she could be committing treason. But would she be? All she'd be doing was telling a man in jail that a monk wasn't coming to give him nightly prayers. Was that a crime?

Lady Alice came down the stairs. "I thought I saw you. What are you doing down here with Sir Clarke? It's late."

"I was giving bread to my father when a knight asked me to deliver a message."

"Sir Clarke. What message did he give you?" Lady Alice asked.

"To tell de Roumare that the brother isn't coming to give nightly prayers."

She scoffed. "Ha. Not a very exciting message, is it?"

"I guess not."

"Well, I am in want of amusement. I shall go with you."

Bronwyn swallowed. Who was she to tell a lady *no*? She led the way down the steps.

Lady Alice lifted her head and held her nose. "What a smell."

She was right. After a pretty smile from Lady Alice, the guards let them through. But there was no denying the smell of rancid straw, chamber pots, and a rat or two scurrying past. Lady Alice gritted her teeth. "On second thought, I don't find this very amusing, after all."

Bronwyn nodded and went up to the guards. "Which one is

de Roumare's cell?"

"Why do you want to know that?" The man looked at her with his eyes narrowed, then observed Alice's rich clothes, fair skin, and jet-black hair, casting her an admiring glance.

"Brother Bartholomew isn't coming to give prayers tonight. I was asked to tell him."

"First cell on your left." He pointed.

Even with the glaring torches hung on the walls outside the cells, it was dark and damp. But as Lady Alice and Bronwyn stood before the cell, she could feel a man's eyes on her. Calculating, discerning.

"What do you want?" the man asked, his voice low and rich in the darkness.

Lady Alice stepped forward, her nose in the air. "We are here to relay a message. The monk isn't coming. You'll have to say your prayers alone tonight and wait till tomorrow for his company."

The man laughed.

Alice stepped back and snorted, raising her chin and speaking loftily. "If that is your attitude toward prayer, I despair of you, for you're in desperate need of the good brother's influence, clearly."

The man laughed and coughed. "Yes, good lady. I'll be sure to say my prayers. Did the brother send you?"

Alice turned to Bronwyn. "No, Sir Clarke did."

The man rose, a solid figure outlined in black against the bright moonlight. He grunted and moved with the ease of a man quick to action, but not without aches and pains. He limped.

"Did he give no other message, girl?"

"No, none."

"Begone. I'll be sure to say my prayers." He snorted and sat back down.

A rat scurried by their feet, and Alice shrieked. "What was that?"

"A rat, I think," Bronwyn said.

"That's it. I've had enough. We are leaving." Without another word, she took Bronwyn's hand and pulled her away, back toward the entrance with the guards. She did not say a word until they were out of the jail and back up the stone spiral staircase. "I will walk you to the gate."

As they approached the castle entrance, Lady Alice shuddered. "What a miserable place."

"Yes, it is."

"What were you really doing down there?" she asked.

"Visiting my father," Bronwyn said.

"He—oh. I remember." She looked away. "I don't think that man really cared about his prayers. It's odd, don't you think?"

"I agree." She paused. "But that was William de Roumare."

"So?"

"You're supposed to know these things, right?"

"What do you mean?" Lady Alice put her hands on her hips. "I am no mind reader. You'll have to tell me what you're thinking."

"You're from Maud's camp. Surely, you would know William de Roumare's role in all this? Like why he's in the dungeon?"

"No. Why would I?" She blushed and looked away. "I was only given the task recently. But I am no killer and cannot bear the sight of blood, so I wouldn't harm a hair on your queen's head. Not by my own hand, anyway."

"You did throw a dagger at Sir Nicholas almost as soon as you met him," Bronwyn pointed out.

Alice tossed her hair over her shoulder. "I knew I wouldn't hit him. I needed a distraction. In any case, this was to be a chance to prove my loyalty to the cause. I don't know who the other players are, only that I must find de Grecy, or barring that, the one he was working with and report back."

Bronwyn cocked her head. What she knew could help Lady Alice, but would it help her father?

"Do you know something?" Lady Alice asked.

"You said if I introduced you to the boy you fancy, you'd try to help my father."

"Yes."

"The boy's name is Rupert Bothwell. He's squire to Sir Baldwin of Clare." Bronwyn paused. "I told him about you. I think he'd be happy to meet you."

"He will?" A smile took over her face and she grew excited. "I mean, of course he will."

"I'll introduce you both soon. But… I need to unmask de Grecy's killer and give him up to the queen."

"Not *my* queen," Alice said.

Bronwyn pointed out, "That's the only way my father will go free."

"Well, I need to find whom de Grecy was working with," she said.

They looked at each other. "Shall we work together?" Alice said.

Bronwyn nodded. "I need to learn which of the knights present at the table could have poisoned the rolls and tried to kill the king and queen, and de Grecy."

"I can speak to them," Lady Alice said, "If you'll help me find out who he was working with."

"What have you learnt so far?" Bronwyn asked.

"Well, his room was empty, and he apparently had no page or squire to speak of. I found no traces of the man he was."

Bronwyn scratched her head. "What will you do when you find out who he was working with?"

"Return to my camp. If there's trouble afoot, they need to know. No doubt whomever de Grecy was working with has already sent word of his death. They may send reinforcements."

"Do you really care so much for the empress?" Bronwyn asked.

Alice raised an eyebrow and looked around to see if they could be overheard. She leaned in close and whispered in the night wind, "It's not her, it's what she represents. Empress Maud is not a woman without fault, assuredly, but she is hard because she has to be. She is ruthless, she is cunning, and she must be, in order to secure her crown. I would do the same thing." She lifted her head. "I wouldn't expect you to understand."

"Why not? When a man runs a market stall and hopes to sell the most, or beat his fellows, is that not the same thing?"

"In a way. But this is different. I speak of crowns—you speak of market stalls."

"We both can help each other," Bronwyn said.

"Yes. In this case, beggars cannot be choosers." Lady Alice's eyes were downcast.

"Or in this case, bakers." Bronwyn extended her arm.

Lady Alice grasped it and turned away. "Who are the knights you seek?"

"Gilbert, Bors, Clarke, Grossetete, and Gabriel. I need to know who could have reason to want de Grecy dead. I have spoken to Sir Gilbert and Sir Bors, but I'm not convinced either of them had anything to do with his death."

"I'll see what I can find out. Fare thee well."

Bronwyn shuffled home through the darkness, gritting her teeth against the chill wind.

Chapter Ten

THE NEXT DAY, Bronwyn was kneading dough in the castle kitchens when a clear feminine voice called out, "Hallo there."

She looked up toward the source of the voice, as did a bunch of the cooks and servants. Lady Alice stood in the entrance and walked forward, no doubt seeing she was becoming the center of attention. "I have need of a servant."

Odo came up to her. "Begging your pardon, lady, but we here are cooks and scullery, not pages. If it is a servant you seek, I'd say—"

She interrupted him, sticking her nose in the air. "No, no. My maid was lost to me, and I need a new serving girl to wait on me for a few weeks until I find someone appropriate. The other girls are already taken, and the queen said I could choose anyone I want." Her eyes fell upon me. "That girl there. She'll do."

Odo glanced at Bronwyn. "Ah, you don't want her. She's a baker. The queen wants her here, in the kitchens, where we can keep an eye on her. Trouble, she is."

Bronwyn's cheeks turned pink as she slapped the dough hard on the worktable, envisioning Odo's face as she did so.

He laughed and continued. "She's just a baker. She's never waited on anyone before. She's got rough manners."

"*No* manners!" a boy called out, and the others laughed. Bronwyn's cheeks burned.

Lady Alice said, "Then clearly, it's time she learnt some. You, girl."

Bronwyn looked up.

Alice strode across to her and whispered, "Play along." Loudly, she said, "Stop what you're doing and clean your hands. I need you to wait on me."

Odo frowned. "Now see here…" he started.

"Do I have to tell the queen you refused to give me a servant, when she said I could choose any I wanted? Do you want to refuse the queen's order?" Lady Alice asked.

"N-No, my lady," Odo said. "But the queen did want her here. A stranger did poison some rolls, as I'm sure you've heard, but her father is being held in case he conspired with him. Are you sure you want such a girl working for you?"

"Well, *she* didn't poison anyone, now did she? So that's none of my concern. But I have need of a maidservant and I want her. I'll keep an eye on her, if that's what you're worried about. At least with me, she won't have time to take after her father."

Bronwyn dropped the dough, her temper rising.

Odo started. "But, my lady, a servant is not something to be taken on lightly. You must speak with her family, and…."

"Oh, I see. You want me to skip down to the dungeons and ask her prisoner father if I might improve her life by taking her as my maid? What do you think he'll say?" Lady Alice's voice dripped with sarcasm.

Odo heard a snicker. He turned and said to the boys, "Keep turning the spit. Go back to your work." To Alice, he said, "I'm just saying, there are agreements to be made. You can't just take any girl and put her to work for you. Not when she's been assigned here. It's not right."

"It won't be for long. It's only temporary, until I find a proper maidservant. Funny, I didn't think she was that important to you. Or are you in desperate need of clean pots?"

He looked confused.

"Her hands are rough and red—even I can see that from here.

It's clear what you've been having her do, when she could easily be serving me instead. I'll be doing her a service. Now, if there are no more excuses, I'd like my maid to help me." She looked at me. "Well? Did you hear me? Put down that mess of whatever you're cooking. I need you to wait on me. Now."

"But, my lady, I don't, I mean, I haven't—"

"I don't care what you can or don't do. A bad servant is simply one who hasn't learnt how to be a good one yet. Now, will you wash your hands or not?" Lady Alice demanded.

Bronwyn blushed harder, feeling the boys' eyes on her, and went to a nearby bucket to clean her hands. Once she'd washed and dried them, she wiped them clean on her apron. "Lady." She curtsied and almost fell over.

The boys snickered, and Lady Alice's mouth withered. She would make a fine old lady someday. "Well. I can see we have work to do. We'll fix that curtsey first. Come along." To Odo, she said, "I'll send her back from time to time to help you, if that is agreeable?"

"Yes, my lady." Odo bowed.

Lady Alice held her head high and walked out of the kitchens, lifting her skirts ever so slightly to avoid getting anything on her hem.

Bronwyn followed her like a shadow, anxious at being watched. Once they were out of the kitchen, she started to speak when Lady Alice snapped her fingers and said, "Come. Don't talk unless I speak to you."

Bronwyn followed her up a spiral staircase and down a corridor to a room. It was small and narrow, with a creaking, wooden floor, a thin bed that needed making up, and with a rickety, wooden table and bench nestled against the left-side stone wall. The room was cold, but not uncomfortable.

"Shut the door," Lady Alice said, and she opened up a chest of dresses. She picked up one and held it up, then another, finally deciding on one of plain, grey wool. "Here. Try this on."

"But I already have a dress."

She snorted. "You smell like bread and you're covered in flour. If you're going to act as my maidservant, you need to look like one."

"But Odo was right. I *am* supposed to be in the kitchens."

"And I tell you, it doesn't matter what Odo says. As far as he is concerned, you are my maidservant now and you'll do whatever I ask." She shot Bronwyn a look. "And in case you're wondering, I have the queen's permission to take any woman I choose as a maidservant, provided she isn't already in service to someone else. You seemed like the obvious choice."

Bronwyn's eyes widened. Had her circumstances changed so quickly?

"Calm yourself. I don't mean for this to be a long-term arrangement. You're completely unsuitable for a maidservant, and I wouldn't want your company all day long anyway. I'd find you tedious and send you away just to be rid of you."

Bronwyn blinked. *Tell me how you really feel*, she thought.

"I had a think last night about our relationship, and what we both want, and thought we need to stick together if we're going to succeed in both our endeavors. So what better way to keep you near me than to make you my maid?"

Bronwyn almost groaned. Maidservant to Lady Alice? What could be worse?

"Are you going to answer me?" Alice asked. "If this is going to work, you need to understand when I'm simply talking and when I want a response from you. For instance, right now, I—"

"I understand," she said.

"I don't like your tone," Lady Alice said, crossing her arms. "Put on the dress. And take off that disgusting kerchief. You're not in the kitchens anymore." She rummaged through a collection of small items on a small table nearby. "Here."

Bronwyn unbound the kerchief that held back her dirty-blonde hair and accepted the wooden comb from Alice's outstretched hand. "Thank you."

She turned her back and quickly changed out of the woolen

dress she had on, pulling the new one over her shift and hose. It went to her ankles and needed tying up with string at the bosom, but it fit well enough. As Bronwyn began to comb her hair, raking the wooden comb through knots and tangles, Alice watched.

"You're almost pretty. You'll do very well."

Bronwyn looked up at her.

"A maidservant is a reflection of her mistress. In this case, you reflect me and how I am to be perceived by others at court. Which is why I need you looking good." She stood by and once her hair was tangle-free, she helped plait Bronwyn's waist-long blonde hair back in a thick braid so it was out of her face yet still hung prettily enough. In the grey dress, she turned in a circle.

"Pretty. Your hands are still shockingly red and your complexion leaves no doubt as to your profession. It's clear standing in front of an oven all day has done you no favors, but you'll do."

Bronwyn touched her cheeks. *What's wrong with my skin? It's not so fair as that of some of these highborn ladies, but still. My cheeks are my own.*

Alice said, "Now, once we're downstairs, I'm going to need you to pay attention."

"What do I do?"

"As a servant? Keep a distance from me and stay nearby, so if I need you, then you're there, but not so close as to be breathing down my neck. I'll send you on errands if I need something, but otherwise, I'll have you follow me around as I speak to the knights in question. Who are they again?"

Bronwyn repeated their names.

"Why them?"

"When de Roumare's men were beaten, King Stephen imprisoned seventeen of them in the dungeon along with him."

"Wait, what? You mean that man we met last night, the rude one. That was William de Roumare? He's their leader?"

"Yes. You never met him?"

"No," Lady Alice said, putting her hands on her hips, her

wooden comb in hand. "Contrary to what you might think, I haven't met every knight and nobleman in the empress's camp, especially when they're off doing things like taking over castles. I think you'd better tell me everything. I can't look like a fool in front of the others."

Bronwyn leaned against the plain stone wall. "You'll know of course, that when the Earl of Chester and William de Roumare took the castle back in December, the earl escaped and de Roumare remained, along with some of his men. It's why there were something like seventeen knights in the dungeon at one point. I don't know who else is there, only that my papa is there and—"

"Yes, yes. I know all this. I don't need to hear more about your father. I understand this is important to you. But I need to know who is still loyal, and who has forsaken the empress. The information you hold could be essential to me, which is why I need to know everything. Are you often in the way of delivering messages to the men?"

"No. That was the first time I'd been asked to do so."

"Why?" She pursed her lips thoughtfully. "Why you?"

"I was on my way out and bumped into Sir Clarke. He ordered me to deliver the message. Simple as that."

"Perfect. And now some knights are in the dungeon, and others are upstairs with the king. And there's no way to tell who's actually loyal. Just perfect."

Alice glanced at Bronwyn. "We are on opposite sides of this war, but that does not mean we can't be allies. You keep my true loyalty from the queen, and I won't betray you to my betters. And frankly, I can see why you need my help. These are knights. They won't talk with just anyone. You were right to come to me."

Bronwyn tried not to roll her eyes.

"Did the queen really bid you looking into this poisoner? Or is it just an egregious rumor circulated by yourself?"

"It's true. What is 'egregious'?" Bronwyn asked.

"It means 'shocking.'" Lady Alice shrugged. "You might have done this to gain consequence in the eyes of your betters. Get attention, be seen as important for once in your life."

Her jibes, so nonchalant, began to irk Bronwyn. "Well, I didn't. But thanks to a court gossip, everyone knows. Brother Bartholomew is asking around, and Sir Nicholas too."

She smirked. "Sir Nicholas. He was the one you barged into de Grecy's room with before, wasn't he?"

"Yes. He's had the entire castle guard looking for you."

"How strange, I've been with the other ladies right under his nose," Lady Alice said.

"I don't think he got a good look at your face. It might've been the disguise you wore when we first found you, or the knife you threw at him."

Alice smiled. "Yes, well. It was his own fault for getting in my way."

"Were you really aiming for his head?"

Her smile widened. "Enough chatter. Let us go downstairs." She crossed the room and stood in the doorway. "Bronwyn."

"My lady?"

"I rarely miss." She giggled and led the way out of the room.

Light rain pattered outside. Bronwyn watched as Alice picked up her skirts as she walked, and something about her stiff back, her head held high, and her straight gaze ahead caused servants to move and get out of her path, and for other members of the court to stop their conversations and watch as she passed by.

Gazes landed on her too, and Bronwyn ducked her head. She wanted no share of their attention. The way Alice moved, it was like she wanted, nay, *demanded* to be seen, recognized, and acknowledged as the noblewoman she was. Bronwyn felt her part as a mere servant in her shadow and kept her gaze pointed downward as they walked through the castle corridors.

They entered the main hall, where the ladies sat and talked, some men played a board game whilst others warmed themselves by a large fire in the hearth, and King Stephen sat back with a smile and toasted the men with a cup of wine. Some men rolled dice, and Alice said casually over her shoulder, "We shall visit the knights and converse with them. If you spot anything amiss, offer me some refreshment."

"Yes, my lady."

Alice boldly entered the room and made her way to the queen, who sat surrounded by a few of the ladies present. Alice did not speak to the queen but curtsied and waited to be acknowledged. "Curtsey," Alice hissed to Bronwyn.

Bronwyn curtsied and stood in place, keeping her eyes facing the ground. But she wobbled slightly, earning some amused glances from the ladies present.

"Lady Alice, I see you found a maidservant to your liking. Let us see her," Queen Matilda said.

Bronwyn rose and tilted her face upward. Queen Matilda's eyes widened. "Why, if it isn't our little baker. Whatever are you doing out of the kitchens?"

"I—"

"She was being wasted there, my lady," Alice said. "The men had her scrubbing pots and pans and I thought her too pretty for such work. Don't you agree?"

Bronwyn looked at the queen's feet. It felt wrong to meet her eyes somehow, as if to do so would be seen as a challenge.

"Give us a turn, girl," the queen said.

Lady Alice stood aside and Bronwyn turned in a circle, her long, blonde braid and grey skirts moving in a slow turn. She stood before the queen.

"Very pretty, indeed. You're right—she's too comely to be a kitchen wench. It was very good of you to take her out of there. Although what I will do without my favorite white rolls with honey, I do not know." Queen Matilda cocked her head.

"I would still be glad to make them, whenever you feel hungry, Your Grace," Bronwyn said.

"Good. I do not approve of raising people above their station, particularly without merit, but as long as you serve Lady Alice well and do not make a nuisance of yourself, I see no reason why you cannot stay. A good choice, Lady Alice."

"Thank you, Your Grace." Alice curtsied once again and Bronwyn followed suit, watching as Alice gracefully rose, a bit like a flower. Bronwyn rose stiffly, awkwardly.

The queen smiled. "You will of course teach her how to properly curtsey too, I take it."

"Yes, my lady." Alice's voice held a note of civility, but she shot Bronwyn a dark look.

Bronwyn followed Alice to a corner of the room where on the long table normally used for dining, there were small plates and platters of food for nibbling.

Alice helped herself to some bread. "Which are the knights you seek?"

"I don't know. I've not seen all of them before, except…" She glanced around the room. She spied Sir Clarke standing apart with Bors and another man dressed in a knight's tunic. They lounged by the fire and played dice. "Over by the fire is Sir Clarke, Sir Bors, and a man I do not know, but I bet is another of them."

Two other men entered the room and joined them. Would it be so obvious for the new allied knights to stay in each other's company, or would they try to join the others and make a place for themselves in King Stephen's retinue?

"Can you play chess?" Lady Alice asked.

"No."

"Me, neither. Let us ask the men to teach you."

"Me? Why me?"

"Do not question me. I don't have the patience for it. Come." Lady Alice walked over to the men, who all looked at her.

"My lady?" one asked.

"Which one of you knows how to play chess?" she asked.

Alice was a sight, wearing a dark-red dress that spoke of wealth, her jet-black hair curled and pinned back into two long braids that hung to the middle of her back. Her eyes darted and challenged. "Well?"

The men exchanged looks, and one said, "I will play you a game."

"Oh, it's not for me. I want my maid to learn. Will one of you be so good as to teach her?"

The men looked from her to Bronwyn, who kept her gaze down, demure. Then she thought, *Alice was challenging, so why mightn't I be too?* Her eyes flickered up to the man who'd spoken, and she met his gaze.

He was a man in his thirties, with cropped, brown hair, a round face, and a chin with a divot in the center. But his expression was friendly, despite the stiff, military bearing he carried. He smiled at her. "All right."

The men made space on the long table and brought over a board and set up pieces. The man introduced himself as Sir Grossetete and bid them hallo. He held up each piece as he explained their names and what they did and began to tell Bronwyn how each worked.

They played a game and she lost, badly, but he didn't seem to mind. Indeed, he rather seemed to enjoy winning.

Alice chattered away to the other men, offering smiles and teasing jokes, when they were joined by Brother Bartholomew. "Playing games, are we?" he said.

"What does it look like?" Alice said.

The men smirked. He recognized Bronwyn, and said, "My, my, we have come up in the world. Did you know you're playing against a baker, Sir Grossetete?"

Sir Grossetete gazed at her. "You bake?"

She nodded. "My papa is a baker."

"Oh, but not right now. He's languishing in the cells, along with your friends. She goes down there to visit every day, instead of going to church or attending to her work in the kitchens," Brother Bartholomew said snidely, crossing his arms. His face took on a pinched look and he said, "Remind me, why is your father in the dungeon?"

Bronwyn's cheeks grew hot, and she made another move in the game. She looked up to see Sir Grossetete watching.

Sir Grossetete's hand froze over the board, just for a second. "Your father is the one imprisoned? The poisoner?" His voice was deep.

"He is no poisoner," she said.

He hovered over the pieces and took her pawn. But his hand trembled and he knocked a few of the pieces over by mistake, sending them flying. "Forgive me. I've lost my taste for the game. Excuse me." He rose and left, leaving her to pick up all the scattered pieces.

Bronwyn glared at Brother Bartholomew, who smirked as she knelt to the floor and picked them up.

"That was rude," Lady Alice said.

"It's the truth. The man should know whom he's playing with, don't you think?" the monk said.

"Trust you to ruin a perfectly decent game of chess," Alice replied.

"I might ask you why you're trying so hard to involve your-self in courtly affairs when you are new here. It is most odd. Perhaps you want to pick up where de Grecy failed?" Brother Bartholomew said.

Alice laughed. "And just what is that supposed to mean?"

"We all know he joined the king's retinue under, shall we say, suspicious circumstances? Not so dissimilar to your own situation, I'd say. You only joined us recently. I wonder if you are truly as loyal to the king and queen as you profess to be."

"You speak in riddles, Brother." Her face took on a bored cast. "Or is it that you seek to throw suspicion from yourself by accusing others?"

They stared at each other when one of the knights ap-proached. "Brother, I should've known you'd find the prettiest young women in the room. Cannot you understand, they are not interested." The man looked the monk up and down, his upper lip curled in a sneer.

"Sir Gilbert. Why does it not surprise me that when the conversation steers toward traitors, you are near?"

Sir Gilbert stepped toward him, getting in his face. Brother Bartholomew was tall, thin, and gangly, whilst Sir Gilbert was broad and stocky.

A loud clap interrupted them, and silence cut through the room. Heads turned to reveal King Stephen, who rose from his chair and approached. He set down his cup and clapped a friendly hand on the monk's shoulder. "Now, now, I'll have no fighting among my men. Brother, you know the castle better than most. Tell me, what is the best way to—"

King Stephen steered Brother Bartholomew away, as Sir Gilbert muttered, "That man is impertinent."

Alice said demurely, "Thank you. He was bothering me."

"Then he should be punished for his impudence." Sir Gilbert looked down into her eyes. "I don't believe we've met."

"I am Lady Alice Duncombe. And you are?"

"Charmed," he said. "I am Sir Gilbert Allenham."

She tittered. "It is a pleasure to meet you, Sir Gilbert."

"The pleasure is all mine."

Bronwyn subtly removed the board and pieces from the table, setting them on a side table in a corner of the room. When she'd finished, she observed Sir Gilbert and Lady Alice chatting together, side by side.

A young man approached Bronwyn. "You shouldn't mind Grossetete's manners. He never likes to lose a game. You were probably beating him."

Bronwyn smiled.

"I'm Gabriel. Are you a lady here at court?"

The slim, young man was in his twenties, with dark, curled hair and broad shoulders that bore his tunic well. He had a worn belt and sheathed sword at his waist, and he moved with an assurance that spoke of confidence of battle.

She shook her head. "I'm a baker. I mean, a maidservant. I, uh…"

He laughed. "Are you sure? Would that all maids and bakers were as pretty as you. I'd buy bread every day if you were selling it."

Bronwyn blushed, her cheeks betraying her, and he laughed again. "Well, it's nice to meet you."

Her cheeks definitely felt hot. "You look young to be a knight."

He grinned. "I bet you say that to all the knights."

She giggled.

He continued. "I'm the youngest. We were members of Maud's camp, but then we got dragged into this foolish scheme and now the others are paying the price for it."

She cocked her head. "Do you mean when de Roumare took the castle?"

"Him and the Earl of Chester, yes. But more fool us for sticking around. We should've known the people would rebel. No offense. It was no surprise to me when Stephen's forces routed us. It's clear to me which side was winning, so when Stephen gave us the chance to support his cause, I agreed." He buffed his nails on the side of his tunic and glanced at them. "It beats freezing in the cells."

That reminded Bronwyn of her father, who was doing exactly that. Her face fell.

"Oi, are you all right?" he asked. "I didn't offend you, did I? I always put my foot in my mouth when I talk to pretty girls. It always gets me in trouble—"

"All right, Gabriel, who's this pretty maidservant the men are talking about?" a familiar voice asked and a man clapped Sir Gabriel on the shoulder, leaning in to take a good look at her. Rupert's eyes grew wide. "Bronwyn?"

She ducked her head. "Hallo."

"You know this girl?" Sir Gabriel asked.

"Yes. She normally works in the kitchens." Rupert shot her a questioning look.

"Then it's true, you are a baker. What are you doing here?

Inspecting the food for His Grace?" Gabriel asked with a teasing smile.

She shook her head.

"Bronwyn, where are you? I need you," Alice called.

"S'cuse me." Bronwyn hurried past the men and darted to Alice's side.

She whirled around. "Where were you?"

"Just putting the chess pieces away."

She snatched Bronwyn's wrist and pulled her off to the side. It didn't matter that they had captured the gazes of some of the men in the room, for Alice seemed to ignore that entirely. "He's here."

"Who?"

"You know. The squire."

"Oh." Bronwyn's stomach sank. She watched as Rupert stood nearby, looking for his master, when he noticed Bronwyn and his eyes widened. He glanced at her, then Alice, and started to approach.

Alice elbowed Bronwyn in the side. "Introduce me."

Bronwyn winced and put a hand to her side, as Alice stepped forward. "Hallo."

They locked gazes. "Hallo there," Rupert said.

"Lady Alice, this is Rupert."

"My lady." Rupert swept her a courtly bow. "I am Rupert Bothwell. Squire to Sir Baldwin of Clare."

"I know who you are." She shot him a coy smile.

"Rupert, this is Lady Alice Duncombe. My… mistress."

"Your mistress? You're in her service? I thought you worked in the kitchens. When did that change?" His eyes widened.

"Today. I needed a maid and dear Bronwyn was good enough to accept my little offer of employment." Alice tossed her silky, black hair over her shoulder and shot Rupert a sultry smile.

"You are new to court, I think. I would have remembered," Rupert said.

"Yes. But I fear I am often getting lost amongst the corridors.

So many twists and turns."

"Then allow me to show you around."

"I would like that."

Bronwyn watched grimly as together, Alice and Rupert began to walk around the room, talking. Alice's face grew animated and she laughed at something Rupert had said, touching his arm. Rupert flexed his muscles and carried on talking.

But then Rupert was called away to attend Sir Baldwin. Bronwyn heaved a small sigh of relief as Alice returned to her. "Oh, he's just what I thought. Charming, honest, loyal, and oh-so-handsome."

"You got all that from one conversation?"

Alice shrugged. "I have no doubt we'll see each other again very soon." She smiled, clearly pleased with herself. Once she was sure of not being overheard, she asked quietly, "What did you learn?"

"Not a lot. Sir Grossetete seemed to want to get away from me once the brother mentioned my pa was in jail for the poisoning, and Sir Gabriel is friendly enough. I don't think he'd want to kill anyone."

"Hmm. I wouldn't be so sure. Even if he is friendly to your face, he might change when faced with battle. Sir Gilbert is…" Alice touched her black tresses that shone in the torchlight. "He is likely smitten with me, so I'll have to tolerate his attention."

"Did he say anything about the night de Grecy died?" Bronwyn asked.

"No. But he thinks Brother Bartholomew is a bit impudent for insulting my maid. I'll weasel out what he knows."

"That leaves Sir Bors and Sir Clarke."

Lady Alice gave an unfriendly look to a person behind Bronwyn. "Sir?"

Bronwyn turned to find Sir Nicholas standing there.

"I overheard what you were saying and can tell you this: Bors and Clarke had every reason to want to poison the king and queen. But it seems more like they were not the intended targets, and I'm inclined to think de Grecy was instead."

Alice pursed her lips. "I do not know you, sir."

"Nor I, you, but you seem familiar somehow. Have we met before?" he asked.

Lady Alice shook her head demurely. Bronwyn almost snickered.

"Never mind. It will come to me. I am Sir Nicholas. I have a care for His Grace's person, and I am looking into this matter of de Grecy's death."

Her reaction was subtle, but Alice tensed ever so slightly. "And what makes you think those two knights would want to hurt the king?"

"They are both still loyal to the empress."

"But how can that be? They joined the king."

He gave a small shake of his head. "They profess to have done so, but they keep to themselves, and Sir Clarke is the worst of the lot. He's the right hand of de Roumare and is not to be trusted."

"I think I can decide for myself who to trust."

"Mind you don't make the same mistake de Grecy did. It would be unfortunate to see a young woman like you dead on a slab."

Alice's face suffused with anger. She huffed and left in a swirl of skirts, leaving Bronwyn standing with Sir Nicholas. He frowned after her. "That girl is trouble."

Bronwyn said nothing.

"Why are you posing as her maidservant?" he asked.

"She asked me to."

"But you're not a maid, you're a baker. Is she helping you with your inquiries?"

"We thought it was the best way for us to look into this matter. She can speak with people I cannot."

He ran a hand through his hair. "Are you sure you can trust her?"

Bronwyn swallowed. She didn't want to reveal they had

agreed not to make each other's lives miserable. "She wanted to help."

"I'll believe that when I see it. She looks like she only wants what's best for herself. She's even been walking around with Rupert. I thought he liked you and you, him. Was I wrong?"

Bronwyn looked away. "She is speaking to Sir Gilbert, and I spoke with Sirs Gabriel and Grossetete. Then there's Sir Bors and Clarke. What makes you so sure they are untrustworthy?"

"How do you know they aren't?" he replied.

"I'll help," Rupert interrupted. "Pardon me, but I'm a part of this too. My master switched allegiances as well, and I can speak for his loyalty."

"That seems false, considering he changed sides so quickly," Sir Nicholas said.

Rupert squared up to him, his expression even and calm. "He is an honest man. I think he did not like this posturing and gloating over the men taking over the castle and treating the local people like dirt. Men are allowed to make mistakes."

Sir Nicholas met his gaze. "I do not trust a man who changes his allegiance so easily, nor his squire."

"Fine, then tell me this. What reason would he have to want to have to kill His Grace?"

"The same reason as any member of the French wench's court," Sir Nicholas said. "He may have pretended his allegiance had changed, but it may have only been an elaborate falsehood, to get into this court. But that is moot, for we are no longer of the opinion that the attack was targeting Their Graces, but in fact, de Grecy. He so recently joined the court, of course, he would know the imprisoned knights. It would be simple, a plot concocted by de Roumare and his men to ruin the baker's rolls and poison them. They might have even suggested he purchase the rolls."

"But surely, if my master was working with de Grecy, they would have offered the king and queen the poisoned rolls first."

"Perhaps de Grecy was greedy and didn't know it's only right and proper for the king and queen to eat first. He would not have known they were poisoned," Sir Nicholas added. "He might have outlived his usefulness to Maud's men. His own greed marked his end.

So either someone decided to kill both de Grecy and the king, or they aimed for the latter and he got in the way. In any case, he was expendable," Sir Nicholas said.

"If it will help, I will speak with my lord," Rupert said.

"No. He will know what we are about. You will give us away," Sir Nicholas said.

"The entire court knows your plan. Brother Bartholomew took care of that." Rupert glanced at Bronwyn, nodded, and left.

Their eyes met, and Sir Nicholas said, "You know something, don't you? Something you're not telling me."

"Walk me back to Lady Alice's room?"

He followed her out of the room. Once alone, she whispered, "There's rumor of a rebellion."

He grew serious. "Where? When?"

"I don't know. Right now, it's just a rumor. My father told me. He heard the knights talking about it."

His eyes clouded. "But this is just hearsay. The men might talk of anything. Lord knows they've had little else to think about in the cells."

"My father is worried." She looked at Sir Nicholas. "I believe him if he says they are thinking of rebellion. Can you tell the king?"

"I need more than that. For him to take action, we need more than a mere rumor, we need facts. Proof. Evidence. Get me something I can take to the king, and I will."

She gripped the sides of her dress. "How am I supposed to do that? They'll think I'm a spy, for King Stephen or for the empress."

"Aren't you?" He gave her an even look. "The queen has tasked you with finding who killed a man in her court. That requires some element of spycraft. Go see to your mistress," he said. "I'll find you later."

Bronwyn returned to Alice, who sat in her room before a polished piece of shined metal, gazing at her reflection. "Come comb my hair," she said.

Bronwyn took up the small, wooden comb, undid Alice's two long braids, and began to comb her silken, black hair from the ends, working her way up. "How did you know you were supposed to meet de Grecy?" she asked.

Alice cast her eyes downward. "My parents had thrown in their lot with the empress and asked her assistance in settling a matter of land markers. Our neighbors, the Shardlows, were determined to let their sheep graze on our land and declared it theirs, so we brought the matter to the empress. She agreed to settle the matter in our favor, provided that I join her retinue."

Bronwyn combed, gently taking the wooden comb through Alice's silky, black tresses.

"At first, I thought it was a great honor, to be one of her ladies-in-waiting. But when I arrived, the empress had forgotten about me entirely and blamed my family for the dispute in the first place."

"What? But you seemed so loyal to her. I thought—"

"That she is a warrior amongst women? She is," Alice said. "And I support her and what she stands for. But she will get what she wants by any means necessary." She breathed in through her nose and let out a deep breath. "She told me that if I were to avoid returning to my family in disgrace for wasting her time and earning her displeasure, then I would do her a favor. I agreed immediately. I couldn't refuse an empress."

"What did she ask?"

"That I travel to Lincoln Castle and once there, meet up with her man de Grecy, who would tell me what news to relay back." She set down the small bit of polished metal. "But it's gone all wrong. I'm here, he's dead, and the queen doesn't trust any of her ladies."

"What do you mean?" Bronwyn asked.

Alice turned to face her. "One of the girls thought it funny that the queen asked a baker to deliver sweet rolls herself, rather than have a page or maidservant do it. Another one of the girls said it's because that man was killed with rolls, so now the king and queen don't trust just anyone to deliver rolls, especially now that the man who did it is in jail. I suppose they trust you because if you tried to poison them, both your and your father's lives would be forfeit."

Bronwyn clenched the comb, her face twisted in displeasure. Her father's predicament was proving nothing more than idle castle gossip to these women.

"Do not take out your anger on me. *I* didn't say anything. But the ladies were talking and somehow, it came out that you are looking into this. They knew from their maids, anyway, but this just confirmed it. They exposed the queen's little plan and now she daren't ask you for rolls anymore, or she'll be the subject of gossip."

Bronwyn bit the inside of her cheek and put the comb back on the table.

"Some of the ladies in her retinue find Brother Bartholomew amusing, even if he is a stuffed toad. But, Bronwyn, I don't like this. Someone is spreading tales, and they treat all this as if it's a game."

"Who do you think is spreading the gossip amongst the ladies?" she asked. "Who are they?"

Alice ticked off her fingers. "Me, Lady Hawise, the Countess of Cambridge; Muriel the chatelaine; and Lady Maud, the Countess of Chester. The queen keeps us all close but takes no one into her private counsel. I doubt even her maids can be trusted."

"Who among them would have reason to want to hurt her?"

"No one except me," Alice said unhappily. "The Ladies Hawise and Maud were used as pawns by their husbands in their plot to take over the castle and so would have no love lost there. Muriel de la Haye keeps her foul temper in check when the queen is around but otherwise has a face like an axe and whimpers all the time, never mind having a nasty tongue for the other ladies, and Maud is too young and stupid to appreciate she's a pawn too. She smiles and laughs and brings good humor to us all, but she is silly. I was never that naive at her age."

"What is your age?" Bronwyn asked.

"I have seen twenty winters this year. Still in my prime, thank you. I could have been married by now, but none of the men were suitable." Alice sniffed.

Bronwyn's mouth quirked in a smile. "It all sounds like whoever was behind this, the women wouldn't have knowingly taken part unless they were coerced to by their husbands. If anything, it seems they would support the king and queen."

"I agree. Unless the women willingly took part in the plot and wanted to do more to hurt Their Graces," Alice said.

"Would they? Lady Hawise seemed cold, and I wonder if she's that innocent in all this."

"I hardly know. But she is cold toward everyone—that is simply her way. I would not take it as a personal slight. But… from what I have seen and heard, I have no reason to think they would be involved in all of this. If anything, Lady Hawise and Mistress de la Haye seem more unhappy about being used."

"What information could de Grecy have had for you?" Bronwyn asked. "He and the other spy? Did the empress really keep you in the dark as to who the other spy was?"

"Yes. It is too dangerous if the names are commonly known. If that sort of information got out, it would mean our deaths if fallen into the wrong hands. It's why I made sure to burn the scrap of parchment in de Grecy's room when I got the chance. All I know is he was working inside the castle with someone. I can only guess they were working on some plan to take away King Stephen's power from within his court and destabilize it so the empress could take over. But the more I learn about de Grecy, the more I find he was considered a braggart and a fool. I think the rolls provided an opportunity for the other spy to get rid of him."

"What makes you say that?"

Alice looked at her. "These men are knights, in the truest sense of the word. They have their own sense of honor. If they thought another man had besmirched that honor, they'd simply challenge them to a duel. None of these secretive attacks behind the scenes. I suspect they would think it beneath them."

Is it not beneath you? Bronwyn wondered.

That afternoon, she stood by Alice's chair at the dining table and looked around, assessing the people there. Who could have used her father's rolls to kill? Who would have been so bold to try, and who would have been so daring as to believe they could succeed? She could almost admire the cunning, except that her father's life hung in the balance. A page burst into the hall. "Help! It's Roger! He's dead!"

People stopped what they were doing and froze. Alice looked at Bronwyn, her eyes wide. "Go," she mouthed.

Bronwyn was among the first in the room to respond. She cornered the page. "Where? Show me."

The boy could only have been around age ten or so, and he ran as fast as his little legs could carry him. Bronwyn could hear men shout, the pushing back of benches and chairs and men fast behind her, but she ran after the boy, lifting her skirts as she hurried.

He took her out of the castle proper and over to the riverbank. The boy huffed and puffed, out of breath, when he took her to a bit of the river and pointed. "There," he said, breathing hard.

"What? I don't see anything," she said.

"Look." He pointed.

Bronwyn looked. There toward the edge of the riverbank was the water, frozen over with ice from the cold night. But beneath the clear, glassy surface, was none other than Roger, wrapped in his green cloak, his face frozen in silent horror.

Chapter Eleven

BRONWYN AND THE page were soon joined by Sir Nicholas and a handful of armed guards and men at arms. Bronwyn put an arm around the boy as he wiped away tears.

Sir Nicholas demanded, "How did you find this, boy?"

The boy sniffed and shivered. "Today. I went out to fetch water for the kitchen and I saw him. He's dead."

Bronwyn held him close. "Sir Nicholas, can he go back to the castle?"

"Yes, yes, go on. Bronwyn, stay a minute." Sir Nicholas's expression was grim.

She let go of the boy. "What's your name?"

"Cuthbert. People call me 'Bert,'" the boy said. He stood short in brown, woolen tunic and leggings, his light hair cut close to his head. But his face was a shade too pale and he wiped his nose on his sleeve. "Am I in trouble?" he asked, his eyes wide.

"No. Go on now."

He ran, and she faced Sir Nicholas. He stared down at the floating corpse, stuck in the ice, and instructed the men to start hacking at the ice. He motioned her to join him a few feet away from the men and said gruffly, "Well, this is a sorry mess. What do you make of it?"

Bronwyn scratched her head. "I saw his face. That's Roger."

Sir Nicholas froze. "No. It can't be."

"It is. We met once. He was unpleasant." Her mouth twisted

at the memory, recalling his quick smirk and sneering face. "He's Sir Bors's squire."

"Yes, I know. And here is Roger, in his cloak. But I thought it common knowledge that the boy's cloak had been stolen and he was looking for the thief." He scratched his head. "Why would he be dead? Could it have been an accident?"

"I'd like to think so, but…" She shook her head. "It's too odd. He looked surprised and scared."

"That's hard to tell from the ice," Sir Nicholas pointed out.

"Still. When we met I… accused him of messing with the rolls and killing de Grecy," she said.

"You what?" His voice rose.

She winced. "I know I was wrong. But he came in wearing the same green cloak as the man who I saw messing with the rolls that night."

"How can you be sure? Green cloaks are not uncommon."

"His was. I haven't seen any since then, not until he turned up. He came and when I said he must've done it, he got angry and said *no*, his cloak had been a gift from his lord and was stolen, he hadn't seen it until he returned from his mission."

"What mission?" Sir Nicholas asked.

"He said he was looking to recruit more men to fight for King Stephen. He was a bit secretive about it. But when he returned Roger found the cloak in his room, so he wore it again."

Sir Nicholas's eyebrows furrowed in thought. "So he came back wearing the same cloak as the killer, you accused him of the crime, and now he's dead. Have I missed anything?"

Bronwyn bit her lip and shook her head. "That reminds me. When I met Lady de la Haye later, she had a piece of hair that I thought was a ribbon. But it was black hair."

He let out a breath. "What of it? She is odd."

"She said she collected it when de Roumare scared her that night, and it was his hair. She said it was proof it was him. So you see, she did see someone that night. Whoever he was."

"And why didn't she come tell me herself or why didn't *you*, for that matter?" His eyebrows met into a scowl.

"She was afraid of not being believed by anyone."

"This is serious, girl. The queen should never have trusted you with a task like this. You're accusing people right and left and look what happened. A boy is dead, thanks to you."

"This isn't my fault. I didn't kill him," she said.

"You might as well have. Whoever did steal the cloak that night may have wanted to pin the crime on poor Roger and what happens? You accuse the boy when he returns, and now the lad's dead. Maybe the killer thought Roger would go looking for him, sticking his nose into people's business, just like you have."

"What? The only reason I'm here at all is because of my father—"

"Yes, a man who's certainly not starving down in the cells. He looks remarkably well-fed compared to the knights down there. If you ask me, that's where *you* belong, not him."

She glared at Sir Nicholas. Knight or not, he'd crossed a line. "What did you just say?"

"You heard me, girl. This all stinks of a plot, and you're at the heart of it. Maybe that was your plan all along, to deflect attention from yourself by trying to solve a murder. How do I know you didn't plan all this from the start and your poor father is paying the price for your treachery? Maybe you should be the one in the cells." He sneered. "You're hiding something from me, I can tell. What is it? Did you switch sides and now serve the French wench? Did she promise you your papa's freedom?"

Her cheeks felt hot. She felt her hands curl into fists. "My father is innocent. He didn't kill anyone, and neither did I."

"And yet Roger is dead. You seem fairly calm to see a young man dead who you were just accusing of murder a short while ago. Why is that?" He glared at her and blinked hard. "I find it hard to believe anything you say. How do I know you didn't just find out for yourself who killed de Grecy and now Roger, and that you've made a deal with the empress's spy for your father's release?"

She stepped toward him, her voice rising. "I didn't. You want to blame me, fine. Go ahead. I'm sorry Roger is dead. I'm sorry I accused him of murder. I made a mistake. You want to put me in the cells, go ahead." She turned away.

"Bronwyn, don't you turn your back on me."

She stomped away.

"Girl, you come back here," Sir Nicholas called, but she didn't care. She left him to the sound of the guards chopping up the ice with their axes in the bleak, afternoon sun.

Bronwyn wiped hot tears from her eyes. Since when did she suddenly become guilty of murder? Sir Nicholas blamed her for Roger's death, but his anger seemed irrational almost, like he was lashing out at her for no reason. But she hadn't killed him. He hadn't even had black hair. So who was the man who'd worn Roger's stolen cloak?

As she trudged through the slushy roads back up the hill, she mentally eliminated the kitchen staff from suspicion; they had all been there for ages cooking or cleaning and whilst many of them gossiped and openly debated who could have done such a vile deed, none of them seemed to have any idea as to who could have done it. That left Roger to have talked about it with the other squires, or his lord. He would have wanted to clear up any suspicions around his disappearance. And what was this secret mission he'd been sent on, that he had alluded to earlier? Who had he told, and who might've been listening?

When she returned, Alice was sat in the dining hall with the other nobles, nibbling on a bit of meat. She caught Bronwyn's eye and turned in her seat. "Well? Is everything all right?"

"A squire died." Feeling others' eyes and ears on them, she added, "Drowned."

"Oh, how terrible," Alice said, touching her collarbone.

Bronwyn stood by and remained silent as the men and ladies chatted amongst themselves. The mention of death cast a somber tone over the meal.

"It's a waste of good help," Sir Bors said, drinking his cup and spilling wine down his front.

Sir Nicholas entered the room, scanning the crowd. He strode over to Sir Bors, and whispered something in his ear. Sir Bors started, setting his cup aside. He quickly followed Sir Nicholas from the room.

Brother Bartholomew rose from his seat. "I shall give the boy last rites."

King Stephen nodded his assent. Queen Matilda glanced at Bronwyn, a slim eyebrow raised.

Bronwyn ducked her head and stayed quiet, grateful for the idle chatter of the nobles, interspersed with having to refill Alice's cup of wine or take her plate away. After a time, Alice waved her away and bid Bronwyn come to her the next morning.

As Bronwyn walked home that evening, the day's stresses weighed upon her and gave a half-hearted wave goodnight to the guards, feeling low. Weariness and sadness dogged her every step. It felt like for each positive moment she'd had, a young man calling her pretty, being raised above her station, there had been a time of darkness to counteract it. Seeing Roger trapped dead beneath the ice, Sir Nicholas berating her in front of the men. Was it really her fault he was dead?

She walked slowly through the castle gates and approached the top of Steep Hill, when she heard the sound of footsteps behind her. She kept on, ignoring them, when something hard struck the back of her head.

Bronwyn crashed to the ground. Snow, slush, ice, and dirt hit her face and neck, seeping through her coat. A swift kick to her side made her cry out, when a male voice hissed in her ear, "Quit nosing around de Grecy's death, or you'll be next."

The footfalls retreated, and she breathed and coughed, spitting out snow and dirt. She slowly got up and brushed herself off, looking around. She was alone. She walked down the slushy, dirty hill, grasping at the walls of buildings and looking over her shoulder as she went. Bronwyn slipped and slid a few times, shivering with cold but hurried as fast as she dared. Her hot breath streamed from her mouth against the chilly air. Her side ached painfully and eventually, she reached her home, knocking on the door.

Margaret opened the door and bid her come in. "You're later than I thought you'd be. What took you so long?"

Bronwyn shut the door behind her and latched it closed, leaning against it hard. It offered little protection from the outside, but it was something. She gingerly pulled off her coat, shedding bits of dirt and dropping slush on the floor that melted instantly.

"Why, you're filthy," Margaret said. "Bronwyn Sibyl Blaken-hale, what happened to you?"

Bronwyn looked up at her and began to cry.

Margaret took her in her arms.

Bronwyn reflected that Margaret had never been very affectionate toward her, but in that moment, she didn't care and crumpled at her stepmother's touch.

Margaret rubbed her arms and listened as Bronwyn relayed what had happened. She was too tired to lie any longer. She was tired of keeping secrets. She was an adult who did not want to be coddled, so Margaret probably wouldn't like it, either. Bronwyn had to stop hiding the truth.

"Someone attacked you? Who?" Margaret asked.

"I don't know."

"I cannot believe this. Well, that's that. That is the last day you're working at the castle."

"But, Mama, I can't disobey a royal order. That's a death sentence. And I'm a serving girl now. I'm serving Lady Alice. And we're closer to finding out who killed de Grecy and proving Papa innocent. I have to go."

Margaret grumbled, "Well, I don't like it. Your father is imprisoned and now you're attacked in the night. Where was Alfred? Why haven't I seen him walk you home after the other night we had him over for dinner? Why isn't he with you?"

Bronwyn shrugged. "Mama, I don't fancy Alfred. Not like

that. He's more like an older brother to me."

Margaret stared at her. "You rejected him? Did he make you an offer of marriage?"

"No. But he told me how he felt. I just don't feel the same way about him."

Margaret frowned. "So that's why he's been in a foul mood."

"I'm sorry."

"Well. It's not for me to say, I suppose. But I think you should think long and hard about it before you make a decision like that. He's a good man, and he'd look after you. He'd look after all of us."

Bronwyn looked at the floor.

Margaret took her chin in her hands, tilting it this way and that. "You need to bathe, again. You're filthy." She turned Bronwyn around and gasped. "You're bleeding."

Bronwyn touched the back of her head and felt matted, sticky blood on her fingers. "Oh."

"Oh, nothing. That's it. You're getting in the tub, right now. This is dangerous, Bronwyn. Must you go back?"

"I have to, Mama. For Papa."

Margaret and Wyot pulled up the wooden tub and filled it with the leftover water and a few herbs so it looked reminiscent of the French bath in herbs that Odo and the senior cooks would poach fish cutlets in. They pulled it near the ovens to get warm, and Mama sent Wyot to bed as Bronwyn stripped and sat in the tub, feeling the water and herbs against her bare skin.

There was no privacy to be had, ever, and their home was no exception. Margaret sat nearby, mending a shirt for her to take to her father the following morning. "Alfred came by earlier, looking for you."

Bronwyn leaned back and gently washed her long hair, feeling the water sting against her scalp and the bloody wound. It hurt.

"You should rethink Alfred's offer. He could protect you. Especially if—" She paused, her voice tight.

Bronwyn sat up and looked at her as her stepmother held up father's shirt by the dim candlelight.

Margaret let out a noisy breath and said in a shaky voice, "I think you need to have a think about what will happen when your father dies."

"He's not going to—"

"I mean it. The queen was foolish to send a girl to do a man's job, finding a killer. It's laughable, and only cruel as it extends your father's life for a few weeks whilst you're doomed to fail. If she were here, I'd give that queen a piece of my mind."

Bronwyn rested her hands over the side of the tub. "You realize you could never say that in front of other people, right? Some people could think it's treason. I'm going to solve this, Mama. I promise."

"Are you sure? You already have one boy sniffing around you. Who is this other lad Alfred told me about? Some ugly squire? Rufus?"

"Rupert." Bronwyn smiled. "And he's not ugly. He... likes another girl, anyway, so it doesn't matter."

"Well, never mind. But all this attention is just going to get worse, mark my words. And with you serving the lady, you're going to be noticed by other men. A young, pretty girl like you is bound to catch someone's eye." She added firmly, "No. I need you married off, and soon."

"No, Mama. Not yet. That won't solve anything."

"It would keep you safe."

"It won't help Papa," Bronwyn said with finality. "Until this is done, I don't want to hear any more about Alfred, men, or marriage."

Margaret shot her an even look but held her tongue.

THE NEXT DAY, Bronwyn dressed and hurried to the castle, finding her way to Alice's room. After a quick knock, she walked in and stoked up the fire in the room.

Alice yawned, stretching in her fine blankets. She eyed Bronwyn and sat up, then stared. "Oh, my God. You look terrible."

"Thanks." Bronwyn looked away, slightly hurt.

"What happened to you?"

"Someone attacked me in the road last night."

Alice stood, wrapped a robe around herself, and examined her face. "You can't serve me at table like that. You've got cuts on your face."

Bronwyn frowned. "What would you have me—"

She *tsked*. "Go back down to the kitchens for today. I'll make do with someone else. I can't have people thinking I beat you."

Bronwyn raised an eyebrow.

"The mark of a good master or mistress is how well their servants are treated. If they look poor, sick, and beaten, it is a sign their master is bad. I can't very well let you go walking around like that." She frowned. "Are you… all right?"

Bronwyn gave her a small smile and nodded. "I'll be in the kitchens if you need me."

Alice waved her away and she left, entering the kitchen as if she'd never left. She quickly tied her hair up and put on an apron, joining the potboys in cleaning dirty pots. She busied herself, and after some time, Odo came up to her.

"So, she couldn't keep you away from us, eh? You're a baker's girl, through and through." He grinned and saw her face. "What happened? Did she do that to you?"

"No. I… had an accident walking home last night. I slipped and fell on my face."

He came close and said quietly, "You'd tell me if she hit you?"

Bronwyn glanced at him. He'd been distrustful since the start, but since then he seemed to have softened toward her. Now it was almost like he was looking out for her, like she was one of his own. A funny feeling warmed her inside.

"I would. But she didn't. It was an accident, truly."

He grunted. "Don't be clumsy here, girl. Can't have you spilling sauces or tripping on things. Get back to work. We've got the feast to prepare for. In less than a week, it's the feast of the Purification of St. Mary."

Bronwyn tensed. In all her walking about and focusing on the murder and boys, she'd lost track of time. That was the day Her Grace had given as a time by which to find de Grecy's killer. She needed to solve this crime before it was too late, and her papa hung from a scaffold.

She scrubbed and cooked, stripped the feathery carcasses of capons, descaled fish, and prepared pottage for the cooks' luncheon.

She was just sitting down to eat when Sir Nicholas came by the kitchen. He motioned to her, and she rose, going to him. She cast a longing look at the stale bread trencher she'd left behind, knowing it would be wiped clean by the scullery boy she was supposed to be sharing with.

Her stomach grumbled as she approached Sir Nicholas, who stood in the entrance. "Sir."

"Bronwyn."

Neither said anything.

He looked down at her with a glare, his bushy, dark eyebrows pointing at her in accusation. "I've been asking around about Roger's death. It seems the lad came back and after he met you in the kitchen he left, and no one heard from him again." He looked down. "Seems he wasn't popular in the castle. I've not heard a single nice word about him."

She was about to demand to know why Sir Nicholas was so fixated on him and had ripped into her yesterday, when an idea occurred to her. "You knew him."

Sir Nicholas glanced away. "Yes. He was my nephew. I knew him since he was a child."

They were related. No wonder he'd gotten so mad. She shifted her weight from foot to foot. "I'm sorry about what I said. I shouldn't have accused him like that."

"No, you shouldn't have." His voice was hard.

Their eyes met, and his angry expression wavered. He cracked his knuckles. "I… shouldn't have yelled at you. Women don't like to be yelled at."

She looked up at him. "No, we don't. And speaking for my sex, we also don't like to be accused of spying."

He met her eyes. "I had no evidence of that, anyway. It's clear that whoever did this is still at large." He let out a noisy breath. "Now I have to arrange the boy's funeral."

"I'm sorry," she said, then paused. "What about de Grecy? Did he have a funeral?"

"No, not yet. The ground is too frozen to bury anyone, so we put him in cold storage. He and Roger will lie there until the spring, then we'll bury them. We'll have the funerals then." He grunted and left.

She stayed in the kitchen most of the day, dipping out during the noon Mass to bring bread to her father. But as she passed the cells, William de Roumare called to her. "Girl."

She stopped.

"Come here."

She took a step forward, then paused.

"I want to talk to you." He limped forward, his limbs stiff with cold and lack of exercise. He was not unattractive, but time in the cells had not done him any favors. He had wavy, black hair and a coarse beard that needed a trim. His eyes were dark and calculating, fierce with intelligence.

She stepped closer and met his gaze. She felt rooted to the spot by him. "What is it?"

He beckoned her up to the cell bars. "You deliver messages. Don't you?"

"I, no, I…" She had done, but he was trouble. He had taken the castle once and was in jail for it. What did he want with her?

"Tell the good brother we will be ready. By the time my lady's Welshmen are at Danesgate, we will be ready."

"For what?"

"Don't play dumb. You know what," he said. "I'm not going to spell it out for you. Just tell him." The man ran a hand through his scruffy, black hair and sat back on a seat in his cell. "Do it."

Bronwyn nodded and brushed away strands of thread that had drifted from the cell bars to her dress, then stopped. This was everything. Could it be that the holy brother was not as innocent as he seemed? Whom should she tell? But she needed proof. She wanted to turn around and accuse de Roumare and Brother Bartholomew directly but couldn't. She needed to think.

She walked on to her father and gave him the bread she'd taken from the kitchen, off cuts that the cooks deemed too poor to give to the aristocrats, and smuggled it out.

He took them hungrily and ate, noticing her face.

"What happened?" he asked.

She told him.

"You must stop this, Bronwyn. You have to. There's no sense in keeping on like this. Stop your hunt. You've riled someone up now and it's got to stop. I don't want to see you get hurt."

"I already did."

"You know what I mean."

She nodded. "I have to go." She had to do something about the monk working with de Roumare. Her mind spinning, she ran up the spiral staircase and ran into Muriel, the chatelaine of the castle. "Hello, Mistress de la Haye."

"Hello, Mistress Baker. Have you seen Brother Bartholomew? He wasn't at Mass today."

"No, I haven't." Bronwyn's shoulders slumped. Where could he be?

"Strange. He's usually there. I wanted to speak with him. I thought he might be giving prayers to the prisoners, but perhaps not."

"Could he be in the privy?" Bronwyn asked.

A smile crossed her face. "Men often are. He did rather eat his fill last night. It wouldn't surprise me."

She left, and Bronwyn returned to the kitchen when she

pulled on her coat, taking a basket in her hand. She'd visit the monk under the guise of gathering herbs.

"Where are you going?" Odo asked. "I need you here."

"I need to get some fresh herbs. I'll be back."

"Well, hurry along. Don't tarry," he said.

She hurried, darting around people, almost running when she smacked into Rupert, practically hitting him with her straw basket. "Oh, where are you off to in such a hurry?" he asked. "Bronwyn? Are you all right? What happened to your face?"

"I got hurt on the way home last night. Someone hit me in the back of the head and I fell on my face."

Rupert's frowned. "Are you all right?"

"Yes. I'm fine."

"I should've walked you home. You're not walking home alone again. It's not safe."

"I'll be fine."

"You say that, but we both know that's not the case. You've stirred up trouble, Bronwyn. Someone wants you to quit digging into this matter with de Grecy. Will you quit?"

"No. I can't."

"I didn't think so." He let out a small sigh.

"Do you have a horse?" she asked.

"Yes. Why?"

"Can I borrow it?"

"What for?" he asked.

"I need it. I need to see something. Can you take me to Danesgate?" If she couldn't find the monk at the castle, she'd need a different plan.

"You're serious," he said.

"Yes. Please."

"All right, I'll take you. Come on." He led the way to the stables and had a groomsman saddle his horse, a tall, brown stallion with a black mane that flicked his tail.

"Shh." Rupert fed the creature a carrot. He took him out of the stables and with a hand on his bridle, said, "Well?"

"I, uh… don't know how to ride."

He rolled his eyes. "And you were going to take one yourself. You wouldn't get as far as the stable door. I can't believe you. What is this about, Bronwyn?"

"I need to go. Help me up, please." She set down the basket and placed it against the side of the building.

He put two hands down and as she put her foot in them, he boosted her up and climbed onto the saddle, clutching the horse's mane in her hands. Rupert handed it up and mounted behind her. He smelled of horse, stale ale and hay.

They rode, a light canter out of the castle gates, out toward Danesgate, and down the road toward Motherby Hill. They rode down and out of the city, going until Rupert asked, "Any specific place near Danesgate?"

"No, just head in that direction. I have a funny feeling."

He nudged the stallion with his heels and kept going, down roads and atop hills, until they were out of the city, when he stopped short.

"What?"

"Look there." He pointed.

She looked. It was still miles away, but in the trees and forests, they could see an encampment. Tents, and rows of men, fighters, warriors, more than she could count.

"Who are they?" she asked.

"Trouble."

Chapter Twelve

B RONWYN TENSED IN the saddle.

Rupert said in her ear, "They're camped all the way out here for a reason. If they were loyal to Stephen, they would've come close and made themselves known. Come on."

"But…"

"Quick, before we're seen." He nudged the horse, turned it around, and off they went, back toward the castle.

"I don't understand," she said. "There's so many of them."

"Yes. dozens. Scores, maybe. Maybe even hundreds."

"You think so?" she asked.

"I don't want to know. We need to hurry back." He nudged the horse onward, faster.

They rode back quickly, taking the horse at a canter. Bronwyn clung to the stallion's mane as they thundered through the muddy roads.

"Roger is dead," she said.

"I heard. Found drowned in the water."

"That's right."

He heard a note in her voice and asked, "You think it wasn't an accident?"

"I don't know."

"I feel bad about it."

"Don't. Roger had no friends. All he was bothered about was becoming a knight. He had no time for anyone else unless it suited him in some way."

She thought about what he said. "Then why do I feel so guilty?"

He shrugged behind her. "Maybe you didn't kill him, but someone did. It's natural. But you're a woman. You shouldn't have to be put in this position. The queen should never have asked you to get involved."

She stiffened. "Maybe the queen thought I could find the killer."

"Maybe she thought you were expendable. You and your papa."

She turned her head to glare at him, then turned back, as she was too unsteady in the saddle. Her legs already felt sore and her muscles ached from riding. She'd never ridden a horse before.

"Maybe I am," she snapped, "but that doesn't mean I'll fail. I will find out who did this. Who killed de Grecy, and Roger."

"Then do it," he said back. They rode in silence, then a minute later, he asked, "What will you do now?"

"A few people have told me that de Grecy wasn't easily welcomed by the people here."

Rupert said, "He was more disliked than the other men. The king likes people in his court to be at peace. De Grecy seemed almost like a bad apple in the midst of an orchard."

"I wonder what he gave them to make the men trust him," she said.

"That's easy. He'd have given them information about the empress's forces. Something real, something that they could check. Something that would prove he wasn't lying."

"Like giving them the identity of the spy in Stephen's camp?"

"Or the date of when the empress's forces would be here," he told her. "We all know they're coming, it's just a question of when. And how many."

They arrived back at the castle. Rupert said, "I have to go tell His Grace about the forces camped outside."

She said, "Wait. Once you do, can you find me Sir Gabriel

again? The man who spoke to me yesterday."

"Why? Bored of me already?" he teased.

"No, it's just, I want to talk to him."

"Why?"

"I want to know who knew that de Grecy was buying rolls for the dinner. I feel like he'll talk to me."

"I'll talk to you. Why him?"

"Why not? He's a knight and he was there the night de Grecy died, wasn't he?"

"Yes." He nudged the horse into the castle courtyard and toward the stables. He pulled the horse to a stop, dismounted, and stood by the house, his face distant. "Does that mean you believe my lord and me to be innocent of all this?"

"Maybe." She glanced at him from atop the horse, then slid off and almost fell over. Her legs and thighs ached all over. She groaned. "Everything aches."

He smiled. "You'll get used to it. Don't forget I'm walking you home tonight."

She watched him go and spotted a groom leading a horse out with closely cropped black mane. She paused. As the groom and horse approached, she said, "Why is its mane cut so close?"

The groom glanced at her and stopped. He put a hand on the horse's back, stroking it gently. "Don't rightly know. A few weeks past, we found him with his mane all chopped off. We don't know who might've done it or why. One day he had a full head and tail of hair, the next, he didn't. Suppose someone might've been wanting to stuff a chair or a pillow."

"That seems odd, just taking the horse's mane like that," Bronwyn said.

"Aye, it does."

An idea occurred to her. "What about a wig?"

"Eh?"

"A wig. Could the horsehair have been used to fashion a wig? For a man?"

"Suppose so." He shrugged. "But why take the mane for that?

It's odd."

She found her way back to the kitchens and worked solidly, hearing the news as the rumors of the empress's men camped outside the city spread like wildfire. It was on everyone's tongue. Odo took no chances and began barking orders at the cooking staff, from sauce-makers and spit-turners down to the meanest potboy and scullery maid. Everyone had a task to do, including her. With the others, she was preparing little parcels of food, to be taken and packed away at a moment's notice. She realized Rupert had never sent Sir Gabriel her way but decided she was too busy to talk. Any hint of idle hands got a person a sharp retort from Odo. Night came. When she put on her coat and went outside, a familiar face was waiting by the main gate.

"Alfred? What are you doing here?"

He squared his shoulders. "I'm here to take you home. Margaret said you were hurt last night."

"Bronwyn, there you are. Ready to go?" Rupert said behind her, but his easy smile fell at the sight of Alfred. "You're here."

Alfred frowned and turned to her. "You're walking back with me, yeah?"

She looked from one boy to another. What a mess.

She said, "I… "I'm fine." She saw the hope on Alfred's face and didn't want to hurt his feelings more than she already had. She'd let him down gently. "Neither of you have to. It's fine."

Both protested at this, speaking loudly at the same time. She winced.

Alfred got in Rupert's face. "I have known Bronwyn since we were children. Her family trusts me with her safety. I've spoken with her mum and she expects me to walk with her."

Bronwyn tensed. Margaret had spoken with Alfred? What about? Was that why he looked so hopeful and glad to see her?

Rupert's chin rose. "I made a promise to look after her. She trusts me to see her back home."

They glared at each other.

Bronwyn started walking. She hated that they were arguing,

wasting time over a stupid matter like escorting her home, when she had more important things to do. She didn't want to think of how her world might change if she needed an escort just to walk home.

In moments, both caught up to her. "What are you doing?" Rupert asked.

"Walking home. What does it look like?" she snapped.

"Why are you angry?" he asked.

"You have angered her. It's your fault for butting in," Alfred said.

"I'll show you—" Rupert started.

She whirled and faced them both. "For God's sake!" Her face was pale in the moonlight. "Stop this fighting. I can't stand it. I will walk home. You can walk with me, or not. I don't care." She gritted her teeth. She wanted her independence. To be able to go wherever she liked, whenever she liked. To not be able to walk about in her own home city… It suddenly made her feel very small. She hated that feeling.

"But, Bronwyn, you were attacked. Your face…" Rupert started.

"I know what my face looks like." Her right hand drifted to her cheeks.

"We would not want that to happen to you again," Alfred said.

"Then walk with me. But if you can't be civil toward each other, then hold your tongue. If I wanted to hear arguing, I'd go back to the kitchens."

She could sense Rupert smirk. "As you wish, mistress."

They walked, and amusement filled her. How ridiculous the situation was. A slight giggle left her throat, and she clapped a hand over her mouth.

"Bronwyn? What amuses you?" Rupert asked.

"It just struck me. You are both walking behind me like some sort of escorts, like I'm some kind of fine lady, when I'm nothing but a baker. Not even. A baker's daughter." She giggled again.

"Perhaps to us, you are more than that," Rupert said.

She said nothing in return. They passed through the roads, staying close and in open spaces that were well-lit by the moon. It was not long before they approached the familiar street that her family's bakery stood on.

She knocked on the door. Her stepmother opened it and she slipped inside, shutting the door in both the boys' faces.

THE NEXT DAY, her face looked better, albeit still bruised and scratched, but the puffiness had mostly gone away. Bronwyn slipped into the grey, woolen dress Lady Alice had given her and went to her room.

She opened the door at her knock and said, "Well, you're looking better. Today, I will spend time with the ladies and later play games with the men downstairs in the hall. Join me after luncheon and I will see what we can learn."

Bronwyn nodded and spent the time in the kitchens helping to bake, when Sir Nicholas said behind her, "Girl."

She turned from her baking, as she'd just been inspecting a bowl of dough that was proofing. "Sir Nicholas."

"Come with me. There's something you should see."

She put a damp cloth over the bowl, wiped her hands on her apron, and followed him, out through the corridors and down a stone stairwell, but in a different direction from the dungeons, and apart from the cold pantry storage, where milk, butter, and cheese were kept.

"Where are we going?" she asked him. A lick of cold dread curled down her spine as the air turned cooler, damp, and less fresh. She suddenly felt very aware that their previous words had been in anger, and whilst they had made peace, she wondered if perhaps she'd been mistaken. Had he come to punish her in private, away from those who might help?

She touched the sloping, stone walls as she followed him into an underground chamber, lined with stone. The faint sound of dripping and cave stone nearby hit her ears, so quiet it was. There was no light at all except for the sputtering light from a torch Sir Nicholas held.

He led the way into a room and stood aside. "Come."

She walked in and stopped. It was a sort of cold store, but worse. She shivered, for there on the storage shelves lay bodies. Three of them, each covered with a sheet. The sight was unmistakable. The large form would be Godfrey, the other de Grecy, and another was thinner, narrower. It could only be Roger.

"What are we doing here?" she asked, her voice quiet.

"I thought you might like to see them. See the corpses."

"Why?"

"Because, baker's daughter, sometimes a body holds signs, marks that tell us something of how they died."

"What signs?"

"That is for us to see." He stepped forward into the room and motioned her forward. He pulled a sheet off one of them. "Look at him."

It was Roger. His body lay on a cold shelf, but he still dripped on the floor. She was glad it was winter, and yet understood why he'd been kept there. Despite being frozen beneath the ice in the river, he'd defrosted, and now was beginning to smell.

She sniffed in, involuntarily, and immediately wished she hadn't. She held a hand up to her nose.

"You'll get used to the smell," Sir Nicholas said.

"I hope I don't have to."

"What do you see?" he asked.

"A body."

"Look again. Closer. Tell me what you see."

She peered at Roger.

"Anything odd."

She gazed at his long body, his boots and dressed corpse that lay on the green cloak he liked so much, which now looked tattered and torn. Reeds, fish, or rocks had torn loose threads and now its fine material wouldn't been seen as good enough for a kitchen rag.

He lay there, one hand dangling by his side, the other clasped to his chest. She did not want to look up at his face, but did so anyway. His skin was pale and waxy, and it had a wet look to it. His mouth was open and his eyes stared straight ahead. It was horrible.

"Cover him, please. I don't want to see anymore," Bronwyn said.

Sir Nicholas covered his face, then pulled the sheet down more, when she held up a hand. "Wait."

"First you want me to cover him, then you don't. Make up your mind, girl," he said.

"What's that in his hand?"

"Eh?"

She pointed. "He's holding something."

They both peered closely at Roger's right hand, that at first appeared to be curled at his chest but instead was clutched around something.

"What is that?" she asked.

"Open his hand and see."

She stared at him. "I'm not touching a dead body."

He laughed, a thick, snorting sound that made her wonder if he had a cold. "You'll have to do worse than that in this lifetime, girl. Just open his hand. He won't bite."

She glared at him. "Can't you do it?"

"I'm holding the torch and the sheet."

"You could put those down."

"Aye, I could." But the look on his face said he wasn't going to.

Creeping sensations crawled down her shoulders and spine, as if mites or spiders were dancing down her skin. It made her shiver and want to shriek. Instead, she gave her head a little shake and reached for the item in Roger's lifeless hand.

She gently touched his bare skin and yelped, snatching her hand back.

"What? What's wrong?" Sir Nicholas asked.

She wiped her hand on her apron, rubbing it. "I touched his skin."

Sir Nicholas exhaled a deep breath. "Is that all? Go on, girl."

She wrapped her hands in her apron and, ignoring Sir Nicholas's sound of disgust, lifted Roger's fingers open. A noise escaped her throat as she touched his fingers, even with the apron's cloth.

"There's something there. He's holding on to something." She tugged, but the apron got in the way. She slipped her hands free and pried his fingers away, loosening them just enough to let whatever it was fall from his hand and onto the floor. It clattered with a *thud*. The object was small, but the quiet of the room and bare, stone walls made it sound huge.

She bent down and picked it up.

"What is it?" Sir Nicholas asked.

Bronwyn picked up the wooden object, noting the thin cord it was attached to. Roger must have pulled it from his attacker and tried to fight when he was pushed into the water, never fearing it would be his grave until it was too late.

"Bronwyn?" Sir Nicholas prompted. "You all right, girl?"

She held up the wooden cross, which bore a single shined piece of glass in its center. "I know who killed Roger, and I think de Grecy, too."

Chapter Thirteen

T HAT DAY AT the castle was a tense affair. More scouts had seen the outskirts of Maud's encampment, and there were countless numbers of fighting men and archers, waiting. The king had decided to wait and keep the castle on alert. No action would be taken yet, but scouts were posted on watch, and more guards monitored the city streets.

Bronwyn was jumpy. Her fingers practically itched with anticipation. She ate a quick meal with the cooks and servants, then shed her apron, unbound the kerchief around her hair, dusted herself clean of flour and walked toward the main room.

Inside, Alice sat by a circle of other ladies near Queen Matilda and waved Bronwyn over. "Ah, there you are. Pour me some wine."

Bronwyn replenished her cup and handed it to her. Alice gave her a sweet smile. "How lucky you are that you have a pretty face but no title. It saves you from unwanted suitors."

Lady Hawise laughed. "Speak for yourself, Lady Alice. You know very well that young knight's been looking for her. He's like a pup, that one."

Bronwyn looked at the lady in question, confusion on her face.

The lady turned to her. "Sir Gabriel's been asking for you." She motioned with her head behind her. "He's over there. You should see if he needs something." She smirked.

"Lady Hawise, please do not order my girl around. Bronwyn, attend me," Lady Alice said.

Bronwyn stood by her, politely keeping a distance but ready if needed.

"Have you baked any more rolls recently, Bronwyn?" Queen Matilda asked.

"No, Your Grace."

"A pity. I should like some of those sweet ones with honey, if you have any."

"Yes, my lady." She bowed.

"I should like one too," Muriel said.

"And I," Maud said, looking very young and no doubt hoping to be included.

"Make some for us all," Lady Alice said.

Bronwyn curtsied and walked away. She crossed the room and was almost at the exit, when Sir Gabriel stopped her. "Hullo there, Mistress Baker."

She looked up at him, unable to hide the shy smile on her face. "Hullo, Sir Knight."

He snorted. "What do you do here? On an errand already?"

She nodded. "I need to make sweet rolls with honey for the ladies."

"May I come?" he asked. "I should like the company."

She raised an eyebrow at him. "Sir?"

"No need to call me 'sir.' Just Gabriel."

She shook her head. "Sir Gabriel—"

"Yes?"

"It wouldn't be right."

He leaned against the wall, ever so slightly blocking the exit. "What? Me in the kitchens?"

She grinned. "It wouldn't be right. It'd be… unseemly."

"Why is that?"

Sir Gabriel was a handsome man. Today, he wore a tunic of light brown, with a belt and sheath at his waist. He was clean and smelled little, which was pleasant.

She blushed, surprised that his smile had that effect on her. "The kitchen is for cooks, like the battlefield is for warriors and knights. I wouldn't go out there. It's not my province. The kitchen is not yours."

He nodded. "But food still is necessary on the open road. Your talents would be useful there."

"Oh?" She was skeptical and he no doubt knew it.

"It's true. A man needs to know what he can and can't eat, especially if there's a long march ahead of him. If a man eats the wrong thing, he can get sick or even die," he told her.

"And do you know which foods are safe to eat?"

"Not always. But I know more than I did. Brother Bartholomew told us. Me and some of the others, not that they paid much attention. More fools, them."

"He taught you what was safe to eat?"

"Yes." Seeing her facial expression, he said, "Your mind is speeding faster than my charger. And before you jump to conclusions, yes, he taught us about mushrooms. It was those that killed de Grecy, right?"

"Yes. How did you know?"

"I was there, remember? Saw the whole thing. It all happened so fast, though. It was hard to believe he'd actually died from mushrooms, especially when we'd learnt about the dangers of them. You think he'd have paid attention."

"Oh?"

"I mean, really, any of the fellows who paid attention when the good brother was talking would have known. Me, Sir Baldwin, Sir Bors. I'd say Gilbert as well, but I doubt he was listening. Oh, and Master de la Haye, the castellan of the castle, would know. He wasn't with us, but I heard him later talking about it—he claims he knew right away those mushrooms were false." He scratched his head. "I suppose he was trying to make himself look innocent before the king, in case he was suspected of doing something. Not that the king would accuse him of anything after what's happened. He's too…"

"What, Sir Gabriel? What am I?" Master de la Haye said.

Sir Gabriel instantly turned red. He fumbled for words and his eyes widened.

Bronwyn saved him. "He was saying you're too smart for that, Master de la Haye. Too smart by half."

Both men looked at her.

She ducked her head. "Excuse me. I've got rolls to make." She darted away, back to the kitchens.

As she tied on her apron and wrapped up her hair, she began to think. A green cloak, black hair, almost like horsehair, a dead squire, poisoned rolls and a handful of knights who'd recently switched sides. The castellan, the knights Bors, Baldwin, Gabriel, and Brother Bartholomew.

She prepped the dough and made them sweet, making ten for the ladies, and a few more for any men who might decide to help themselves. Once they were ready, she tidied her appearance and brought them on a serving platter, entering the room.

The smell of the smoky fires and the warm torchlight filled the room. She carried the rolls in, the sight instantly attracting interest from the men and women present. Ignoring the curious looks of those present, she went straight to the ladies, offering the platter.

The queen took one, and the ladies followed suit, waiting for her to first take a delicate bite. She swallowed and said, "Delicious."

The ladies nibbled at their rolls and murmured in agreement, nodding and chatting amongst themselves.

Bronwyn breathed a tiny sigh of relief as Alice said, "She does make excellent rolls. It's why I took her on. I think all servants should have a skill at something, don't you?"

Bronwyn waited for each lady to help herself to a roll, then removed the platter and stood back, as a few of the men looked on with interest, and one beckoned her forward. She coughed. "My lady."

"Yes, what is it?" Alice asked.

"I do believe some of the men would like a roll as well. May I?"

"Only if the queen wishes it. Your Grace, would you care for another roll?" Alice asked.

Queen Matilda shook her head. "I am well. Please, do share them."

Alice bid her away with a wave of her hand, and Bronwyn took the platter across the room, where Sir Gabriel greeted her with a smile. "Hullo again, Mistress Baker."

"Sir Gabriel."

He helped himself to a roll and was soon joined by Sir Baldwin, Sir Gilbert, and Sir Bors. They took the remaining rolls and chewed, talking amongst themselves.

Sir Baldwin looked like a kind gentleman, with a stocky figure and short, brown hair. He'd helped himself to two rolls and held one up. "Good rolls."

Soon only Sir Gilbert and Sir Gabriel remained, but at a pointed look from Gilbert, Gabriel disappeared.

"Sir Gilbert?"

"You are the maidservant to Lady Alice," he said.

Bronwyn nodded.

"She is very beautiful."

"Yes, sir."

"Is she… That is to say, has her father…" He chewed thoughtfully. "Is the good lady betrothed?"

"Not to my knowledge, sir." Seeing his look of quiet dejection, she added, "I think if she were, I would know."

"Ah, yes, servants always know these things, sometimes before their masters do." He looked at her. "I like a servant who is discreet. Know what that means?"

Bronwyn shook her head.

"One who can keep a secret. And I gather you are very good with secrets. You'd have to be if the queen herself trusts you to investigate a murder."

"I…"

He cut her off before she could say more. "I should like to court Lady Alice. You will tell me if she is seeing any other man."

Bronwyn paused, her mouth open. Then it occurred to her, she could use this to her advantage.

He saw her expression and said, "I will reward you for your loyalty."

She swallowed. "I wonder if you might answer me a question, Sir Gilbert."

"What?" He, broad-shouldered and bulky, looked down at her. He was not a man to be trifled with, that much was certain. "I see, you want information. For your lady, no doubt. All right. Ask and I shall tell, if you are not impertinent."

She cocked her head at the word.

"Cheeky." He told her.

"Oh. You were there the night the knight de Grecy died."

He scratched his chin and brushed his chest, scattering crumbs from his tunic. "I was, but you know that already. What of it? The man ate a roll that disagreed with him. That's what you get for ordering expensive rolls and trying to impress the king with your pomp and fancy ways."

"What do you mean?"

"He came here acting like he was better than the lot of us, but we knew him from before, Maud's camp. When he disappeared, I thought he'd died. We were all surprised to see him here, acting the lord, as if he had the king in his pocket. We knew him for the turncoat he was."

She thought that was rather hypocritical of him, considering that out of the knights who had changed allegiances, de Grecy was the one who had remained true to the empress. "Do you think he meant to kill the king with his rolls?" she asked.

"No. De Grecy always had an eye for what was good. He always thought someone else had it better than him. He liked to show off. If you ask me, he thought he had it good here. In King Stephen's camp, he could make himself out to be important. Never mind that he didn't know his arse from his elbow. What is it you wish to know?”

“Did he tell many people he was buying rolls for the king?”

“De Grecy? Hmmm.” He thought on this. “No. He wanted it to be a surprise. But he was a vengeful sort, so he did tell a few of us. Those who had joined the king’s camp recently, so we would know he had one up on us. You understand?”

“Who did he tell?” she asked.

“Let’s see. Myself, Baldwin, Bors, Grossetete, Gabriel. The good brother advised him not to be so vain and like a braggart, but de Grecy wouldn’t listen. He especially wanted Grossetete to know. They were always at odds in Maud’s camp, so he particularly wanted Grossetete to have to know and to sit at dinner whilst the king enjoyed the rolls and bestowed favor on him. It would be like de Grecy to do that to a fellow knight.” He looked ready to spit on the floor, then thought better of it. “Is that all you wished to know?”

“Yes.” *For now*, Bronwyn thought.

“Well, help me with Lady Alice and I shall help you. Now, tell me. What does she like?”

She looked at Alice. She knew very little about her, aside from her beauty, her true loyalty, and her vanity. She did like gazing at her reflection.

“She likes pretty things,” Bronwyn said.

“Pretty things,” he repeated. “Like flowers, jewelry…”

She nodded.

He gave her a stern look. “I’ve answered your questions. Keep my secret, girl. It’s the sign of a good servant, that.”

She bowed her head and waited for him to go, when she was met by Sir Nicholas.

“Bronwyn,” he said.

“Sir Nicholas.”

“I have word that the good brother has been fasting and preparing for the feast day celebrations, which is why we have not seen him. When he appears, and I have no doubt that he will, beg Their Graces for an audience, and I will support you.”

She nodded, nervous. "Why not you, Sir Nicholas?"

"It is not I the queen has charged with being her investigator. Besides, I am to keep control of the guard. I will stand by you, but I cannot be everywhere at once. Take courage, girl." He clapped a hand on her shoulder and left.

Gabriel approached her. "What did he want?"

She shook her head, feeling Sir Gilbert's eyes on her. "Nothing I can say."

He quirked an eyebrow.

"What is it you are thinking now? Go on. I can tell your mind is miles from here," he said with a smile.

She glanced at him. "Is it true that de Grecy and Grossetete were at odds?"

"Huh? What do you mean?"

"It's just that I heard—"

"Oh, I see. Asking questions about that again. "The man is dead. Let the dead lie, I say."

"But is it true?" she asked.

"Well…" He glanced around and took a spare cup from the table, filling it with wine. "I don't like to speak ill of others, or the dead. It's not very Christian."

"I'm sorry. I just wonder if what I heard was true. Were they enemies?"

He cleared his throat. "It's not for me to speak so about my fellow knights. That's idle gossip, and not for servants like you to dabble in." His expression turned surly. "Perhaps you ought to speak to the good brother. I think you could use a lesson in humility."

As if conjured by magic, the brother in question appeared behind her. "Who needs a lesson in humility?"

Bronwyn stiffened.

Seeing Sir Gabriel's glance at her, Brother Bartholomew said, "Ah. Let us have a little talk, you and I." He took her by the arm and pulled her away.

She tried tugging free, but his grip was strong as he ushered her toward the exit. "I am serving my lady," she said.

"It looks to me like you were trying to charm King Stephen's knights. And worse, I find you gossiping. A girl like you needs to be doing penance in church. I see the Lord has smiled upon you and given you a place in the good Lady Alice's service. But what do you do? You waste your good fortune."

"Let me go," she said.

He jerked her harder. "Not until you are back in the kitchens where you belong."

"No. Let go of me." Her voice carried.

Men and women were looking at them now.

Brother Bartholomew said, "Your little search for a murderer has turned up nothing. The queen should never have wasted her time on sending a girl to perform a fruitless errand. You belong in the cells with your father, the traitor."

She lost her composure, God help her. She spat, "My father is not a traitor."

Silence filled the room. Even the music had stopped.

Queen Matilda's voice rang out, "What is going on here?"

Brother Bartholomew's look was snide. "You're going to get what's coming to you now, girl."

Bronwyn glared into his cold, blue eyes, so light and pretty, like ice on the river in the morning.

Queen Matilda was upon them. "I said, what is happening here? Tell me."

Brother Bartholomew presented a picture of quiet piety and bowed his head. After raising his gaze, he called out, "Sire, a matter to lay before you. I have found this girl nosing around your court, spreading lies. Allow me to take her away."

Queen Matilda's face turned pink, for he had spoken to her husband, as if she were not standing there before him.

In that instant, Bronwyn could well see the quiet rage simmering inside her. She, a queen, who if the rumors were true, had literally led armies, had been duly ignored in favor of her husband by a mere monk. The audacity.

Her eyes were like daggers.

Bronwyn could well understand her rage, for it mirrored her own. How dare he? For the queen to be overlooked as if she were nothing, not even a servant. It was not to be borne. She said, "My lady, I beg an audience before you."

"Why?" The queen's voice was hard.

Her heart beat in her throat. She could feel her pulse jumping. "Because I have found the answer to the matter you asked me to look into. The issue of de Grecy's death."

Queen Matilda called to her husband, who sat across the room. "My lord."

"Yes?"

"We have a request for an audience. I have a mind to hear this one," she said, her voice careful. However light, it held a serious note that caught her husband's attention.

"Very well, my lady. Come, let us adjourn to the inner chamber. Sir Nicholas, escort them if you would."

"Wait," Alice said.

"Lady Alice?" Queen Matilda said, her voice stinging.

Alice bowed her head. "Forgive me, my queen, but this girl is my maidservant. I would accompany her to this audience, if you will allow it."

Queen Matilda's face was stern. "You speak for this girl?"

"I do."

"Very well. Come along."

In no time at all, and under many aristocrats' watchful eyes, they were escorted by Sir Nicholas and a handful of armed guards into the throne room, where the king and queen took their seats.

Bronwyn stood before them with her hands clasped and head bowed, her eyes to the floor.

The doors shut, and the room was silent, although many were listening. In the room were the king and queen, with Sir Nicholas and Brother Bartholomew off to the side. Guards lined the walls, spears and swords at the ready. Also present were Alice, who stood behind Bronwyn, and the knights, Sirs Gilbert, Bors,

Baldwin, Clarke, Gabriel, and Grossetete.

"Speak," King Stephen commanded. "Who called for this audience?"

Bronwyn spoke up. "I did, Your Grace."

"Why?" He glanced at his wife as if to say, *We are accepting audiences from servants now?*

The queen silenced him with a look and said to her, "Talk."

"I know who killed Sir de Grecy and the squire, Roger," Bronwyn said.

"Who?"

"Brother Bartholomew."

Silence. Then a snicker. A laugh.

Brother Bartholomew clapped and joined in the laughter. "That is a good jest, girl, but one in poor taste. Now be off with you. Go back to the kitchens, where you belong."

Bronwyn ignored him. "It is true."

"What proof have you?" King Stephen asked.

"I have spoken with the knights and learnt that of the men who knew de Grecy was buying rolls to please my lord and lady that night, Brother Bartholomew was among them."

"But so were a handful of knights," the monk said, interrupting. "And that is hardly proof of anything. What you pose as fact is merely hearsay."

"Just so, only the kitchen servants, a few knights and Brother Bartholomew knew of the types of mushrooms that were safe to eat and those which were poisonous. And in fact, Brother Bartholomew taught the knights this."

"Who told you this?" King Stephen asked.

She looked at Sir Nicholas, who gave her an encouraging look. "Sir Gabriel, Your Grace."

Heads turned and the knight said, "It is true, my lord. I did tell the girl this. I did not lie."

Brother Bartholomew shook his head at the man. "Shame on you and your wagging tongue, Sir Gabriel. I expect you to see me for penance once we are done here."

The man blinked in surprise, then hung his head.

Bronwyn swallowed. "There's more. The night that de Grecy died, my father and I made the rolls at home and took them into the castle. But in the kitchens I spotted someone in a green cloak adding mushrooms to the rolls we'd made. I raised a fuss, but the men didn't believe me, and you know what happened. This man had black hair, and he scared Mistress de la Haye, who was certain de Roumare had escaped from the cells. She was so certain it was him, she even grabbed a piece of his black hair from when he fled the kitchen. But it's not human hair at all, but horsehair. From a horse Brother Bartholomew clipped and sheared for its hair, to make a wig."

"Bring the good lady here," King Stephen ordered.

In moments, the chatelaine was present. She looked nervous and twirled and untwirled the piece of black hair around her fingers.

The king repeated the charge laid against the brother. "This baker says you found a piece of hair from the night the man escaped from the kitchen."

"You mean this?" She held up the hair.

"Give it here."

Sir Nicholas took it from her, and passed it to the king and queen. "It does indeed resemble horsehair."

"It was not until Roger returned from a secret mission that I discovered he didn't have black hair at all. He couldn't have done the crime, for he had been sent on a secret mission earlier that day. He wasn't even in the city when the murder took place."

"What secret mission is this?" King Stephen asked. "Sir Bors?"

"I sent the lad on no mission, Your Grace," Sir Bors said.

"Roger told me so himself," said Bronwyn. "When he returned, he came to the kitchen for a bite to eat, and he told me he'd been on a mission for the king. And he said he was going to speak with a person right away. I didn't know it at the time, but I believe that was the same person who killed him."

Brother Bartholomew snorted. "You are wasting His Grace's

time. Admit it, you and your father served poisoned mushrooms to the king and queen. It's due to their mercy you were not imprisoned as well as your traitorous father," Brother Bartholomew said.

She replied through gritted teeth, "My father is no traitor, and neither am I. The person in the stolen green cloak, with the black horsehair wig, who sent Roger on a secret mission, is the one who killed him and de Grecy."

"But who is that?"

She looked squarely at Brother Bartholomew.

He snorted. "Me? I can understand your anger, but do not aim it at me, girl. You have no proof."

"You stole Roger's cloak," Bronwyn said, "and made a wig from the horsehair. You hoped to impersonate de Roumare for it. No one would suspect it was you, since you have a tonsure."

"I did no such thing."

"When Roger came back he found the cloak in his room and said it smelled like horse, and worse. But no one would have suspected *you*."

"And rightly so," Brother Bartholomew said. "I am innocent."

"But only the person who killed de Grecy and who wanted Roger gone is the one with a reason to want to hurt him. It would've been easy to lure him out to the river. But Roger took something from the killer, in his last moments before he froze beneath the ice."

"What was it?" King Stephen asked.

She turned to the monk. "Brother Bartholomew, where is your cross? I haven't seen you wearing it for some days now."

People looked at him.

"Why, I… lost it. It must have fallen off my neck when I wasn't looking."

"Then why did I find it in Roger's lifeless hand?" she asked, fishing it out of her apron. Amidst gasps and mutters, she held it aloft in the air, the small, wooden cross dangling from her fist. The piece of shined glass at its center caught the light and shone.

"Brother, how do you explain this?" King Stephen asked. "I recognize that as your cross. It is distinctive."

"She must have stolen it."

"She did not. The girl speaks the truth," Sir Nicholas said. "I was with her down in cold storage when she found it in Roger's hand. Unless you think me a liar too, Brother?"

Brother Bartholomew looked askance at Sir Nicholas and licked his lips, a nervous action. "I… remember now. I gave it to the boy. I wanted him to have a cross of his own. A gift."

"You just said a moment ago you lost it. Did you forget?" Queen Matilda asked.

"Yes. Yes, I did. But I didn't kill him. Someone else did."

"Funny, for we found threads from a green fabric in your room," Sir Nicholas said, "and a black wig that looks poorly pieced together. It was shedding all over the place. It does not appear to be like human hair and it certainly smells like… horse."

"You were in my quarters?" the monk asked. "You had no right."

"What's the harm? You have nothing to hide. Do you, brother?" Sir Nicholas pressed. "You are loyal to King Stephen, are you not?"

"Of course I am," Brother Bartholomew said.

"Then why is it that de Roumare bid me give messages to you?" Bronwyn asked.

"*What?*" King Stephen asked.

All eyes were upon Bronwyn. "Since my father was imprisoned, I've been visiting him in the cells. Recently, he warned me of talk he'd heard from the knights also imprisoned down there. He said there was talk of a rebellion from within the castle. We didn't have any proof, but I've learnt that de Grecy was here on false pretenses, Your Grace. He was here and meant to be working with someone on the inside, someone loyal to the empress."

Queen Matilda hissed.

Bronwyn continued. "He was meant to work with them and

together bring about the rebellion, in time for when the empress's forces arrived at Lincoln. With the castle retaken, they would be put in charge and hold the doors open for Empress Maud."

King Stephen's face was stormy. "You speak of things beyond your understanding, girl. How can we know this is truth and not rumor?"

"I can speak for the girl's honesty, Your Grace," Sir Nicholas said. "I was with her when we found a young woman in de Grecy's room, searching through his things. If you recall, we instigated a search for her that very day but could not find any trace of her. From her attack on my person, I can only assume she was a spy."

"A spy? Here in my court?" King Stephen said. "Are you sure?"

Sir Nicholas nodded. "I am, Your Grace. She attacked me and escaped before we could catch her."

"And what of this business with the dead boy, and the mushrooms?" King Stephen asked.

Bronwyn spoke up. "Brother Bartholomew has been down in the dungeon, speaking with the imprisoned knights who had taken over the castle before Christmas. I believe he is the insider spy that de Grecy was working with." She glanced at Alice.

Alice's eyes widened, but her cheeks were like made of stone. Her passive expression did not waver.

"Of course I would be down there," Brother Bartholomew said. "I was hearing their prayers and giving them penance, like any holy man would."

"I did not order you to visit the cells, brother," King Stephen said.

Brother Bartholomew bent his head as if in prayer. "Forgive me, my lord. I felt it would be unkind, nay, un-Christian not to attend to their souls. I would of course relay any useful information to you, if I thought it helpful."

"I thought what a man said in private to a monk was to remain so, and private before God," Queen Matilda said.

"Yes, well, there are exceptions, my lady," the monk said quickly. He wiped his brow.

"Nervous, brother?" Bronwyn asked.

He shot her a glare. "You have no proof of anything."

"You stole Roger's cloak. How do you explain the threads in your room and the wig? The missing cross I found in his dead hand?"

"You make too much of nothing. I merely took the cloak to be a lesson to the boy. He was so proud of it, strutting around like a peacock. He needed to be taught a lesson not to put so much store by material goods. A little humility did him good."

"You took my squire's cloak?" Sir Bors said. "I punished Roger for losing it. You admit to stealing?"

"Isn't that against one of the commandments, brother?" Sir Nicholas asked.

Brother Bartholomew turned red. "Yes, and I will do my due penance. But Roger needed to learn a lesson. I had heard rumors that he was mean and cruel to the other boys."

"That is no reason to steal, brother. That cloak was a gift to the boy for his good service." Sir Bors said. "It would have kept the boy warm at night. Did you send him on a so called secret mission as well?"

Heads turned to look at Brother Bartholomew. "I might have suggested he ride out to survey the area and see if he could find more men to join Stephen's cause. But it was a suggestion only. It was not a secret mission by any means. The boy was telling tales, Your Grace. It's not my fault." A vein on this forehead purpled. "I may have taken the squire's cloak, but I did not kill the man de Grecy. I didn't."

"You did," Bronwyn said. "And you tried to frame it Roger and de Roumare."

"Why?" Queen Matilda asked.

"From what the knights tell me, de Grecy had an arrogant manner. He liked to fancy himself important and when he joined

King Stephen's court, he would gain favor with the king, especially with a treat like sweet honeyed rolls. And because he liked to play both sides, he thought that by working with the spy here, he would prove himself valuable to Empress Maud as well by arranging the rebellion. But he died before that could happen. My guess is de Grecy was overheard talking about the plot by Brother Bartholomew, who plotted to kill him when the chance arose."

Bronwyn added, "Brother Bartholomew heard de Grecy bragging about the expensive order of rolls and decided that was his chance. He sent Roger off on the mission, waited for the right time, and slipped out of the dining hall and put on the cloak and wig. Once he'd put the mushrooms on the bread rolls and shoved me into the potboy, he ran.

"Mistress de la Haye saw him. She screamed and said she'd seen de Roumare, just as he probably hoped—which was why he'd chosen the black wig. While everyone would wonder how a prisoner has escaped, they wouldn't be looking for a monk. But that backfired because no one believed his witness. Instead, she fainted, and Brother Bartholomew was immediately sought—but he was nowhere to be found. Why? Because he'd gone to stow the items back in his room. It's why he wasn't immediately there when the call was raised for him to attend Mistress de la Haye. Later, he stowed the cloak in de Roumare's cell to keep himself from suspicion, then hid it back in Roger's room."

She paused and cleared her throat. "I know Brother Bartholomew is involved because a few nights ago, I was asked to give a message to de Roumare from Brother Bartholomew that he wasn't coming that night. I mistakenly thought they meant prayers, and the men laughed, as if it were a great pretense. They clearly meant something else."

King Stephen sighed and leaned back in his chair.

"You have no proof. No proof of any of this," Brother Bartholomew said. "I am no killer. I am not a traitor."

"Perhaps not, but you have been led astray, I think," King

Stephen said. "Monks do not steal or strive to teach others cruel lessons in humility. But I also do not think you are a murderer."

Brother Bartholomew smiled in triumph.

"What of the girl, sire?" Sir Nicholas said.

King Stephen tapped his chin. "I am not sure. How can we be sure anything she says is truth and not a lie?"

"Exactly," Brother Bartholomew said. "The girl is in league with her father, who is a traitor. He tried to kill you. He killed de Grecy and now is connected with de Roumare, who bears you no love. Please sire, you have known me for years. Would you take the word of a mere girl over me?"

King Stephen looked at them both. "I believe anyone can be honest. And I also believe people can make mistakes." He expression hardened. "This young woman knows far too much for an ordinary baker. I believe *she* must be the one working with a spy, not the good brother."

"What? No!" Bronwyn froze.

"Guards. Take this girl to the dungeons," King Stephen said.

Brother Bartholomew smiled, rubbing his hands together. "Very wise, my lord. She's caused enough trouble for one day." To Bronwyn, he said, "You understand what the penalty is for collaborating with spies, don't you, girl? Death by hanging."

Bronwyn's blood ran cold, and she swayed on her feet. She would hang?

Queen Matilda touched her husband's arm. "Milord, is this the right decision? I do not think—"

"Do not question me, wife. I will not ask why you keep counsel with humble bakers and traitorous women," King Stephen said, his mouth firm. "Take her away. She and her father will be hung at dawn."

"Your Grace, please. Let the girl stay in my care. She is young and stupid. She knows not what she says. I can—" Alice began.

"I have made my decision," King Stephen said.

Bronwyn's eyes watered. Her face felt hot, but she lifted her chin and remained mute as the guards led her from the throne room.

Chapter Fourteen

BRONWYN WAS LED at spearpoint through the corridors. Word spread of the girl baker being imprisoned and so servants and nobles stopped what they were doing in order to see.

She kept her gaze straight ahead as she was marched through and down the spiral staircase, to the cells. She met the surprised expressions of the guards to whom she'd slipped coins to for weeks, all of whom now shot her glances of suspicion and distrust as she was led at spearpoint past them.

She was let inside the same cell as her father, who hugged her, then looked on in dismay as the cell door was locked behind her. "Bronwyn, what are you doing here?"

"Papa." He felt so cold, and thin. His beard was long and scraggly with grey hair. He'd grown a mustache and he desperately needed a haircut, not to mention a bath. His small cell had rushes on the floor, a mouse here and there, and the smell of urine in the air. The space itself was filthy, but they were together again.

She hugged him tightly. "I'm glad to see you again."

"And I, you. But what are you doing here? Why did they let you in? Am I to be freed?" he asked.

"No. Father, I'm…" She told him everything.

When she'd finished, he said, "Oh, Bronwyn…" He sat down on a small pallet he'd made in the corner. "My girl, what have you done? You've doomed us both."

"No. I haven't, I swear. Someone will come." She looked at the door to the cell. "Someone will."

They didn't have to wait long. The guards came through with a pitcher of wine for them to drink from to slake their thirst and some stale bread for them to share. A gift from Lady Alice, they said.

Bronwyn said she was full from luncheon and gave her half to Papa. He at first made a token protest but seemed so hungry that in the next five minutes, it was gone.

An hour later, a familiar face appeared. "Bronwyn?"

Bronwyn met him at the bars, holding the metal with her hands. It was cold, but her heart gave a treacherous flutter. "Rupert."

He looked at her, taking in her appearance and cell. "Are you all right?"

"Yes. I'm fine. What's happening upstairs?"

Rupert looked away. "Brother Bartholomew has the king convinced you were behind it all. Sir Nicholas and Lady Alice are pleading your case. I could only get away for a few moments. We're trying to get you freed."

"What about my papa?" she asked.

Rupert glanced behind her and spoke quietly. "Bronwyn, we're doing all we can to save your life. If we were to create a distraction, would you go?"

She swallowed and looked back at her father. To run would be to court death. They could never return home. They would be hunted like outlaws.

She shook her head. "We'd need time. And I'm not leaving my papa."

Rupert nodded and covered her hand on the bars with his. He started. "You're cold."

She shrugged. "It's a bit chilly down here." She tried not to shiver.

"Come on. You've had enough time. Get out of here, lad," one of the guards called, marching over.

Rupert patted her hand. "I'll be back. We'll get you both out of here, I promise. Don't lose hope."

The guard clapped a hand on his shoulder and jerked him away.

"I mean it, Bronwyn. Don't lose hope!" Rupert called as the guard marched him away by spearpoint.

Once Rupert had left, Bronwyn sat by her father and they chatted, sitting beside each other as they shared a blanket for warmth. Bronwyn felt her father was desperately tired, and so cold. In such conditions, a chill had seeped into his bones and she could feel him trembling beside her.

The night wore on and a coldness emanated from the dank, stone walls. It seeped from the very bones and bedrock of the castle, reaching for their warm skin like ghostly tendrils. To say they were cold was not enough. They froze, huddled together for warmth, and Bronwyn came to know what it felt like to have ice in her veins.

She did not know how much time had passed, but when she looked up, another familiar face stood there at the bars, watching.

"Alfred?" she asked. "What are you doing here?"

"I paid the guards to let me in." He held a candle and beckoned her forward.

Her father called, "Alfred, son, how did you get into the castle?"

"Never mind that. Bronwyn, I've come to take you home," he said.

Hope rose in her. "Home? But how? Did King Stephen pardon me?"

"No. Nothing like that. When the king pronounced sentence on you, a sir, some knight or whatever, Nick?"

"Sir Nicholas?" she said.

"Yeah, him. He and that squire, they came to your family's shop, spouting some nonsense about you being imprisoned and sentenced to death."

Bronwyn shushed him. She hadn't told her father. She didn't

want him to know.

Alfred raised an eyebrow at her and said, "Well, your mama had a fit. Wyot was in tears. They sent me here to plead your case."

"And?" Her father had joined them now. "Good to see you, Alfred. I hear you've been helping out at the shop." He extended a hand through the bars.

Alfred shook her father's hand. "Master Blakenhale." His eyes widened to see her father's appearance now. Alfred said, "We've scraped together some money to pay a ransom toward you."

"But we're not being held for ransom," Bronwyn said. "If that were the case, we'd have paid to get my papa out before now."

Alfred shot her a look. "Your mama and I, we pleaded to the king. She begged the man."

Bronwyn stared. Her mother had come and begged the king for their release. She felt like a child. "Go on. Where is she? Is she here?"

"No, she went back home. She said we needed you back to help at the shop, or else the family wouldn't survive. She offered to make a gift of money, all we have saved, and to work in the kitchens herself if it meant you could come home."

"What did the king say?" Bronwyn's father asked.

"He thought on it, and hearing the counsel of Sir Nicholas and that squire," Alfred said with a frown, "he agreed to let you go."

"He did?" Bronwyn's eyebrows rose.

"Yeah, he did."

"Then get the keys and let's go. Call the guards. Guards!" Her father called.

"Master Blakenhale…" Alfred hung his head. "They're not coming."

"What do you mean?"

He looked up, meeting Bronwyn's eyes. "The king only agreed to let one of you go."

She gasped. Disappointment was sketched across her father's

face. "Papa, you go."

"No, you. You go on, child. Go." He nudged her toward the bars.

"Stop, the decision is made," Alfred said. "He's allowed Bronwyn to be released."

To live, he meant, she thought. "Why? Papa has been here longer, too long. Take him."

"No, Bronwyn, the king has decided," her father said, but there was a note of doubt in his voice she could not ignore.

"Why?" she asked Alfred. "Why me and not Papa?"

Alfred let out a breath, and the candle almost went out. "Here, hold this." He handed it to her father, who took it eagerly, letting the candle warm his bony hands.

"Because…" Alfred started.

"What?" Bronwyn asked, her voice hard. She'd never forgive herself if she went free whilst her father stayed in the cell to rot.

"I told the king we were affianced," Alfred said.

"What?"

"Engaged," Alfred said warmly. "That if he let you go, I'd keep you out of trouble and you'd spend your days far from the castle and never come back. You'd work in the bakery with me, as my wife."

Bronwyn's jaw dropped open. "Your wife."

"Yes." Seeing her face, he said, "I know you're surprised, but, Bronwyn, it's the only way. It was the only way they'd let you go. It's your life we're talking about here. Your mother, Wyot—they need you. *I* need you." He reached for her hand through the bars and gave it a squeeze. "Jesus, Mary, you're cold," he cursed softly.

"Alfred, I—"

"Say *yes*. Say *yes*, and this nightmare will all be over. We'll go home and I'll move into the bakery and we'll all live there together."

Bronwyn stared at him, her eyes wide. She swallowed. "I'm too young."

He laughed. "You're eighteen. You're past the age of consent, and I know you're a woman. I was there when you first started your monthly courses and you thought you were dying. Remember? I know you."

She shook her head.

"Come off it, Bronwyn. You can leave here, free. You wouldn't have to worry about murders, or deaths, or brothers poisoning knights or whatever. You could live at home, with me. The queen should never have trusted you with a task like that, anyway. She'd have known you would fail."

"I didn't," Bronwyn said.

"Huh?"

"I didn't fail. I figured out who killed de Grecy. They just didn't believe me."

"Well, that doesn't matter. More fools them for not believing you. Anyway. You won't have to worry about any of that anymore. Not once we're married. And you're a fine baker, Bronwyn. As my wife, you'll be able to bake whatever you want."

It was true. She could see them now, living together as a large family, baking and making money. Staying and baking in Lincoln the rest of their lives. Feeding the people, high and low. She'd have children and Margaret and she would be bouncing babes in their arms as Alfred and Papa… No, wait. Papa wouldn't be there. Alfred would take his place as man of the household. Was that what he'd wanted all along?

And what about Rupert? Where would he be in all this? If she was married to Alfred, he wouldn't come and tease her or chat to her anymore—Alfred would make sure of that. She'd miss him. Bronwyn blinked. She liked Rupert. She liked his smile. The way his eyes crinkled when he laughed and joked with her. How he'd escort her everywhere, as if she were a grand lady, and help her out at a moment's notice. She didn't want to leave this world without seeing him one last time. Rupert and her father meant so much to her. But only one of them would hang in the morning.

"What about my father?" she asked.

Alfred turned his head, eyes flicking to her father, who

clasped the candle like it was a holy relic. "What about him?"

"What happens to him if we marry?"

"Well, he stays in here."

"He'll die tomorrow."

"Yes. But that's not my fault. I was able to make a deal for your freedom, and I did. You should say thanks. You should be thanking me," Alfred pointed out, running a hand through his hair.

She almost laughed. Instead, she looked him in the eyes. She didn't want a life of safety, if it meant being with a man who stole kisses rather than asked for them. Who forced affection on her when she did not want it. And who overlooked the love she had for her father, when it mattered most to her, more than her own life, at that moment. Alfred offered her a life, but what was a life without true love?

"Alfred, do you love me?"

He blinked. "Of course I do." He said it so quick, in the same tone of voice he might place an order of cod from the fishmonger.

"Do you?" she asked.

"Yes, I do. I have, ever since we were kids. Now come on, Bronwyn. What do you say?"

That was his attempt at a betrothal. Why did she feel so uninspired? There must have been many girls who would have jumped at the chance to be with Alfred. What a shame, she reflected, that she was not one of them.

She slowly withdrew her hand. "I'm not leaving my father."

Alfred's face crumpled in hurt, then anger. "You're being stupid."

"I don't care."

"Bronwyn, no. Don't be foolish," her father said, touching her shoulder.

"I mean it, Papa. I won't leave you."

"You really are dumb," Alfred spat. "Here I come all the way here to the stinking dungeons to rescue you, and you want to stay here. You're nuts. Why won't you come?"

"I told you, I won't leave without my papa," she said.

He paused. "I promise I'll be kind to you. Is a life with me really so bad?"

She looked at him. Really looked at him. Alfred, the tall, sometimes giant-like, blond, broad-shouldered man built like an ox who could carry heavy loaves of bread and move a heavy cart with ease. Alfred, whom she'd known like a friend, practically an older brother, for years. Who had always teased and elbowed her with a joke, until he'd recently taken issue with her looking into de Grecy's death and had kissed her without asking. Who now was asking for her heart. And was willing to give her a life in return.

It might have been tempting, once upon a time. It wasn't now. She cared for Rupert. Fancied Rupert. If there was ever a man she wanted to consider having a future with, it would have been him. Not Alfred, who stood there looking at her, waiting.

She didn't love him, and it felt wrong to say *yes* to a man asking for so much.

"No, it wouldn't be. But I don't love you," she said.

"Bronwyn," her father chastised.

Alfred's smile disappeared. He looked at the earthen floor. "You could learn to love me."

She shook her head. "No."

He looked up, his expression a sneer. "So you'd rather stay here and die in the cells or tomorrow on the gallows than have a lifetime of happiness and safety with me. I knew some girls were foolish, but you really are the limit. You know what? Fine. Have it your way. Stay here and rot. I don't care. I'll take back the ransom and sod the both of you."

"Bronwyn, don't do this," her father said, "Take his offer. Say *yes*."

"No," she snapped. "I'm not leaving you."

"You're not leaving me—you're leaving to keep on living. Obstinate child, won't you go?"

She shook her head again. "Mama would never forgive me." *And I would never forgive myself,* she thought.

"It doesn't matter." Her father gripped her hand. It felt warmer now that he'd been holding the candle. "I don't want you to die. Go with Alfred. Please. I give you my blessing. Go."

"Papa," Bronwyn said, giving his hand a squeeze. "No. There's still a way out of this."

"How? Alfred has bought you a another chance at life. Do not turn it away." He looked at her, his eyes dark and hollow. "Please, Bronwyn. It is the only way. I would rather see you alive and wedded than dead for a principle. Please, girl. Use your head."

She looked back at the man who could be her husband and savior. And possibly jailor. "Goodbye, Alfred."

He spat on the floor. "Goodbye, Bronwyn. I hope you realize you're making a big mistake."

"That is between me and God."

He snorted. "I would have treated you well, you know." He blinked hard and sniffed. "Last chance."

She dropped her father's free hand and looked at Alfred. His every word and arrogant expectation, his anger and dismissal of her feelings, made her close off her heart to him all the more with each passing moment. She did not want him and never would. She refused to commit them both to a life without love. That would be a torment.

"Alfred? Look after my mama and Wyot, would you?" she asked.

"Stupid girl," he muttered as he walked off, his heavy footsteps echoing down the hall.

The dungeon was quiet, but for the muted mutterings and chatter of the knights within. She heard the restless moving and shifting of the men trapped in the cells and felt a tension there. It didn't matter to her if they'd heard their exchange or not. But she did not want to be near when the next day came. If her suspicions were right, then Empress Maud's company would be upon the city within hours.

Papa refused to talk to her, only muttering how she'd lost track of her senses. He sat, holding the candle Alfred had left them and its small, sputtering warmth, until it burnt down and blew out, leaving a wispy trail of smoke in the air. Darkness filled the cell, but for the dim, sputtering torches sparsely hung outside on the walls.

Some hours later, her father slept, when a figure came and stood before their cell. "Girl."

She rose and went to the bars, then stopped. "Brother Bartholomew. What do you want?"

He carried a candle that played shadows on his face, revealing a nasty smile.

"Come to gloat?"

His smile widened. "You are exactly where you belong."

Her hands clenched into fists. "Is that why you've come? To point fingers and laugh at me?"

He laughed. "I don't need to. You dug your own grave, girl. You and that wagging tongue of yours. If only you'd kept quiet, we might have come to an agreement. But now it's too late. You and your father will die."

She glared at him. "You convinced the king."

"Of course. The king is too much of a trusting fool to believe the word of a mere girl, and besides, I have given him counsel. His forces have frightened the good Lady Maud and she is hiding elsewhere. She is weak. Why else would her knights switch allegiances to his court?" He smiled. "He trusts me. Much more than that Sir Nicholas fellow."

"What did you do?"

"Nothing—yet. But I've got plans for him." His eyes glittered with excitement.

She banged her fists against the bars, smarting her skin and earning a call from the guards, "Quiet down there!"

Seeing her expression, he said, "Face it, girl. You are alone. You have no friends, only enemies. And now you will rot in that cell with your father. Although not for very long. If you do not freeze tonight, on the morrow you will face the noose."

"You're still going through with the rebellion."

"We've had this planned for weeks. If it weren't for de Grecy, it might've happened sooner. But either way, tonight is the last night Stephen will rule in this castle. This will soon be Maud's and you'd better pray to God that you do not live to see her."

"Why is that?" she asked.

"Because, of the many enemies you have managed to incur in your pathetically short life, I am the nicer of the two of us. Pray that you never meet her."

She lunged for him, straining against the bars. He fell back on the floor, the candle falling away. The monk cursed and picked it up before it could catch on any of the dirt or rushes on the floor. He cleared his throat. "Yes, well. Goodbye."

With his nose in the air, he left, carrying the light with him. They were left in the darkness, with naught but the sputtering torch on the side wall. The air instantly felt colder.

Bronwyn heard her father's racking coughs as he trembled beneath the thin blanket. She wrapped her arms around him and they slept until morning. When they woke, their breaths formed white plumes of vapor in the chilly morning air.

It was a fine day to die.

Chapter Fifteen

ALL WAS LOST and Bronwyn knew it. That day should've been a feast day, for it was the feast of the purification of St. Mary. And yet she was filled with dread.

The guards came down to deliver breakfast, day-old bread rolls and stale ale. "Gifts from upstairs," one said, passing them rolls and filling their cups with ale.

Bronwyn's stomach had been growling for ages. She'd been lifting a roll to her mouth and paused. The outside was covered with crumbled-up mushrooms. She dropped the roll. "Where did these come from?"

"Brother Bartholomew. Why?"

She glanced over and her father had a roll half in his mouth, about to bite down. "Papa, no!" She lunged at him, knocking him to the ground, along with the ale and bread.

"Bronwyn!" he cried out as the guards threatened them with violence for causing a fuss.

"Don't eat it. It's poisoned," she said, tossing the roll away.

"What? Oh. You mean…" He glanced at the roll, now being feasted on by two rats.

"Poison mushrooms," she said. "A little gift from Brother Bartholomew." She looked back at the guards. "Could we have some more ale?"

The guards shook their heads. "You spilled it, you lose it." They walked on, noses in the air.

She let out a small sigh. Both their cups of ale had spilled. There was not even a drop left.

The church bells rang, signaling the start of Mass. But within the hour, the peace was shattered by shouts, the thunder of horses' hooves, the call of battle trumpets and horns, and the clash of spears and swords.

The guards at the dungeon entrance cried out and were quickly subdued, their cries renting the air. Bronwyn and her father stood by, tense, watching from the shadows, their eyes wide. In moments, the imprisoned knights had escaped the cells, shouting and hollering, cheering and laughing as one by one, they were let out. Following William de Roumare, one paused before Bronwyn and her father's cell.

"Leave them. The king was going to hang them anyway. The good brother told me of her meddling about in our plans. Let 'em rot," de Roumare said.

She gazed at him with quiet stoicism but said nothing. As much as she wanted out of the cell, she did not want to be within arm's reach of the men. They were warriors, fighters, hungry and hard, and each was bigger and stronger than her.

The knights left, and she let out a small sigh of relief. The sounds of battle raged, and her father paced the small space of the cell, looking up every time there was another loud crash of noise. Then he paused. "You were right."

"About what?"

He pointed. There in the corner of the cell, lay the two rats who'd eaten his breakfast roll.

The sight of it sent a shiver down her spine.

They were interrupted later by the sounds of footsteps hurrying down the spiral staircase. "Bronwyn? Bronwyn? Are you there?" a voice called.

"Alice?" Bronwyn went to the bars, gripping the cold iron. "Alice?"

She came darting down the steps, her face wild. "Thank God you're alive. Uh, how do I get you out of here?"

"Who are you?" Bronwyn's father wandered up to the bars.

Alice glanced and rolled her eyes, glancing at his dirty appearance with her upper lip almost curling into a sneer. "I'm sorry, but I'm here for her. Now, Bronwyn, we have to get you out."

"That's my father you're talking to," she said.

"Fine. Hello, I am Lady Alice. We have to get out of here, now." She held up a knife. "I thought this could help open the lock somehow." She tried forcing the lock, but a moment later, let out a grunt in exasperation.

"Alice, why are you here?"

"It's chaos up there. At Mass, we were all present when the king accepted a candle and it broke apart in his hands, into three pieces. People were shocked and some say it is a bad omen. But that's not the worst of it. The Empress Maud's men are here, outside, this very minute."

Bronwyn tensed.

"The monks begged for King Stephen to aim for peace, to negotiate, have peace talks, but his knights and men at arms urged him to fight, so he's taken his knights out there, beyond the castle, to face Robert of Gloucester's men." She paused. "Rupert is out there."

"But, Alice, why aren't you with the empress's forces?"

An unhappy look flitted across her face. A second later, she said, "You're my maidservant. I need you."

"Alice, what about the guards? How did you get past them?"

"They're…" She swallowed. "They're dead. Someone killed them. I think there was something wrong, because the rats are dead too. There are some bread rolls next to them." She shivered.

"Brother Bartholomew," Bronwyn said grimly. "Alice, can you look on their persons and see if they have keys to the cells?"

"Me? No. I'd have to touch dead bodies. I couldn't. Can't you do it?"

She cocked her head and gave Alice a look.

Alice gave a long-suffering sigh. "The things I do. All right, but you owe me for this." She left and there was some scuffling, a squeal or two, and she came back, wiping her hands on her dress.

"What's happened upstairs? Is everyone all right?" Bronwyn asked.

"No. It's all gone to hell," Alice said, trying one key after another. "The Earl of Chester has arrived with his forces, including his father-in-law, Robert of Gloucester, the empress's right-hand man. You may not remember, but his daughter is the young Lady Maud, who is being held here as a sort of political prisoner amongst the ladies."

"I remember."

"Well, they've come and they don't care who has sided with whom. They're killing everyone in their sight. It is horrible." Alice's face was pale as she tried another key. "These men have lost their minds. They're slaughtering everyone. Nowhere is safe."

"But I thought you were loyal to the empress," Bronwyn said.

"I am. But right now, I'm more concerned with saving my own hide, and yours." She gave the key a hard turn and with a satisfying noise, it unlocked the door. "There. Now are you going to just lounge around in that cell all day or are you coming with me?"

In seconds, Bronwyn and her father were out. Her father clutched her arm and said, "We must hurry."

But he was weak. Together, the three of them made it up the spiral, stone staircase and into the corridor, when Alice stopped. "What do we do? It's not safe."

"We have to get out of the castle and back into the city. It's our only hope of escape," Bronwyn's father said.

"How?"

Bronwyn picked up a sword from a fallen knight. "This should help. Let's stay together."

Together, they dashed past servants, hurried past ladies and through the downstairs areas into the kitchens, where there was a back entrance for deliveries. Farther along it led to an open courtyard, but if a person wasn't in service, they might not have known the way. Having worked in the kitchens, Bronwyn did.

She spied potboys and scullery hands hiding, and even Odo trembling in a corner. "Go, go. Get out of here," he said, seeing them. "Go and God help ye."

They hurried past when they were stopped by Brother Bartholomew, who stood by with two guards. He jabbed his finger in the air. "Get them! They're traitors!"

The guards rushed at them. Alice and Bronwyn's father fled. Bronwyn held out her sword when Odo lunged at one of the guards with a small cooking spit, impaling the man to the wall.

Bronwyn screamed and fell back. The other guard slipped and fell on the wooden floor, now slick with blood and mud, and fell on her. She yelped and scrambled to fight back, shoving and pushing, when she realized he did not move. His eyes were open and his mouth hung ajar when it hit her, the man was dead.

She remembered then she was holding a sword in her hands. He'd fallen on it and died. Blood was spilling onto her dress. She grunted and shoved the dead guard off, giving the sword a stiff yank. It was stuck, seemingly fixed in place by the man's blood. Putting her weight into it, she tugged and finally pulled the blade from his body.

She looked up to see Odo facing the traitorous monk. Odo was bigger, stronger, and wider than the religious man, and he glared at him with a face closer to hell than a happy baker. "You and your interfering ways. You ruined everything. I never thought I'd lay a hand on a man of God, but I might make an exception for you. Get out of here before I run you through," he said.

Kitchen boys came up behind him, armed with forks, knives, and rolling pins. Brother Bartholomew fled.

Bronwyn let out a sigh. "Thank you."

Odo gave a nod. "That way is full of fighters. You'd best go out the privy."

"What?"

Alice and her father caught up to her. "Are you all right?"

Alan asked.

"I'm fine. But Odo says that way is too dangerous. He says we should…"

"Go out the privy," Odo confirmed. "It'll take you out the back way and no one will see you."

Alice balked at this. "I am a lady. You expect me to go down…"

"Go to the garderobe down the hall and out the hole. You'll fall into the cesspit and can get out that way."

"But we'll be covered in filth. It's called a *cesspit* for a reason," Alice said.

"Would you prefer to take your chances up here?" Odo asked.

Alice made an unhappy noise in her throat and said in a resigned voice, "Lead the way."

Odo took up the cooking spit and with a courageous cook or two, led the group down the corridor and to the garderobe, which was little more than a wooden shelf above a hole that stank.

He lifted up the shelf, his voice strained. "You should be able to squeeze through."

"But we're high up off the ground. We could die," Alice said.

"You'll die if you stay here."

"I can't. I'm afraid of heights. No. I can't do it."

He faced her. "My lady, you either go out that hole or you can stay in the kitchens and wait to see if the new masters will keep you alive or kill you. They will always have need of a servant. Do they need *you?*"

Alice's mouth opened in indignation and then shut. She turned to Bronwyn, "You go first."

Bronwyn turned toward the garderobe hole, when her father first climbed through. He was slim and was in desperate need of a bath, but they all would be, considering the means of their escape. He climbed through and was out without a sound.

"Oh, my god," Bronwyn said.

"Sweet Jesus," Alice said. "I can't. I can't do this."

"Come on, Alice. We'll go together."

"Ew, no."

Bronwyn took her hand. "Help me down." She climbed through and bracing herself against the sides, feeling damp, stone cold and wet with urine and the smell of dried and wet refuse against her dress, she said, "One thing."

"What?" Alice asked.

"About that squire you like."

"Yes, what about him? This isn't really the time," she said.

"There's something you should know. I…"

"He doesn't have another admirer, does he? I have a very jealous nature."

Bronwyn stopped what she was about to say. There would be time to tell Alice later how she felt. "You'll have to come with and find out." Bronwyn reached for her hand but missed and slipped down the hole, sailing down to the cesspit below.

She landed with an awful splash, and it was as foul and disgusting as one might imagine. She inhaled mouthfuls of liquid refuse and coughed up breaths stinking of urine. She clawed and breathed, breathing in wet bubbles of filth, scrambling for air as she floated in a puddle. Finally, she got her head above it and coughed and hacked, retching as she spat and breathed in mouthfuls of sweet air.

A moment later, Alice screamed shrilly and landed with an almighty splash into the pit nearby, sending a small wave of the foul-smelling muck to hit Bronwyn in the face.

Fortunately, it was not very deep, and once they'd coughed, retched, and climbed out, with the help of her father, Bronwyn looked up. They must have fallen about twenty feet into the muck. It was wet and soft in the worst way and had cushioned their fall, sort of. The three of them stank and were covered with all sorts of refuse she did not want to name.

Alice coughed. "That dirty rat pushed me! I'll have his guts for garters. The sorry fool." She cursed the entire way as Alan helped her out.

They were on the other side of the castle, toward the back, away from the fighting, but still needed to go around and down the hill to make their way from the city. They emerged and ran from the castle courtyard and out, back through the city. It was chaos.

Fires roared, thatch rooves burned and crumbled, wattle and wooden structures crashed, sending sparks and shafts of wood into the streets. Smoke filled the air, men-at-arms marched, and men on horseback rode through the crowd of people. There were people everywhere, crowding around, stinking of sweat and urine and fear, terror etched on their faces as they fell into a mass crowd and kept moving.

Alice trembled and they held hands, along with Alan, who stayed close. "Let's go to the shop. I want to find your mother and Wyot," he said.

Bronwyn clutched his hand. "What if I lose you again?"

"You won't. We didn't come all this way to be parted." He stroked her cheek, despite the filth that was there.

How wrong he was. They held hands as long as possible, but the push and shove of the crowd soon separated them. Bronwyn cried out for her father, but he was gone in the crush of people. Alice and she clung to each other as they were swept out in the mass of people, almost like a wave, and then they were out on the streets, running, stumbling, picking each other up and trudging down Steep Hill, almost like they were drunk. They kept moving, for not to move was to court death, and death was on the hunt that day.

Bronwyn started to recognize her surroundings and pulled Alice aside, as more people shoved and ran past. People looted shops, others ran, carrying anything they could hold in their arms. She saw mothers run past with children clinging to their backs, men bearing whatever weapons they could, and children hiding in the shadows, some so young as to be clueless as to the danger that had befallen the fair city.

They made it to her family's shop and Bronwyn banged on the door, pounding on it. "Mama! Mama, let me in!"

But as the door gave way, she saw they were too late. Mama, Wyot—they were gone. And Papa wasn't here yet. The place was abandoned.

"Now what do we do?" Alice asked.

"I don't know." She shut the door and locked it for a moment, thinking.

"We need a plan," Alice said.

"I know."

"We need to do something. It's not safe here. I saw the knights a few streets away. They're coming closer. They were burning shops, with torches."

"Right." Bronwyn looked around her family home. Would it, too, fall beneath fiery destruction today?

She quickly glanced at the room. There were a few cooked bread rolls. "Come here. Put these in your dress."

"What?" Alice said as she gave her three rolls.

"Just do it," Bronwyn said, stuffing some into my dress.

"I've already swum in feces today. What more can I do? Might as well hold food to my body like some tradeswoman." Alice said, stuffing the rolls in. "Now can we go?"

"I hear voices inside," a man said outside the door. "Women."

"Open up! In the name of the empress!" a man said, pounding on the door.

"Don't open it. They'll kill us!" Alice hissed.

Bronwyn pulled her hand and dragged her over to the oven. She placed a hand to its surface. It was cool. Whatever plans Margaret had meant for it that morning had been stopped by the battle outside.

"No. No. They're burning down houses and you want me to climb in an *oven*? Are you mad?"

More banging on the front door. It shook and rattled in its frame.

"They'll never look here." Bronwyn tugged her hand.

"No. Absolutely not. I refuse."

"You can refuse to die too, but I don't think they'll listen," Bronwyn said, meeting her eyes.

Fists banged the door, rattling it. The men then took swords and axes to it, chipping the wood. Smoke drifted through the cracks, seeping into the shops. Buildings were burning outside.

"Come on." Bronwyn pulled her to the massive oven and Alice pushed back. "No."

"Fine." Bronwyn hid in the oven and pulled the sliding panel closed. She'd shut herself in darkness, and felt ashes coat her refuse-covered clothes. She heard a rustling and then quiet, just as the sound of splintering wood and loud noises came through.

"Where are they? There were voices in here," one man said.

"I thought I heard a woman," another said.

Bronwyn bit the inside of her cheek. Where had Alice gone? Would she be found?

"Search for them. Look. There's a trap door in the floor. They're probably hiding down there."

Bronwyn heard the men pull open the door in the floor, leading to an ordinary storeroom.

She didn't move. Quiet as a mouse, she waited as the men rustled through the shop, knocking things over, kicking things.

"It stinks like bread and a cesspit. Never thought a bakery would smell this bad," one man said.

"People probably used it as a privy."

The men talked a few minutes more. Bronwyn held her breath, breathing so quietly, she barely made a sound.

Then a sneeze.

"What was that?" a man said.

"Somebody sneezed. Find out who."

The men scouted around, when one said, "Well, look what I found."

"No! Let me go!" Alice cried. "Let go of my arm. Do you know who I am?"

Bronwyn's hands curled into fists. Alice had been caught. What to do? Would they hurt her?

"No, but I'm looking forward to knowing you better. What do you say, boys?" a man jeered.

"Yaaah!" a man shouted. "Get away from her!"

"Who's this?"

The men fought against a new foe as Bronwyn slid the oven panel aside.

One of the men said, "What the—?" and she charged at them like a feces-covered spirit.

The men were all fighting. Alice jerked away and ran to Bronwyn's side. Bronwyn picked up one of the long, wooden peels with a flat, shelf-like side and brandished it like a weapon.

Alice stared at the newcomer. "Rupert?"

He looked up.

Alice gripped Bronwyn's shoulders. "He's here. He's come to rescue me."

There were three men facing Rupert. He held a sword with both hands like he knew how to use it, but Bronwyn decided to even those odds. She took the peel and tripped one of the men, tangling the pole in his legs. He fell and dropped his sword.

Alice quickly picked it up and held it aloft. "Don't move!" she said. "Don't or I'll run you through."

The man looked up from the flat of his back and laughed, getting up. "I'm not afraid of two women."

Bronwyn jabbed his stomach with the pole. "Don't move."

The man coughed and sneered at them, as Rupert took on the other two. Bronwyn didn't dare look up, keeping her gaze trained on the man on the floor, watching for any sudden moves.

"Why are you two covered in muck?" he asked. "You stink."

Alice lifted her chin slightly. "We fell in a cesspit. What's your excuse?"

A corner of Bronwyn's mouth curled in a grin as she waited for the man to realize he'd been insulted. She mentally counted the seconds. One… two… three…

The man on the floor got up and approached, menace written on his features.

Alice backed up. "Don't come any closer." Her voice trembled.

The man gave her a leering smile. "Come here, pretty girl. Mud or not, I'll—"

Bronwyn jabbed him in the stomach with the peel, then again in the balls. He grunted and clutched his crotch, stumbling to his knees.

"Ha!" Alice said. "Take that!"

Rupert was doing all right against the others, but not amazing, for it was two against one. Bronwyn smacked one in the back of his head and he fell like a stone.

Alice dropped the sword she held and ran into Rupert's arms. "Oh, Rupert, you were wonderful. Thank you. You saved our lives."

Rupert's eyes widened at suddenly having his arms full of Alice, and he awkwardly put a hand around her back. He looked at Bronwyn, wrinkled his nose, and said, "You both really stink."

Alice hugged him tighter.

"You don't want to know," she said.

"We need to leave. It's not safe here," he said.

The man who'd been hit in the balls groaned.

Bronwyn said, "Alice, let's go."

Alice managed to somehow look up at Rupert, even though they were the same height. "You won't leave me, will you?"

He shook his head. "No." He led her out by the hand, or rather, she clutched his hand and refused to let go, Bronwyn noticed.

It bothered her, seeing them holding each other like a courting couple. An angry, ugly feeling sprouted inside her, like a nasty weed. She wanted to feel for Alice, but instead just felt annoyed she was touching Rupert. Like she owned him, almost. Maybe Bronwyn would never have a chance with Rupert. Not when a lady like Alice showed interest.

Bronwyn took one last look at her family's shop and holding the sword, followed them out into the road.

The sky was grey and dim with smoke. Fires roared and the buildings held an unholy, orange light as wood, wattle, and daub walls and thatch rooves burned steadily. People yelled and cried, running.

Bronwyn followed Rupert and Alice as closely as she could, but it was like walking through a hailstorm. People ran and shoved, and at every step she was pushed, nudged, bumped, sometimes brushed and even knocked past. It was dangerous and she felt cold inside, despite the warmth of all the bodies pressed around her in a tight knot, each trying to escape the hell that was Lincoln's streets.

They ran, dashed, and moved with the crowd, until they exited the main city and faced the Fosse Dyke, but Bronwyn stopped dead in her tracks. The waters of the dyke glittered in the sun, bearing boats.

"Look, there're boats! We can escape." Alice pointed.

"Wait. Stop," Bronwyn said, dragging Alice and Rupert over to stand by a wall as people dashed past. Some fled without even stopping, not even caring as they ran.

"Why did you make us stop?" Alice asked.

"Look."

There were boats floating in the river, a few skiffs. But they were already crowded with people and the crew was trying to set off, waving people away. It didn't matter. The people of the city were so terrified, they fled, casting all cares aside as they ran for their lives. The people flooded the streets like water, the crowd was so massive. Bronwyn had never seen anything like it before.

This was more than a crowd, or a bunch of people celebrating at a feast day. It was worse than a mob, more tightly packed. It was grim. It was a dead weight. And the ships couldn't take it for much longer.

They watched as people cried the boats were full, to stay away, but their cries fell on deaf ears. For every man, woman, and child who stood on the skiffs, dozens ran, pushing and shoving to take their place. It was horrifying as soon, people overloaded the boats and even more jumped on as the boats cast off, floating so heavily, and the ships began to....

"They're sinking," Alice said, her eyes wide. She clung to Rupert as the boats' wooden hulls groaned, creaked, and eventually sank, with hundreds of people on them. "Oh, God." She hid her face against Rupert's chest and he put an arm around her as she trembled with fear.

Rupert touched Bronwyn's shoulder. He didn't say a word, but their eyes met, and something passed between them. A feeling of sadness, understanding—maybe something more. They had survived a siege together, but a horrid feeling sat in Bronwyn's chest, tight, making it hard to breathe. She wanted to go home to her pallet in her family's shop and go to bed. But that was no longer an option. Not anymore. Was this just the beginning? Would life ever be the same again?

The terrified moans and ragged cries of people dragged her attention from his face. Bronwyn couldn't look away. Hundreds of poor souls met their maker that day, and as warm tears coursed down her stained face, all she could do was watch, hope, and whisper a prayer to God that her family wasn't amongst them.

Epilogue

B RONWYN HEARD LATER that five hundred people in the city had died that afternoon on the river, overloading the boats. As they had been outside of the city, they'd met with other townspeople, now refugees, as Empress Maud's armies had taken Lincoln.

They had learnt that King Stephen's forces had gone out to face Maud's armies, facing Robert of Gloucester's men with Ranulf de Gernon, the Earl of Chester, and Welsh mercenaries they had hired and who were loyal to Maud.

To hear the men tell of it, they said these fighters had broken the king's line of defense and some of the king's knights had fled in the face of the bigger armies, deserting him at the most inopportune time. King Stephen had apparently borne an axe in the style of the kind Northmen carried and fought with that and his sword until both had been shattered in the fight, one after another.

Bronwyn had heard different accounts, one that he had been struck by a stone and fallen, another that he had been cornered by a knight and declared beaten. Either way, the accounts end the same way: Robert of Gloucester had ordered that King Stephen and his knights be taken prisoner, and the day had been won. King Stephen and those who followed him had been on the losing side.

Rupert's master, Sir Baldwin de Clare, had been captured

alongside the king, as well as his men, all of whom were taken prisoner.

Alone and yet crowded in a refugee camp outside the city, Bronwyn felt useless. Rupert was without a master, she had no family, and Alice didn't stay at Bronwyn's side for long.

Maud's victorious army had sacked the city. Everything they could destroy, they'd ruined or burned. The people who'd remained had been put to the sword or killed in different ways. Bronwyn heard it said the men had taken pleasure in devising new ways to kill the city's remaining few. She hoped that Odo and the potboys and cooks had survived, but part of her also wondered if perhaps it wouldn't be a mercy if they hadn't.

She, Alice, and Rupert joined the camp of refugees outside the city, mixed with Maud's army. She joined the kitchen staff and spent the days cooking, cleaning, doing anything she could to survive.

Rupert got work amongst the men at arms and fighters at the camp, but his duties often took him elsewhere for periods of time. Alice, ever resourceful, found her way to Maud's court and inserted herself amongst the ladies at the empress's side. Bronwyn wanted to call her a traitor, but they both believed in their own side, so she supposed that they looked like traitors to each other. Bronwyn did not know what happened to the ladies and the queen still in the castle. She did not see Sir Nicholas, Alfred, Sir Gabriel, or Brother Bartholomew again.

It wasn't until she spied a middle-aged, well-dressed woman urinating by a tree that she saw a man sneaking up on the woman with a sword. Without thinking, Bronwyn rushed and knocked him over, both crashing to the ground. The woman screamed, the man and Bronwyn fought, and she earned herself a few bruises and cuts, until the man shuddered and stopped.

She looked up. They were both at surrounded by guards and at spearpoint. She froze, and the man bled on her, for he had fallen on her dagger and now bled out. Another man dead, by her own hand. She shrieked and shifted away, shoving him, as blood stained her dress. Her eyes wide, she swallowed as one guard with a spear held it close to her throat.

"Back off, you'll kill her," the woman snapped. She stood and arranged her skirts, standing to her full height. She surveyed her with hard eyes. "Who are you? What do you want?"

"Nothing. I'm Bronwyn Blakenhale. I'm nobody."

The woman wore a dark-crimson dress, and she had a veil and circlet over her hair and a thin belt to accentuate her waist. She was very finely dressed and stunningly beautiful. Her skin was clear and fair, her eyes sharp with intelligence. For a moment. Before she snorted and said in French-accented English, "I'll be the judge of that. Your name. Welsh?"

"No, I'm English. But the name is."

"Good name. The Welsh are good fighters." She felt at her pockets but had no coin purse. Her face darkened. "What were you doing there? Were you spying on me?"

Bronwyn shook her head. "No. I saw the man start to sneak up on you. It looked like he was going to attack, so I jumped him."

The guards exchanged uneasy looks. The woman shot them all an annoyed look. "That is what happens when you're not alert." She tossed a long, thick, light-brown braid over her shoulder. "God, I hate the outdoors. Give me a castle any day. You, Bronwyn Blakenhale. Come along. You're with me." She snapped her fingers and walked off.

Bronwyn watched her go and got to her feet. She asked one of the guards, "Uh, what?"

One glanced at the woman departing and said quietly, "You're not nobody anymore, not now. That was the empress. You just saved her life."

From that day onward, Bronwyn's life changed.

The End

Historical Note

It's always difficult to write in the context of another time period, and even harder when the story is set centuries ago. As amateur historians, we have to be diligent in our research of the smallest details and try to portray accuracy of not just the major events of the time period, but also of the minutiae of a person's daily life.

For instance, this story predates *The Assize of Bread and Ale,* which governed the weight and costs of bread in villages, hamlets, and towns, so I've taken artistic license with my descriptions here. You'll have to forgive the modern-style language I use as well! Additionally, with the system of measurements, as the Roman system was reintroduced by William the Conqueror and not revised until the thirteenth century, I've stuck with using measurement terms rather loosely.

Starting a life in service as a servant, page, squire, etc., was something to be agreed with and not done lightly. Lady Alice has rather flown in the face of convention by stealing away Bronwyn for a short time. I appreciate this would have been inaccurate but thought it necessary to flag.

Similarly, when I visited Lincoln and made the trek up to see the castle, I was struck by the signs for Steep Hill. Aptly named, I inserted that into my novel, but apologies to any true historians who may find this to be historically inaccurate.

One of the cool things about doing historical research is finding out little nuggets of information you can insert in the story. In this case, I found multiple contemporary accounts mention the church service where King Stephen has the candle break in three pieces in his hands, and people think it is a bad omen of what's to come.

I've read a few different contemporary accounts of the Battle of Lincoln but am sure I still have some details wrong. Allegedly, we do know the names of some of the men who abandoned King Stephen in battle, and apparently, he did fight with an axe and was taken prisoner. Sadly, multiple sources also mention the death of five hundred of Lincoln's townspeople overloading the boats in the river and drowning, more of whom died there than in the actual battle.

All inaccuracies are mine; if I have missed some details or if you want to share some great historical sources with me, please do. I'd love to know what you think.

Sources Consulted

Primary source

Potter, K.R., and R. H. C. Davis (eds). *Oxford Medieval Texts: Gesta Stephani.*

Oxford University Press: Oxford Medieval Texts, 1976. Digitized 2020. DOI: 10.1093/actrade/9780198222347.

Secondary sources

Anderson, Carolyn. *Narrating Matilda, "Lady of the English," in the Historia Novella, the Gesta Stephani, and Wace's Roman de Rou: The Desire for Land and Order.* 1999.

Mirov, Lev. *"Our Beloved Protectress": Lordly Women and Military Activity in the Anglo-Norman and Angevin World of the Twelfth Century.* Undergraduate thesis, 2011.

Townsley, Lida Sophia. *"Twelfth-century English queens: charters and authority,"* MPhil thesis, 2010. Trinity College, Dublin.

"How rich medieval people spent their money." Medievalists.net. 2023. *https://www.medievalists.net/2023/12/medieval-spend-money/?utm_source=gravitec&utm_medium =push&utm_campaign=Push%20Notification*

"The Battle of Lincoln (1141) from five sources." DE RE MILITARI, The Society For Medieval Military History. 2014. *https://deremilitari.org/2014/03/the-battle-of-lincoln-1141-from-five-sources/*

Acknowledgments

This book has gone through multiple revisions, and it would not be as strong a story without the skilled editing of my fantastic, patient, and good-natured editor, Amy McNulty. Thank you to the wonderful team at Dragonblade for their constant support and belief in me. Thank you also to Aviva Orr and Theresa Green for the writing sprints, as well as to my family, my bandmates, and my lovely readers. Thank you all.

About the Author

E. L. Johnson writes historical mysteries. A Boston native, she gave up clam chowder and lobster rolls for tea and scones when she moved across the pond to London, where she studied medieval magic at UCL and medieval remedies at Birkbeck College. Now based in Hertfordshire, she is a member of the Hertford Writers' Circle and the founder of the London Seasonal Book Club.

When not writing, Erin spends her days working as a press officer for a royal charity and her evenings as the lead singer of the gothic progressive metal band, Orpheum. She is also an avid Jane Austen fan and has a growing collection of period drama films.

Connect with her on Twitter at twitter.com/ELJohnson888 or on Instagram at instagram.com/ejgoth.